DESIGNED BY FLAWS

MARTELL L. HARRIS

BEYOND CONTESTATION

I want to thank my entire family for their constant support and belief in me. Laura, my mother. Her love for books ignited my creativity and motivated me to pursue a writing career. Through her love of reading, she introduced me to a multitude of worlds full of possibilities and diverse viewpoints. Neshai Harris, my dear sister, has always been there to cheer me on. I want to express my heartfelt gratitude to both of them, with love and in memory of Neshai Harris.

CONTENTS

CHAPTER ONE

THE PAWN ADVANCES

*I*f you try to measure your life, you'll find the margin for error to be infinite!

Reo sprints along the aging bridge, grappling with his mother's last words. He reaches the center of the majestic, bustling overpass. The howling gusts fade as he halts and gazes into the distance.

Stinging sweat clouds his vision, trickling down his temples and catching in his dark brows. His breath stains the crisp autumn air in heavy white puffs. He wipes his eyes with the rough fabric of his sleeve, blinking away the salt burn before checking his vitals on his sleek digital smartwatch, its display glowing an ethereal blue against his skin.

The bustling bridge buzzes with people, half of whom can't take their eyes off their own smartwatches. The other half can't take their eyes off him. He leans on the rail and basks in the dying light.

The glistening gold gives everything an invaluable appearance. The restless breeze carries the sweet scent of flowers, filling his lungs. His eyes feast on the moment as his hands glide over the rails, gripping them. He stands at the railing as if he owns it. A shiver runs up his left arm. He inserts a small clear dot behind his ear and touches his watch.

"Moshi, Moshi, TJ. How are you, my friend?" His low, silvery voice is calm.

"Hello, senpai. I am okay. Otis has your current location in Kyoto. I see you're on your last mission. Would you like to continue speaking in Japanese for your situation report?" TJ asks with a raspy tone.

"We should be okay to continue in Japanese. No one is looking my way to hear me. Have you found Tristian?" Reo asks.

"Yes, Tristian is hiding here in America! He is the leader of a Yokai-worshiping group called the Dark Suns. They are not a threat, just a bunch of Yokai enthusiasts. I've tracked his last known location in San Francisco, and I've also found their stash house for artifacts. I've confiscated all the items there. Before you ask: no, the weapon was not there, but I'm getting close. Although, I may have stumbled upon something much bigger..."

"It's been two years since he took it. You must find him before it's too late. Millions of lives depend on us, and we don't have time for anything else. Remember the rules: the mission always comes first," Reo says.

"I'm doing my best here, but I got sidetracked by intel coming out of Washington State. Listen to this..."

"That's enough, TJ! Getting that weapon back is paramount, or all is lost!" Reo interjects, switching to English as people start to stare.

TJ takes the hint and follows suit. "Tristian betrayed us all. Our brothers and sisters were murdered! We both want him to pay. I know what's at stake here, but damn it, just listen to the intel I have!"

"You're right, TJ. I apologize for my outburst. I just can't help but feel this is due to my short-sightedness. Please tell me what you found."

"I think I may have found Myou, but I can't confirm it."

Motionless at the railing, Reo watches the last shimmer of daylight disappear. His chest thumps wildly as his breathing grows labored. He clenches his fist and hits it against the metal bar, scoffing to himself.

The peaceful chatter of the crowd on the bridge shatters as chaos erupts around him. People scatter in terror as some maniac brutally snaps the necks of three men while trying to grab a small girl. Snatching his victim, the attacker disappears into the thick bamboo grove at the bridge's southern edge.

"TJ, you've done well, but I have to go now. Stay on the Myou intel. I'll get the confirmation we need. She won't escape this time!" Reo says into his earpiece. His gaze fixes on the bridge's far side. Pressing his smartwatch to disconnect, he draws a deep breath. With measured steps, he pushes through the frenzied masses toward the shadowy bamboo thicket. The throng's hysterical shrieks overwhelm the child's cries, obscuring any trace of their path.

Twin trails diverge where the bamboo begins—one illuminated by lanterns, the other cloaked in shadow. Reo shuts his eyes as the wind whistles past him, though the distant crowd's hysteria breaks his concentration. Crouching low, his fingers brush the earth for a long moment while he samples the air currents. Rising, he opts for the unlit trail, tracking the child's lingering fragrance.

A path of shattered lights leads further into the grove. Rustling bamboo stalks bend with each gust, beckoning him forward. His calculated stride soon narrows the gap to the kidnapper, who grips the small girl from behind, squeezing her neck with gnarled fingers.

"If you come any closer, her death will be excruciating!" One corner of the man's mouth lifts. "Now, tell me who you are."

Reo doesn't respond; he continues to stroll deliberately toward the man, his dark eyes fixed and unblinking. Each footfall lands, silent as death, on the earthen path, his posture relaxed yet coiled with lethal purpose.

"Hey! I said stop right there, or I will rip the little bitch's head off!" The man's nails draw blood from the little girl's neck.

Reo remains unfazed. He advances like a predator closing in. Tears cascade down the child's terrified face as she attempts to cry out, her voice trapped in her throat.

The assailant hoists her into the air, his fingers clenched around her neck in a brutal grip. "Her death is on your head!"

Reo freezes mid-step as he observes the display of raw power. Standing a mere thirty feet from the pair, his knuckles whiten as he goes rigid. The swaying stalks of bamboo intensify their whispered symphony, their deadly standoff bathed in moonlight. "I was enjoying the sunset, and you ruined it. Let the girl go; she holds no sway over your fate!"

The man foams at the mouth, viscous saliva dripping down his chin in thick rivulets. His teeth elongate and sharpen into jagged daggers, gleaming wetly in the moonlight as his transformation accelerates. His skin burns a deep crimson, as if molten lava flows beneath the surface. His already imposing frame stretches impossibly upward, muscles bulging and twisting, until he towers over them like an ancient temple gate. With sickening cracks, ivory horns burst through his skull, curling upward like those of a demon straight from the darkest legends of old Japan.

"Who are you to interrupt my meal? I've been feeding at this bridge for hundreds of years!" the monster declares.

Reo tilts his head forward, his dark eyes narrowing as he studies the grotesque creature before him. His jaw tightens, muscles flexing beneath skin that bears faint traces of ancient battle scars—permanent reminders of countless encounters with beings like this one. The moonlight casts stark shadows across his youthful features.

"I am Uchima Reo, the Yokai Executioner! Do I have to repeat myself? Let her go, Oni!"

The Oni falls to his knees as he releases the girl, his massive form trembling like a mountain in an earthquake. His widened eyes lose their fierce glare, the intense crimson glow dimming to a dull ember. A wrinkled expression of recognition and fear consumes his craggy face at the sound of the name. Ancient legends of the Yokai Executioner's merciless justice flash through his centuries-old memory, each tale more terrifying than the last.

"Please, I didn't know it was you. I will let her go! Please let me go, and you'll never see me again!" the Oni pleads.

"Letting her go was your path to heaven!" Reo responds.

The Oni sighs in relief and lowers his head.

The girl runs past Reo, but his eyes never leave the Oni. "Taking her in the first place, Oni, was the path to hell!"

He continues to trail the Oni through the shadowy bamboo alley, his footsteps silent and calculated like a predator stalking its prey. The Oni raises its massive horned head, its fiery crimson eyes piercing through the darkness with demonic intensity. In one fluid motion, born from centuries of martial arts mastery, Reo executes a devastating hip toss, his hands gripping the demon's coarse hide as he sends it crashing to the rain-slicked ground with bone-jarring force. He follows through without hesitation, forcefully stomping on the creature's thick wrist, causing a sickening crunch that echoes through the bamboo forest. As Reo plants his right foot firmly on the Oni's muscular neck and leans over it, his face a mask of cold determination, a horrific cry escapes the creature's lips—a sound that mingles pain and terror in equal measure.

"That was not smart, but I may let you go if you can answer my questions. Where is the Umbra?"

"Alright, alright. Ah! I heard they all went to America two years ago. They knew you could not leave Japan because you had to hunt and kill the evil Yokai here. So... Ah! They left some Yokai here to keep you busy while they execute their plans in America. They are searching for something or someone. I can't remember."

"What was it? Something or someone? Don't make me ask again!" Reo leans in on the Oni's neck.

"They are looking for someone very special and rare. It's an earthly deity, born once every ten thousand years."

An earthly deity? A half-god, half-human being with extraordinary abilities. If a Yokai were to gain their power, that would be devastating, Reo thinks.

"What do they need this earthly deity for?"

"I don't know, but they systematically removed all the threats to their plans, including your team. You are the only one left that can stop the Umbra from bringing back the Kokuten," the Oni replies.

"That's a big word for such a low-ranking Oni!" Reo stomps on its kneecap, breaking it. Its cry fills the forest. "What state in America are they in?!"

"I-I don't know. She called it the Evergreen place!" the Oni responds.

A penetrating scowl overtakes Reo's face in the moonlit forest. He glares at the Oni, panting as he increases the pressure of his foot on its neck, leaning closer until he can smell the demon's putrid breath. The fallen leaves crunch beneath his weight as he shifts, sending a cascade of autumn debris scattering across the damp ground. His jaw clenches, muscles rippling with years of contained rage.

"She?! You mean Myou? Where... is... she?!"

The Oni stares into his raging face, beginning to sweat and gasp for air as dark rivulets run down its mottled purple skin. Its trembling voice struggles to force the words from its trauma-tized throat, emerging in desperate wheezes under the crushing pressure of Reo's foot. The demon's red eyes dart frantically from side to side, searching the shadows of the forest for any hope of escape, finding only the cold judgment in his captor's merciless gaze.

"She—she was... the first one to go there! I heard they were close to finding the earthly deity near a Shinto shrine in America. If they get it before the next Diamond Fuji, the stars will fade from the sky, and the mountain will rise to devour the lands and its people, and there is nothing anyone can do to stop it, not even you! That's everything I know; you said you would release me if I answered your questions. Now, please let me go!"

Reo removes his foot from the Oni's throat and takes a step back. The Oni clutches its throat and coughs up blood while squirming on the ground.

"How many others begged for their lives, only to be eat-en by you?!" Reo steps forward, forcefully stomping on the Oni's other kneecap, causing it to emit an ear-piercing sound that echoes through the bamboo forest like a thunderclap. The inhuman shriek sends shivers down the spines of the people standing on the other side of the bridge, where they watch the young girl make her way back toward them. The primal fear that grips them stops the men from going to help her cross the weathered wooden planks that creak beneath her feet.

The young girl finally reaches the other side of the bridge, her kimono damp with sweat as she wipes away her tears with trembling fingers. A mixture of relief and determination flashes in her eyes, though her face remains ghost-white with terror. Overwhelmed and exhausted, she sinks to the ground, her small frame collapsing against a moss-covered stone. Her teeth chatter uncontrollably, sounding like scattered pebbles. Each scream from the bamboo forest seems to reverberate through the surroundings, growing in volume and horror until the very air vibrates with malevolent energy.

Two men, dressed in simple farming clothes, help the young girl to her feet, supporting her weight between them. She looks at them, complexion pale as fresh snow, her lips quivering with unspoken horrors. Although it takes several minutes, during which more screams pierce the evening air, she finally speaks, her voice barely above a whisper.

"It was an Oni. A man saved me. I heard him say the name Reo, but they were speaking in a different language. I don't know what they were saying," the young girl says.

A huge gasp rises from the crowd.

"An Oni?! You mean the man who grabbed you was the bridge demon of Arashiyama? It can't be. Yokai haven't been around for centuries!" a man replies. The petrified crowd peers across the dark bridge into the bamboo forest. The screams echo across the water as they help the young girl to her unconscious mother.

Reo stands over the mutilated body, glaring at his work. He has painted the bamboo forest crimson, the metallic scent of blood hanging thick in the humid night air. Dark spatters mark the tall stalks of bamboo like abstract art, stretching up into the darkness above. He is drenched in blood as three men enter the forest in hazmat suits carrying supplies: lights, bags, shovels, and clean clothes. Their boots crunch softly against the forest floor as they move with practiced efficiency, their headlamps cutting sharply through the mist that has begun to settle between the towering bamboo.

"Wow, this is worse than your last Oni kill, Reo-sama, but don't worry, we will clean it all up in no time. Here are your new clothes. You can wash up in the river. You've executed the last evil Yokai in Japan; what will you do now that your mission is finally complete?"

"It's not over. They staged these last few years to keep me from looking westward. I will return home to Ise; there, I will replant my mother's garden. I will stay until TJ can find more information about the Umbra's position, then we'll destroy them all."

"How long has it been since you've been home?" asks the man as he shovels the mutilated Oni body parts into the wooden wheelbarrow, his weathered hands gripping the handle. Reo gazes toward the heavens to bask in the starry glimmer, watching as the Milky Way stretches across the ink-black sky like a river of diamonds. His frigid breath fills his view with ghostly white clouds, dissipating into the crisp night air as he searches through years of memories for an answer.

"It's been too long." Reo finally replies, bowing to the men before walking into the darkness.

"I can't believe he saved someone this time!" The man smiles and helps the others shovel up the Oni's remains.

A young man walks toward the gorgeous grand shrine of Ise in the Mie Prefecture of Japan. He stops to wash his hands before entering the massive red Torii gate. He ascends a large flight of stairs that leads to a mansion-sized building. He halts at a shrine in front of a large room and prays.

"Amaterasu, goddess of the sun. I have confirmed that the Yokai are in Seattle, Washington. I ask that you protect the people of the United States, for they will need it," the man says, bowing before leaving.

A shinshoku hears the prayer and relays it to the high priest, who makes his way toward a traditional house nearby.

Reo enters his home after tending to his majestic garden. He appears to be under thirty, with beautiful olive skin and smoldering amber eyes. His chiseled jawline is adorned with a five o'clock shadow, and his defined cheekbones complement his perfect smile and flat nose. He is significantly taller than the average male, with the physique of an Olympic swimmer.

Reo sits and meditates in front of a small shrine called the kamidana. Surrounding it are an unsealed old letter, some food, and a beautiful red Tsubaki flower. While praying for his loved ones at the kamidana, he hears the front door slide open and someone enter his home. His gleaming, confident eyes widen as he stands and bows toward the shrine. Reo heads to the main room, where a wise-looking man of considerable age sits in wait.

"Forgive me for making you wait, Shokai. Please, take a seat," Reo says. The shokai sits in the most respected spot in the house.

"Reo-sama, I've been coming here for many years now. I know I am a high-ranking Shinto priest, but you don't have to be so formal in your home. You can call me by name. I also want to practice my English with you," the high priest replies.

Reo sits in front of the shokai and pours tea into his cup. "Very well. It may not be the polite thing to do, but if you wish, I will call you by your name, Makoto-sama."

"Thank you. You honor me. I wish I could say I came for your excellent tea and splendid company, but we have received confirmation of yokai in America, specifically in Washington State. I know you've only been resting for three months since defeating the last evil yokai in Kyoto, but if we fail to act, they will grow and become unstoppable in America."

Reo places the teapot on the table, gazing out at his exquisite garden as he takes a calming breath. "You don't have to convince me how important this mission is, Makoto-sama. This is personal; I am going to stop them. I just need to know where they are."

Makoto pours Reo's tea and sets the teapot on the table. He then picks up his teacup and holds it with both hands, taking a slow sip and smiling contentedly. "Seattle, Washington, is the place. We have contacts at a shrine just outside the city limits. This will be your first time leaving Japan, right? Isn't your student TJ from America?"

"Yes, but he hasn't been my student in more than three years; he calls me senpai now. He's currently on a mission in San Francisco, checking out the sighting reports on Tristian and the order he has created called The Dark Suns." Reo picks up his tea and sips.

"Senpai... upperclassman, huh? You've trained an incredible martial artist, and he is an even better engineer. The physics-defying smartwatch he created can level the playing field when facing a stronger foe. I've read the notes on what it can do, and it will save many lives. I'm just sorry that its inception came at such a high price," Makoto says.

Reo sips his tea and remains silent. He inhales slowly, trying to keep his mind calm.

"I've been a priest for a very long time; I've heard many prayers from many people. Some were happy, while others were terrible. The one thing they all have in common is that they felt a little better letting it out. It helps to talk about it, Reo-sama."

It's all my fault; I was too weak; I couldn't do it!

When Reo doesn't reply, Makoto says, "Very well. The Dark Suns. I've heard of them in a few of our reports. They steal precious artifacts to appease the Umbra, hoping to become Yokai themselves."

"And because they are human, we can't get approval to execute them unless they interfere in a mission. In my opinion, they are worse than the Yokai," Reo replies.

"An earthly deity, half human and half god, is a once-in-a-millennium event. Is it true that you've actually met one?"

Reo nods. "Yes, I have, though their power was dormant. I saw something in their eyes that confirmed they were extraordinary. These earthly deities are said to possess great strength, speed, endurance, and otherworldly abilities."

"Myou cannot be allowed to obtain that kind of power. I wonder, Reo-sama, do Americans even have Yokai?"

"Yes, however, they refer to them as demons, devils, and ogres. I researched them while studying English. Our Yokai make their demons look like kittens. No one on this planet should ever witness the things I've seen them do. But in two days, I will go to America and find the deity before they do."

"Myou's been hunting for the earthly deity for twenty-seven months already. Do you have a strategy for defeating her this time? I'm sure she has grown more powerful since you last faced her. I mention this because we've learned she has the weapon that Tristian stole from you two years ago. We have to assume that she has amassed an army by now, and in your last fight with her, you nearly lost everything."

Reo shakes his head, looking at the pond water and seeing the sun's reflection. He stares at it as he always does, with a puzzled expression. "This time will be different. One of us will die—she or I!"

CHAPTER TWO

THE
EVERGREEN
STATE

A woman in her twenties slumbers peacefully, lost in a nighttime vision. Her subconscious reveals an image of a child, roughly ten years old, strolling along holding the hands of her parents. The father has Japanese features, while the mother's heritage is African American.

"What is this place?" The little girl asks her parents.

The mother exchanges warm glances with her husband as he kneels beside their daughter. "Well, Llia (Lee-Ya), this is called a Shinto shrine. It's one of the oldest in America. In Seattle and across the United States, followers of the Shinto faith visit to pray to the deities for guidance and support in their lives. They also seek blessings for their loved ones." He gestures toward the statues, smiling.

"I can even ask to see my grandparents in Japan again soon?" Llia asks, jumping up and down.

"Yes, sweetheart, you certainly can, though probably not twice in one year. Traveling from Seattle to Japan is expensive, even for the deities," the man replies, while his wife covers her mouth to stifle a laugh.

"Dad, what are these large red poles for?" Llia asks.

"Those are torii gates—they serve as a protective boundary against negative forces. You'll need to cleanse your hands before passing through them. It purifies you of any spiritual contamination so you can step beyond the threshold. Do you see the pair of guardian lions positioned at the entrance?"

"Yes," Llia replies, hiding behind him and clutching his shirt. Her small fingers grip the fabric tightly as she peers around his waist with wide, uncertain eyes at the stone guardians.

"Oh no, come here, sweetie. They are the good guys. They protect the gate from evil. My dad called them defenders. Some even refer to them as Yokai executioners. Nothing bad will get past them. They will destroy any evil Yokai who tries to enter a purified shrine."

"What happens if something bad gets past them, Daddy?"

"Well, Llia, if something bad were to get into the shrine, it would no longer be purified, and it would be nearly impossible to remove the bad thing!" As the words leave his lips, a scarlet torrent bursts from his mouth, cutting off his speech. Crimson droplets cascade down his chin as he collapses, his body seized by violent tremors. A shadowy veil envelops him, bleaching his flesh pale and transforming his eyes into bottomless voids. He lunges with inhuman speed, sending her mother sprawling.

In one brutal movement, he silences her desperate cries with a quick twist of her head. His attention then turns to the child, his lips curving into a gentle grin. Terror freezes her voice as she staggers backward, tumbling down. The man, his mouth now filled with serrated fangs, lunges at her with ravenous intent.

"Daddy! No!"

The woman jolts upright from her terrifying dream, perspiration soaking her clothes. Thunder cracks overhead, making her jump. The deafening hail pelts the metropolis like scattered marbles striking oak planks. Lightning intermittently illuminates her room. Panting heavily, she reaches for a cloth to dry herself off. After turning her pillow to the cool side, she sinks back into her snug, welcoming mattress. The steady drumming of precipitation soothes her nerves, anchoring her thoughts to reality and pushing the dark visions away. She tucks herself into a tight fetal position, gaze fixed on a photograph perched nearby. Shadows of rain droplets trickle across her face as slumber claims her once more.

Morning light brushes against Llia's face as she stirs from her night's rest. Her eyelids lift to reveal serenity outside her window where turmoil had dominated only hours before, causing her to question whether the storm existed only in her mind. The clock on her wall, with its gentle ticking, shows six o'clock. She hesitates, battling internally before mustering the determination to abandon her bed's comfort. Moving through her usual routine, she drags herself to confront her reflection in the bathroom mirror, noting the signs of her restless night.

As a college graduate, her appearance forms a stunning composition—full, shapely lips match her prominent jawline, while her cinnamon skin radiates beneath a charming nose. Golden-brown eyes dance with vitality, enhanced by perfectly arched eyebrows. She towers over her housemates, her athletic physique revealing both strength and elegance. Velvety spirals of dark hair fall past her shoulders, enhancing her natural beauty.

Within her spacious bedroom, she methodically extends and flexes her limbs, dedicating a quarter of an hour to loosening her muscles. Following this, she completes multiple rounds of floor exercises. Her hands and legs slice through the air with swift precision as she delivers rapid jabs and martial kicks at invisible targets. The rigorous training session leaves perspiration streaming down her features as she attempts to purge the lingering fragments of her disturbing dream.

A glance at the clock shows seven-fifteen—her deadline for leaving for work. She steps into the shower, enveloped in the humid mist for fifteen minutes before dressing in another ten.

Passing through the living room, her gaze drifts to the display cabinet showcasing her international karate titles—dual certifications marking her fourth-level black belt achievements in both Kyokushin karate and Tae Kwon Do, alongside numerous athletic field medals. Moving to the kitchen, she is greeted by the enticing fragrance of freshly made cappuccinos wafting through the apartment.

Llia's rustic apartment features two full bathrooms and three bedrooms adorned with expensive wall décor. The apartment even has private roof access that she and her roommates use every blue moon. From the roof, they can clearly see Pike Place Market. Dull hardwood floors run throughout the spacious apartment, and a large window in the living room overlooks the park across the street. They often sit there and watch the sunset in the distance. The space is fully furnished with high-end furniture and decorated with photos of the three girls at various ages. However, Llia's most valued item is her dad's chair, which sits near the large window. It was his thinking chair, and they used it frequently when she was a little girl.

As she grabs a glass from the cabinet while singing "Titanium," she looks in the fridge and stops, noticing there is no milk. Her eyes burn as she frowns.

"Dammit, Rose. Is it too much to ask you to buy more milk after you finish it?"

"She strikes again, I see," says a disembodied voice from the hall.

"Yes, Iris, I swear I'm going to strangle her," Llia replies as Iris emerges and enters the living room.

With caramel-colored skin reflecting her Indian heritage, Iris possesses striking features crowned by bold, elegant brows framing deep chocolate eyes. Her petite figure makes her the smallest of the roommates, standing several inches below Llia.

Plump lips and cascading ebony hair that tumbles to her waist complete her enchanting appearance.

"Well, get in line because she stole my favorite dress to go out last night. But you didn't hear that last part from me. Also, have you been to the new Japanese restaurant near the school? Everyone at work is talking about it, they say it's great. We should go one day. If only I could find some time off work."

"No, I haven't heard about it. I've been busy with all the filing work at the police station. The crime rate is getting outrageous these days. Let's all go out together: you, me, Rose, Moro, Maddix, and Charlie. It's been a while since we all went out together," Llia says while taking a bagel and spreading cream cheese on it.

"Are you sure it's the records clerk job keeping you busy, or are you searching through all those files for clues about..."

"Honestly, it's a little of both. I always feel like, *Today is the day. I'll find what they've all missed.*"

"Llia, it's been years since you've had any time off. You need to take it easy before you burn yourself out. Detach yourself for a while. Maybe go on a date and have some fun."

"We all can't be as lucky as Maddix and find our Charlie," Llia chuckles. Charles, who went by Charlie, was Maddix's boyfriend.

"I guess everything is going well for him now, but it got bad when Jason broke his heart. I thought that was the worst. Sometimes, things work out, though. But seriously, Llia, don't work too hard looking for clues..."

"It's eight o'clock, Doctor Iris," Llia proclaims.

"Oh shit, really? I've got to run. I don't want to be late for my first day of residency at the hospital. My dad is going to stop by the job and take me to lunch today," Iris grabs Llia's bagel from her hand and rushes toward the door.

"Et tu, Iris?!"

"Thanks, I love you. Goodbye!" Iris laughs as she jets out.

"Have a great day, you petty thief," Laughing to herself, Llia prepares another bagel. Iris pops her head back in the doorway.

"Thank you! Oh, and Llia? Don't kill Rosie. We need her part of the rent. Ha-ha-ha. I love you guys. Bye!"

"No promises. Love you too," Llia says as Iris closes the front door behind her once more.

There's movement in the hall.

"Rose, I know that's you."

"I'm so sorry, Llia. The milk was on my to-do list, I swear. I studied last night!" Rose responds, sitting by the counter.

"What about the floor? Is that on your to-do list too? You were supposed to clean it three weeks ago, it's your turn!"

Rose is a little taller than Iris, but she weighs the same and has curves. She is of Caucasian descent, with smooth, milky skin and short crimson hair. Her emerald-green eyes are captivating. She often wears a smoldering expression that most men find irresistible.

"Also, I'm not buying the study excuse. You are the smartest person I know. I mean, you're getting your master's degree in psychology, and 'I was studying' was the best you could come up with? You little liar! You're glowing. It was a date," Llia teases.

"A real master of observation and deduction. I should have known you could sniff out the truth. You can read people like books. It's not your scariest quality, but it's up there," Rose replies.

"I only reveal my scariest quality when I don't have my cappuccino in the morning!"

"Fair enough. And Iris is right, by the way. You work too hard. The human mind was not meant to be fixated on an obsession that ties you to such a traumatic memory. You're literally pouring gasoline on the fire every time you look through those files."

"Thank you, Doctor Eavesdropper. You know, it sucks living with a medical doctor and a psychiatrist sometimes. Iris is all, 'No, Llia, don't eat that, it's bad for you.' And you sound like, 'You need to go out and sleep with someone, you'll feel much better about your life'."

"Okay, that Iris impression was spot on. You can't eat a damn sandwich in front of her. But I sound nothing like that."

"Yeah, yeah, so who did you sleep with last night? And do you feel better about your life?"

"Ha-ha, I went out with a guy I met the other night. We talked afterward, and then he went home. He was a complete gentleman. His name is Mark."

"It's Mike, actually," says a young man as he walks out of the hall and waves at Llia. "Hi, nice to meet you."

"I thought I told you to wait until everyone leaves, and then you could come out!" Rose whispers.

"But I'm going to be late for class..."

"So, Mike," Llia interrupts, "you're in college too? Do you attend Seattle University?"

"Yeah, Go S.U! I graduate this year. I plan on entering the draft, but please don't tell anyone." His unsettling smile makes Llia feel uncomfortable.

"Oh, that's great. Your secret is safe with me. Rose, I'm going to head out and get a cappuccino. I can feel that scary quality emerging!" Llia rolls her eyes as she heads out.

"Wow, she's hot too. Hey, Rose, you think next time we all could..."

"Okay, it's time for you to get the hell out of my apartment! Lose my number, LITTLE MIKE!" Rose shoves him out the door and slams it in his face. The other tenants across the hall stare at Mike as he performs the walk of shame.

"Shrimp dick, asshole!" Rose mutters to herself as she walks back into her room. Her stern look fades into disappointment as she closes the door.

Traffic whizzes past Llia as she pauses at the edge of the road, preparing to cross. She clamps her partially consumed bagel between her teeth before fastening her heavy coat. As she ambles over the pavement toward the shop situated directly opposite her apartment, she messages Moro to explain her tardiness at work. Inserting her headphones, she launches her preferred music collection. The first track happens to be her mother's beloved tune, "Always a Woman to Me," by Billy Joel.

The melody stirs memories deep within her. Through the morning commotion of the city, it weaves a captivating melodic tapestry. During her trek, she encounters various passersby. Her mind drifts to mornings spent in the kitchen, where her mother's voice would harmonize with the song as they prepared breakfast. The recollection never failed to brighten her expression, despite their past quarrel regarding her chronic tardiness at the shop where she used to work. She understood her mother's predicament—running a business without enough employees and requiring her assistance.

The scent of fresh pastries wafts from Pike's Donuts, the same shop her father brought bear claws home from every Friday morning. Detective Moro had insisted on continuing the tradition after her father's passing, though it wasn't quite the same.

She passed the old precinct building where her father and Moro had spent countless hours poring over case files. The weathered brick facade held memories of bringing them lunch during summer breaks and watching them piece together clues while she did her homework at the corner desk.

Seattle University's familiar columns came into view. Her mother had fought her on the criminal justice major, wanting Llia to take over the family grocery instead. "The store is our legacy," she'd said. But Llia's father had backed her choice, proud to have a daughter following in his footsteps.

Pioneer Square's cobblestones clicked beneath her boots. Her mother's store had stood on this corner for thirty years—Kim's Market, with its red awning and hand-painted window signs. Llia had spent her childhood stocking shelves, working the register, and learning the rhythm of retail from her mother's patient instruction. The building now housed an artisanal coffee shop, but she could still picture the neat rows of produce and her mother's meticulous inventory system.

"You're just like your father," her mother would say, shaking her head at Llia's chronic lateness. "Always chasing the next big case instead of keeping regular hours." But there had been pride mixed with her exasperation: pride in how Llia had graduated at the top of her class, just like her father had at the academy.

The Billy Joel song faded out as she rounded the corner. Her mother had played it during long nights of inventory, singing along while teaching Llia to balance the books. The same song had played at her father's funeral, her mother gripping her hand as they said goodbye to Seattle's finest. A text from Moro lit up her phone.

"Don't worry about being late. Your dad was never on time either."

She smiled, tucking the phone away. Some things never changed, even as the city transformed around her. As the sixth track began to play, Llia arrived at her destination. She halted at the entrance, rooted in place. After pulling out her headphones, her eyes fixed on a memorial notice displayed on the storefront: "In loving memory of Daisy Kim Sato."

Her blank stare turned into a trance as the past weighed upon her, leaving her paralyzed with shame and accountability. The storefront's neon lights blurred into a hazy glow, mirroring the fog that had settled over her thoughts. Each breath felt heavier than the last, her chest tightening with the crushing responsibility of choices made and actions left undone. The evening crowd flowed around her like water around a stone, but she remained fixed, anchored by memories that refused to fade.

"Hey, Llia? Llia Ridley?!" a male voice shouted from afar.

Llia flexed her hand instinctively, her fingers curling and uncurling as if trying to grasp her scattered thoughts. She looked to her left, slow and mechanical, to see two young men approaching through the morning crowd. Their silhouettes cut sharp angles against the neon-painted sidewalk as they wove between distracted pedestrians, their purposeful strides carrying them straight toward her.

"Maddix and Charlie, hi. How are you?" Llia exchanged embraces and polite greetings.

"Llia, it's great to see you again!" Charlie says as he walks into the store, turning to Maddix, "I'm going to get us some coffee. I'll be right back."

Towering above most people, Maddix has entirely average characteristics—pale golden locks and ice-blue irises that inspire neither interest nor aversion. His clean-cut visage and gently sloping chin give him an almost boyish look, concealing his true age. Balanced between lean and sturdy, his build projects an everyday physicality. His bearing and demeanor hint at a keen intellect.

"I will never understand why you walk so far every day, especially since you have a store literally across the street from your apartment. I mean, why stop here? You might as well walk to Pike's Place," Maddix laughs.

"I'm coming to see my secret boyfriend," Llia jokes.

"Ah, so you're a jokester today. Anyway, how's everything? Whenever I drop by the apartment, you and Iris are always working. We hardly ever get to catch up like we used to. I'm left listening to Rose unload all her problems. By the way, I think her issues are worsening."

Llia brushes her dark hair from her eyes and scans his face, taking in his casual stance and the slight crease of concern etched across his forehead.

"True, but that's just how she is. Rose is fine. She's been through a lot, so we typically cut her some slack with her decisions. So, try to be kind."

"Sure, but what's going on with her?" Maddix tilts his head, raising an eyebrow.

"How about we skip to the part where you invite us to the Turn Up party?"

"Wait, what?! How did you know that's why I was coming over?!"

"You literally have a card sticking out of your pocket with the words 'Turn UP' written in bold. When is it?"

A group of muscular guys in tight-fitting shirts emerges from the convenience store, their eyes lingering appreciatively on Llia as they pass. One of them, sporting a neatly trimmed beard and designer sunglasses perched on his head, catches Maddix's attention. They exchange knowing smiles, a silent moment of mutual recognition passing between them in the morning sun.

"It's happening in a few days, and you have to come this time. You've skipped it the past two years, for understandable reasons, but we really missed you. It's just not the same without my best friend and everyone is going to be there. Besides, you need a guy! It's been two years since… well, you know. It's about time!"

"I'm not prepared for a relationship at the moment. Besides, I finished college three years ago and it's been two years for Iris. You have to be an active student to go." Llia moves toward the door, but Maddix positions himself in her path.

"Wait, I'm sorry—I'm sorry about the man thing. Okay, look, Rose is still in college for her Ph.D. in behavior analysis. She can bring Iris as her plus one. This is my last year, so you can be *my* plus one. This is the biggest party on the West Coast and it only comes once a year! Everyone will be there. Let's have some fun for a change. You deserve it—it's all work and no play," Maddix tempts, widening his eyes and pouting.

Llia takes a deep breath. *He's not going to stop until I say yes. I'm not going to stop until you say yes!*

"Well, I guess, yeah, I'll go—on two conditions: no hooking me up, no trying to get me laid. I am fine. I don't need a guy in my life right now!"

"Yes and yes! It's a deal. The party is at V.J. Johnson Hall this year, so I'll pick you guys up in two days," Maddix says as Charlie comes out of the store, handing him a steaming cup of coffee. The rich aroma swirls around them, mingling with the crisp fall air. They exchange a quick wave, their breath visible in the cool morning, and begin to walk away, the sound of their footsteps echoing lightly on the pavement.

"Llia, you didn't mention anything about getting you tipsy. Remember what happened the last time we did that? Alright, see you later!" Maddix shouts as he and Charlie head up the street toward the university.

"Damn," Llia exclaims as she remembers the incident, her cheeks flushing at the embarrassing memory. She walks into the store with an expression somewhere between a smirk and a grimace, the bell above the door chiming softly as warm air rushes out to meet the autumn chill. The scent of fresh coffee and pastries envelops her like a familiar embrace.

CHAPTER THREE
THE TURN UP

The girls are racing from room to room, grabbing clothes, makeup, and brushes from each other to prepare for the TURN UP party.

"Llia, I heard you didn't go out with that cute guy I set you up with yesterday," Rose says, glancing in the mirror to apply her eyeliner.

"We all grew up together, we've lived together for several years now, and you still don't know what type of guys she likes, Rosie? Cute dirtbags, right?" Iris teases, applying her eyeliner.

"Well, who asked you, Dr. Love?!" Rose retorts.

"Oh no, the honor of 'Dr. Love' goes to you. You have more dates than a calendar year," Iris laughs.

"Really, dude?! I can see why *you* don't have a man! Not to mention your parents have to approve of him first, but Llia has no excuses. It's not *my* fault I like to have a little fun and explore my sexuality, unlike *you* two who work yourselves to death every day. We are in our prime, and you act like the Golden Girls!"

"Okay, Blanche, chill out," Iris responds as Rose scoffs, amused.

"Guys, come on, you're always fighting. In fact, I'm struggling to think of a time when the both of you weren't bickering... Oh shit! Remember what's-his-name? Um—Dean!" Llia exclaims.

Rose nods. "Yeah! How could I forget? He asked me to the homecoming dance."

"Only after he asked me!" Iris chimes in.

"That's not the point! That's where the fighting started. Remember what we said after we found out he was a loser? Come on, CP Squad, sound off! 'Sisters forever!'" Llia cheers.

"Yeah-yeah, sisters forever," Iris grumbles.

Rose laughs, "Sisters forever... or until I get mad again."

"I don't even know how I let you guys talk me into going to TURN UP," Iris shakes her head, "I have a ton of paperwork to get through for work, and I'm engaged to be married in about eight months!" The room falls dead silent.

"Wait, WHAT?! Iris, you don't even have a boyfriend!" Rose exclaims, standing.

Llia places her hand on Iris's shoulder. "We knew your parents were traditional, but not *that* traditional!"

"Yeah, you said you can only marry an Indian guy, but you could choose that guy for yourself. Although last I checked, you shot down all the local ones."

Iris shakes her head. "If only it were that simple. Remember that lunch I had with my dad the other day? He said I have until

December to find an Indian husband my parents will approve of. He has to be from the right caste as well. If I can't find a husband by then, my father will arrange for me to marry his best friend's son."

"Oh, Iris, I am so sorry. Marrying a man you don't even know or love—I can't even imagine…" Llia says as she hugs her.

"Is he handsome? Or at least rich?" Rose asks. Iris and Llia both shoot her a look.

"Well, my mother said he is very handsome and rich. I think his family is worth a hundred million dollars, but most importantly, he comes from a respectable caste. Our parents are already discussing a potential arrangement. As if I needed any more pressure right now! I barely got out of medical school without pulling my hair out. My dad paid for everything: medical school, our apartment renovations, and the down payment. If I refuse to marry this guy, they'll disown me, and he wants all his money back!"

"So, we raise the damn money and pay him back ourselves. You don't have to marry a complete stranger for their sake!" Rose offers.

"It's three million dollars!" Iris says, lowering her head.

Llia looks at Iris in the mirror and leans toward her. "Oh yeah, you have to marry him. Remember the part about us working to death? That's not in the cards for me." Llia places her hand over Rose's mouth. "Maybe he's kind and honest. Just know that we will be there to kick his ass and rescue you if he isn't!"

Llia places her hand on Iris' shoulder. She does her best to fight back the tears, but her eyes betray her emotions.

"So, does this mean we aren't watching *Married at First Sight* anymore?" Rose asks as she and Llia hug Iris, laughing.

"Oh Rosie, you are such a weirdo. I keep thinking that love isn't something you find, but something that finds you, something that makes you the best version of yourself. Money and looks have nothing to do with it. How can I hope to have that when I didn't even get a choice? He may not even like me! Or maybe he is in love with another woman right now and is being forced to leave her for me!" Iris cries.

"Iris... you are drop-dead gorgeous, you're smart, and you are the strongest person I know!"

"Hey!" Rose scoffs.

Llia amends, "Okay, you are the *second* strongest person I know! Every time we go out, at least five guys ask you out."

Iris smiles and wipes her eyes. "Yeah, but that's only if Rosie isn't around," she jokes.

"That's because I am the prettiest Rose you've ever seen!"

"We know!" Iris and Llia reply in unison.

"Listen, Iris, I know this is a lot and that your parents' approval means a great deal to you..."

"Rosie, it means *everything* to me. In my culture, you don't defy or disrespect your parents. This is how we do things in India. Unlike Llia and me, you wouldn't know how it feels to be stretched by your family and two different cultures."

"You know what? I don't. That's fair. I also know nothing about having a family that loves you, either. But in life, you should be happy. If honoring your parents' wishes makes you happy, then do it. But just remember one thing: we are not in India!" Rose exclaims as she storms out of the room.

"Rosie! I didn't mean it like that!" Iris calls out.

"It's okay. She knows you didn't mean it." Rosie's mom and dad abandoned her when she was six years old, so family is a very sensitive subject for her. "Just let her cool off, she'll be fine. As you said, it's difficult for us because we are trying to please both our cultures without being swallowed alive by one of them," Llia says. Being half Japanese and half African American, she understood the internal struggle Iris was feeling.

"Tradition and your family's expectations can be over-whelming, but what's the point if you're not happy with who you are? I mean, no offense Llia, but you could pass as African American if you wanted. There's no other option for me. I'm unable to break free from traditions. There is only one real choice for me, and I am terrified of it, but I can't run from it either!"

"Are you kidding me? Do you know how often I get asked, 'What are you?' like I'm some sort of object? In Japan, the term is *Hafu*; it means mixed race. The first time I heard it, they said it in a derogatory way. That pisses me off! I think you should just talk to your parents and be open with them."

"Oh, really?! And when was the last time you spoke with your grandparents in Japan after your dad died?" Iris asks as Llia looks in the mirror and then checks her watch.

"I only want the best for you both, that's all. It's time to go. We're going to be late for the party," Llia says as she leaves the room.

Dammit, Iris, you're two for two. I'm so sorry, Llia; I didn't mean to bring up your father. What am I going to do? Iris gazes into the mirror and lowers her eyes. She exhales deeply and leaves the room. They all converge in the living room and stew in the awkward silence.

Where in the world is Maddy? I need a drink right now, Rose thinks. "Hey, has anyone been able to get in touch with Maddy? He isn't responding to any of my messages?"

"Yeah, and he's late picking us up," Iris adds.

"No, I haven't talked to him since a few days ago at the store. He said he would be here to pick us up, but I called us an Uber. Something important may have come up, or he forgot about us again," Llia says.

"He's getting hot and heavy with Charlie, more likely; he might have said, 'Screw those wenches!'," Rose laughs.

Iris chuckles, but Llia smiles halfheartedly and shakes her head. *This is not like Maddix. He is the most punctual person I know. Something isn't right.*

"I am glad he has Charlie, though. For the past six months, to borrow Iris's line, he has been the best version of himself. I imagine love is like being cold your entire life—not because you lack emotions, but because the world can be a chilly place. Then, you meet someone who shares your coldness and fear. Together, you ignite a roaring fire inside each other, like finding warmth in a snowstorm. One day, I hope to find someone who can melt the ice away..." Rose says as she folds her arms and sinks into the couch cushion.

They all stare at Rose as she gazes at the floor.

"I really need to get around to cleaning the floors!" Rose jokes, suddenly embarrassed by her rambling.

"Please!" Llia laughs.

"Well, I know we love you! No matter what. You'll find someone who loves you. They'll be so hot that you'll both sizzle every time you kiss! Hell, I hope we all do!" says Iris.

Their laughter fills the room as Llia checks her buzzing phone. "We can't wait for Maddix any longer. The Uber is here. Ladies, let's go."

The girls head down to the street, load into the Uber, and take off. They arrive at Seattle State University within thirty minutes, despite the traffic. They walk to the heart of the enormous campus toward V. J. Johnson Hall.

Parked cars fill every inch of the endless curbs for miles, and loud music booms around them. They reach the hall's steps, where a throng of people gathers just to get inside. The girls make their way to the front of the line, passing all the freshmen and sophomores. They turn every head in the line, earning eye rolls from most of the girls. They approach a huge double door lined with ten large guys wearing football jerseys.

"You're not on the list, so you can't get in! Better luck next year. Have a nice evening. NEXT!" the doorman says. Two big guys pick up a stunned freshman and throw him out of the line.

"Aww, shit! If it isn't Rose Aday, Llia Ridley, and Iris Khatri. The CP Squad in the flesh. What can I do for you lovely ladies?" asks the doorman, staring at Rose like she was his last meal on earth.

"Jim, how are you?" Rose replies.

"I would be great if I could get that number," Jim says, the corners of his mouth curling upwards as his fellow doormen in the back egg him on.

"Well, I'm sure your girlfriend Stacy wouldn't like that very much!" Rose responds.

"Yeah, she wouldn't, but what if she doesn't know, right?"

Rose glares at him and bites her bottom lip. "Jim! Here's what I'm going to do. I'm not going to give you my number. I'm going to walk into this party with my sisters. I'm going to try very hard not to remember that you slept with Stacy's roommate last weekend behind her back!"

Jim is the only one who hears her because of the loud music. His eyes widen. "Oh shit! Okay, I'm sorry. Here, take this V.I.P. bracelet. Please, I am so sorry. You guys can go in and have a great time."

Rose snatches the bracelet out of his hand and throws up her arm as they enter. The girls walk down a huge hallway leading to the main floor of the enormous building. They witness an ocean of people dancing to a live band, immersed in colorful strobe lights. To the left, a long bar is lined with people and drinks. On the right, on the second floor, is the V.I.P. room filled with bouncers wearing black shirts and showcasing huge, rippling muscles. The music is blasting so loud that the girls have to huddle close to talk.

"What did you say to Jim to get us in? He lets no one in without checking that list!" Iris asks.

"Something his girlfriend Stacy already knows. She's going to dump him tomorrow. Okay, girls, I want to play a game! We'll meet at the bar with our new boy toys in one hour. Whoever pulls the most handsome guy here doesn't have to do chores for a month," Rose declares, holding up her pinky and smiling.

"Uh, you owe us a month's worth of chores right now!" Llia reminds her.

"Fine, two months if I lose, and I'm square if I win," Rose replies.

"Oh, what the hell! I'm getting married soon. I might as well live it up!" Iris exclaims, joining pinkies with Rose. They both look at Llia, who is reluctant to take part.

"Come on, Llia, you used to love this game. You don't have to sleep with the guy. It'll be fun," Rose urges, batting her eyes. Llia finally links her pinky with theirs and exhales sharply. They all smile and go their separate ways.

Iris heads for the dance floor while Rose walks straight into the V.I.P. room. The person behind her gets stopped and turned away. Llia goes to the bar and sits where she can see a clear path to both the dance floor and the V.I.P. room.

"Give me a Kamikaze shot, please, and keep them coming," Llia requests. The bartender mixes and serves the drink. She spots Iris dancing with a cute guy on the floor and pulls out her phone to text Maddix, asking for his location.

"Hey, Llia," calls a familiar voice. She turns and sees Charlie.

"Charlie! Hi... How are you?"

"Not so great."

She looks around, but Maddix is nowhere to be found. "Where is Maddix? He didn't come to pick us up."

"I don't know. He hasn't returned any of my calls. He was supposed to meet me for lunch today but never showed."

Something is wrong. "When was the last time you saw him?" Llia presses, texting Moro with all the information about Maddix.

"He met up with a few friends yesterday to go to that new restaurant near the campus. I think it's called Ma's. He came home late and then he was acting strange this morning. I came here hoping to run into him."

"That's a good idea. I texted Detective Moro what you told me. I'll send a message to the girls and a few friends. We'll all help you look for him."

"Thank you, Llia. You are a great friend."

"I won't be when I get my hands on Maddix for making us worry!"

"I'm going to go to the other side of the room and look there."

"Okay, Charlie, I'll stay here and look. Rose is checking the V.I.P. room, and Iris is scanning the dance floor."

"Brilliant! I'm heading over there. Keep me posted, and thanks again."

"Okay," Llia replies.

Charlie disappears into the crowd. Llia takes a sip of her drink and then knocks on the bar for another shot. The bartender serves her a second one. She scans the room again and spots Rose upstairs with Shane West, the most attractive guy in the entire college. As they laugh and enjoy champagne, she sees Rose hanging onto him. Llia slams her second shot and knocks again.

Two hours pass and a stranger sits not too far away. He locks eyes with her. She struggles to make out the figure through the strobe lights.

"Is that Maddix?!"

She places her hand over her stomach and grimaces as a sharp pain arises. She looks toward the dark figure, whose eyes glow a dim magenta. Rubbing her eyes, she realizes the man has disappeared. Pushing her drink aside, she decides she's done for the night. Someone takes a seat beside her and orders a Captain Coke. Casting a quick glance from the corner of her eye, she scans the individual. It's clear he has put effort into his appearance; his well-maintained physique and neatly pulled-back ponytail showcase his long hair.

Oh, what the hell? Might as well have some fun...

"Hi, I'm Llia."

The man turns his head and shakes Llia's hand. In the dim light, she gets a better look at him and brushes her hair back, smiling.

"Hello, I'm Reo. Nice to meet you."

Holy shit! He makes Shane West look like a third-rate model.

She stares at him, momentarily forgetting that it's her turn to respond. "I've never seen you before, and I thought I knew just about everyone here. Are you a professor?"

He leans close to Llia's ear, and she inhales the scent of his cologne, feeling weak in the knees.

"Apologies for leaning so close, but I've been reading your lips until now. This music is so loud, and it's hard to hear. Wait... you are half-Japanese! *Do you speak Japanese?*"

"Yes, and I'm very impressed that you could tell. Most people can't."

"How could they not? You're so beautiful, it's obvious. I always say that people born of two cultures have the best of both worlds. You are extraordinary."

Llia's enormous smile catches Rose's eye, and she stares in disbelief. She grabs Shane and heads toward Iris.

"You're from Japan, huh? Have you ever been to America before? Your English is great. Okay, spill: what's wrong with you? Are you married? A serial killer? Or are you waiting for someone else?" Llia laughs.

"Wow!" Reo laughs and takes a sip of his drink.

"Sorry. It's been a while since I've flirted. I'm afraid that's not my strong suit."

"Oh, I think you're doing very well, and you're right on all counts, by the way. I hunt monsters in my spare time as well." Reo laughs again.

Cute and a great sense of humor? "Would you like to continue this conversation somewhere a little quieter?" Llia asks.

"Yes, I would love to."

They stand, and Llia turns to grab her purse.

"Where do you think you're going? Oh my God! Hi, I'm Rose, and she's Iris," Rose stammers.

"Everyone, this is Reo. Reo, this is everyone. Okay, goodbye, you guys!"

"Wait, just hold on a minute. We don't know him," says Rose.

"Rose, we're leaving!" Llia winks several times.

"You should have that looked at; it may be serious," Rose says, ignoring the signal.

"MEETING NOW!" Iris yells as she heads toward the bathroom.

Llia turns to Reo, "Please wait right here. Don't disappear."

"I'm not going anywhere. I'll see you when you come back."

The girls make their way to the bathroom, leaving their dates to stand by the bar. Shane looks at Reo and gives him a huge smile. Reo averts his eyes.

The girls find themselves crammed into an empty stall in the crowded bathroom.

"Guys, what the hell! One minute, you want me to get laid, and now, you don't?" Llia looks between Rose and Iris.

"Wait, who said anything about you getting laid?" Iris frowns.

"Can you repeat the question?"

"Both of you shut it. Who is he? Most of the time, when someone looks that great, they're into guys," Rose states.

"Oh, spare us your psychological bullshit, Rosie. You're just mad because someone other than you got the hottest guy in the room!"

"Oh, Llia won the bet by a mile, but you're wrong, Iris; I am happy for her. I'm just concerned, that's all. I want you to have a SAFE and magical night. I love you guys. You're all I've got," Rose tells them honestly, opening her arms.

The three girls come together in a tight embrace, their arms intertwined like vines around each other's shoulders. The warmth of their bond fills the space between them, a familiar comfort that has seen them through countless joyous and trying moments. In this dimly lit room, their sisterly affection creates a small fortress against the world outside, if only for a fleeting moment.

Someone walks through the door with heavy footsteps that echo against the tile, and all of the other girls in the bathroom bolt in a panic, their high-pitched screams piercing the air like shattered glass. Their heels click frantically against the floor as they scramble over each other in their desperate rush to escape, leaving behind a cloud of perfume and the lingering sound of their terrified voices bouncing off the walls.

The trio huddle together in the furthest stall, clutching each other in fear. The deafening rush of fleeing people had emptied the corridor of melodies and voices. Only the echoing taps of multiple sets of feet drawing near the bathroom stall break the silence.

"You guys stay in here no matter what!" Llia instructs. She walks out of the stall with calculated steps, her shoulders squared, jaw set with determination despite the tremor of fear coursing through her body. The fluorescent lights above flicker ominously, casting shifting shadows across the bathroom's cream-colored tiles as if nature itself senses the approaching danger.

"Be safe!" Iris says.

"Try not to kill them!" Rose adds.

Llia sees three burly guys, their letterman jackets marking them as members of the college football team. Two of them appear sickly pale, their faces glistening with an unnatural sheen of sweat despite the cool air. The third has taken on an ashen gray tone. Something is terribly wrong with them. Their eyes seem vacant and unfocused, and their breathing comes in ragged, shallow gasps that echo off the bathroom walls. Without uttering a single word, they shuffle toward Llia with unsettling synchronization, their movements jerky and unnatural, like puppets being pulled by invisible strings.

It's been two years since I engaged in full contact. But this shouldn't be an issue. I won't hold back.

"This is the girls' restroom. You have one chance to leave! And if there's not a hot guy out there waiting for me, I'm going to be furious!" Llia proclaims, assuming a combat position.

The first assailant charges forward with a lurching gait, arms outstretched like a mindless zombie. Llia pivots smoothly, years of training taking over as she executes a perfect hip throw that sends him crashing to the tile floor with a sickening thud. The second attacker moves with unexpected speed, his movements more fluid and predatory than those of his companion. She barely has time to adjust her stance before he's on her, but her muscle memory doesn't fail— a lightning-quick sweep of her leg followed by a palm strike to his sternum drops him hard. The victory is short-lived, though; movement catches her peripheral vision—the first guy is already pushing himself up from the floor, his movements jerky but determined, showing none of the pain or hesitation a normal person would after such a fall.

What the hell? Are these guys on drugs? I know I knocked them out!

She settles into a defensive stance as the last attacker circles her, his movements more fluid and purposeful than those of his companions. There's an unsettling intelligence in his eyes that the others lack. When she launches a probing strike, his counter comes with frightening speed and power, nearly catching her off guard. They exchange a flurry of strikes and blocks, each testing the other's defenses, but neither gaining the upper hand.

Her momentary focus on this more skilled opponent proves costly. The other two assailants, having recovered with unnatural quickness, converge on her from both sides. Their movements are mechanical yet devastatingly effective. A crushing blow catches her ribs, another clips her jaw, and before she can recover, iron-strong fingers dig into her shoulder. The world spins as one of them hurls her across the room like a ragdoll. The bathroom mirror explodes in a shower of crystalline shards as her body crashes through it.

She crumples to the tile floor, gasping as waves of pain radiate through her body. The sharp smell of copper fills her nostrils as something warm trickles down her back. When she manages to reach behind herself, her fingertips come away slick with blood, glistening crimson under the harsh fluorescent lights.

Shit, they are fighting in unison to make it impossible to defend from all angles. I can't risk them taking me out and getting to the girls. I hate to resort to this, but I have no choice.

With a determined expression, she rises with fluid grace, directing her unwavering eyes toward the assailants as they bolt toward her like rabid wolves. Her muscles coil with practiced precision as the first attacker reaches her. The force of her hip toss is so strong that it sends him hurtling through the air like a sack of potatoes, his body crashing through a bathroom stall with a thunderous crack as the door splinters into countless pieces. Without missing a beat, her well-timed side kick connects with devastating precision, sending the second assailant careening backward into one of the pristine bathroom sinks.

The porcelain fixture explodes upon impact, spraying fragments across the floor as water begins gushing from the broken pipes. In a split second, she instinctually blocks the last attacker's wild strike, her forearm deflecting his blow before she retaliates with a devastating spinning back fist. The impact resonates through the room as he hurtles into the wall with bone-crushing force, causing the ceramic tiles to crack and shatter, cascading down to pile on his motionless body like a broken mosaic.

"That's right, Llia, kick their asses! She is really moving," Iris whispers, watching through the gap in the stall door. *But she can't keep that up for long. She's going to have to really hurt them, and I know that's the last thing she wants to do.*

"I am so glad I talked her out of wearing that skirt," Rose whispers. Iris turns and gives Rose a blank stare, her brown eyes narrowing. A muscle twitches in her jaw, but she remains focused on monitoring the brutal confrontation unfolding before them.

They keep getting up! It's now or never. I'm just about at my limit, Llia thinks.

The trio staggers to their feet. Despite their wounds and bruises, they advance menacingly toward her, leaving no doubt about their intentions. She immediately dashes at the closest attacker and disables him with a precise, crushing strike that shatters his jawbone. In one fluid movement, she unleashes a devastating kick to the second assailant's side, rendering him unconscious. The final opponent creeps up from behind, but she whirls around with a fierce spinning kick that sends him crashing to the floor, his head bouncing violently as he is knocked out cold.

Having dispatched the last attacker, Llia bows her head and wipes sweat from her brow. She inhales slowly, then limps toward the restroom doorway. Peeking through the entrance, she spots several individuals engaged in a brawl.

Is that Reo?

Her head snaps back toward the girls huddled in the bathroom stalls, their frightened whimpers echoing off the cold tile walls. The fluorescent lights above flicker ominously.

"Girls, I think I hear the police coming. Stay here. I'm going to take a look."

Llia begins to exit the bathroom when a brutal strike launches her against the rear tiles. She crumples to the ground, momentarily paralyzed. Through hazy eyes, she glimpses a female figure approaching, but another person drags the attacker away. Her consciousness fades as she hears Rose and Iris calling out above her.

CHAPTER FOUR
MOONLIGHT

The steady beeping of monitors awakens Llia in a sterile white hospital room, providing an unwelcome rhythm to her consciousness. Rose and Iris are slumped in uncomfortable plastic chairs by her bedside, their soft breathing the only other sound in the room. Empty coffee cups and snack wrappers scattered around them hint at their vigilant watch. She scans the room, her heart sinking when she doesn't spot Maddix's familiar figure among the medical equipment and generic artwork on the walls.

She tries to move, but the tenderness in her back sends sharp waves of protest through her body, forcing her to remain still against the crisp hospital sheets. "What the hell? What happened?" she asks as she struggles to sit up.

Iris, wearing her white lab coat, raises her head and sees that Llia is awake. She taps Rose on the shoulder. "Thank heavens! You were unconscious for two days. You sustained minor contusions and no internal bleeding. Most of your bruises have already healed, which is unusual. Considering the state of that bathroom, it's a wonder that's all you have. How are you feeling?" Iris inquires, measuring her blood pressure before shining a small light into her eyes.

"I'm kind of foggy. I remember fighting those guys, but after that, nothing. Shit! And my ass really hurts."

"Well, that's what happens when you fall asleep in a public bathroom!" Rose replies.

"Wait, what?!" Llia frowns, confused.

"That's not funny, Rosie! Now is not the time. How about you get Llia something to eat and drink from the cafeteria? While you're at it, let Moro know she's awake!" Iris instructs.

"Okay, I'm sorry. You know that's how I process stuff like this. I'm not good at touchy-feely things when they're directed at me. Some psychiatrist I am, right? But thanks for saving our asses again. I'll be right back with some food." Rose wraps her arms around Llia and squeezes her. Llia feels a droplet land on the back of her neck.

"I am so glad you're okay. I was so afraid that I would lose you too," Rose whispers.

"As if I'd miss out on collecting my winnings from our bet," Llia jests.

Rose smiles and leaves the room.

Oh, Rose, Llia thinks.

"Here's what happened at the party." Iris fills her in, "A group of very disturbed guys attacked the event. They killed a lot of people. We could have been among them if it weren't for you."

"How many people died?"

"About thirty. Some were trampled to death as everyone was trying to get out."

Llia's eyes grow wide, and the beeps from her machine hasten. "Where the fuck is Maddix?!"

"Calm down. He's fine. He said he couldn't get off work for the party. He stopped by for a short while yesterday,. I'm afraid he's currently dealing with some personal issues."

"I had a feeling! Let me guess, he had a fight with Charlie? Is that why he didn't answer his calls?"

Iris's soft eyes meet hers as she grabs her hand. "Llia, Charlie's dead. They killed him at the party."

"No! Not Charlie," Llia exclaims, her lips quivering with the weight of emerging tears. They spill down her cheeks, glistening like jewels in the dim light of the room. With a heavy heart, she lays back down, surrendering to the sorrow that envelops her. Her gaze fixates on the ceiling, where shadows dance, reflecting the turmoil within her soul. Time stretches as they both remain lost in their grief, mourning the loss of Charlie—a friend taken too soon, their quiet sobs filling the empty space around them.

"We all loved Charlie; he was a fantastic person. Right now, I need you to relax and rest. The good news is that you didn't break a single bone. You'll be good as new in a few days. By the way, you were amazing in the bathroom."

"Thanks." Llia wipes her eyes as a man in a dark trench coat enters the room.

"I'll come back later to check on you. Rest up, doctor's orders," Iris says, jotting notes on her chart before leaving.

"You couldn't take one day off without getting into trouble, could you?" the man says as he sits next to the bed.

"Good to see you too, Detective. Did you find anything?"

Moro was a Japanese man in his middle years, with streaks of silver threading through his dark hair at the temples. An air of wisdom surrounded him, earned through decades of detective work on Seattle's most challenging cases. He was of average height, carrying himself with the measured grace of someone accustomed to observing everything around him. His slender physique was accentuated by the way his trench coat hung from his shoulders, a garment that had seen just as many late nights and crime scenes as its owner. His sharp, analytical eyes missed nothing, a trait that had served him well throughout his law enforcement career.

"Llia, how many times do I have to remind you to address me as Moro? I practically raised you."

"Sorry, the painkillers are kicking in. Tell me you got something."

"No, we found nothing. It's like they vanished as quickly as they came. Surveillance cameras showed everything up to the point when the fighting started, and then nothing. They must have had someone on the inside cut the feed, and there's no trace of the perpetrators."

"That makes no sense. I knocked out three guys in the bathroom!"

"When we got there, we found you laid out on the floor with the girls huddled around you."

"Did you ask them what happened?"

"Kid, you forget I'm the teacher and you're the student. The girls maintain the attackers got up and ran away. I know you, so let me stop you right now: don't interfere with this case. Let me work it out. Did you see anyone or anything out of the ordinary? Like someone you've never met before?"

"No." Llia shifts her eyes.

"Now remember, just because your dad was like a brother to me and I'm the one who taught you reasoning, deduction, and observation, doesn't mean you can get away with lying to me! Though you are very talented, I am still the lead detective, and you are a case filer for the police department. I already know about Mr. Reo," Moro says, pulling out his worn orange notebook.

Dammit, Rose! Llia thinks.

"He was just some guy I met at the bar. I didn't see him do anything or say anything out of the ordinary."

"Just as well. He's a person of interest. I will find him, so if you see him..."

"Yeah, yeah, I will call you. Why do you always write in that old notebook? What happened to the one I bought you for Christmas last year?"

"Oh, I still use it. They both have sentimental value. I've been using this one for years. Let's just say I put special evidence in this one. But, as good as you are at changing the subject, just remember that I am immune to those tricks. Now, get some rest, kid. We will talk more another time." Moro rises and places his notebook in his jacket pocket.

He leans over Llia and kisses her on the top of her head before he turns and walks towards the door. "I am so glad you're okay, kid. I will catch everyone responsible for this, and they will pay!"

"Wait! I have to go to work tomorrow. I haven't missed a single day since I started and..."

"I've already spoken to the captain, and you can take a leave of absence. His words were, 'Take as long as you need, and your job will be here when you get back. You could use a break from looking for clues in those cold cases for a while.'" Moro stops before he heads out. "I'll be seeing you tomorrow, kid."

Llia rolls over and stares out the window. She looks at the crescent moon, surrounded by a sea of shimmering sparkles, and allows her thoughts to digest everything she's learned as she gazes at the night sky.

Several hours later, the hospital settles into that peculiar twilight state between shifts, when the bustling daytime activity gives way to the quiet, methodical pace of the night staff. The fluorescent lights hum softly overhead, casting long shadows down the sterile corridors. Llia's room is directly across the hall from another patient's quarters, its door adorned with a stern

"Do Not Disturb" sign that has begun to curl at the edges from constant exposure to the building's artificial climate.

In the dimly lit room, a young woman about Llia's age slowly sits up, her hospital gown crinkling with each careful movement. Her eyes, still heavy with medication, gradually adjust to the soft ambiance created by the faint glow of monitoring equipment. Her hand darts forward, fingers splayed and uncertain, trying to grasp the elusive doorknob that seems to float in the semi-darkness. When she finally finds it, the cool metal against her palm feels reassuring. The door creaks open with a sound that seems thunderous in the night's silence, revealing a vaguely lit room beyond.

The bathroom features all the usual fixtures: a shower encased in institutional beige tile, a standard medical-grade tub with safety rails, and a porcelain sink that gleams dully in the darkness. The overpowering scent of cleaning products fills the bathroom—a distinct mixture of bleach and industrial disinfectant unique to medical facilities, sharp enough to make her nostrils flare in protest.

The young woman shuffles into the bathroom and gingerly lifts her thin hospital gown, the flimsy fabric offering little protection against the chill air. She eases down onto the cold toilet seat with a sharp intake of breath, the porcelain stealing what little warmth remains in her body as she relieves her bladder. A long, weary exhale escapes her lips, her shoulders slumping with exhaustion. With heavy eyes and chattering teeth that echo softly in the sterile space, she misses the telltale warning of the lights flickering above—once, twice, three times in rapid succession. She rubs her goosebump-covered arms vigorously and shivers, the motion doing little to ward off the bone-deep cold that seems to intensify with each passing moment.

"Would you like a red sheet or a blue sheet?" a croaky voice asks, echoing off the bathroom tiles with an unnatural resonance that makes the hairs on the back of her neck stand up. The sound seems to come from everywhere and nowhere at once as if carried on the waves of the intensifying cold.

Her heavy eyes pop open, and her chest pounds with such force that she can hear each thunderous heartbeat echoing in her ears. Cold sweat trickles down her temples as adrenaline floods her system, every muscle tensing in primal response to the otherworldly presence lurking in the shadows.

"Who—who's there?" the young woman asks, thinking it might be a nurse bringing in fresh sheets or something.

"Would you like a red sheet or a blue sheet?" The unnerving, ethereal voice slithers through the air, now mere inches from the bathroom door.

"Do you have a white sheet instead, sir?" The flickering bulbs stabilize into a constant illumination. Quietness blankets her surroundings as she hears the lock on her room door engage from where she sits in the bathroom.

An icy tremor courses along her spine, making her breathing ragged and shallow. "Show yourself!" she calls out, frantically scanning for the intruder. Without warning, darkness engulfs the bathroom, and a powerful bang against the door makes her tremble.

With every beat, her heart somersaults within her chest, threatening to burst through her ribcage. Despite her best efforts to cry out, her voice betrays her—the scream for help dies in her throat like a whispered prayer. A frigidness creeps through her veins like liquid nitrogen, making her limbs feel numb and foreign. The bathroom door creaks open with agonizing slowness, the sound of squeaking hinges piercing the silence like rusted daggers.

The temperature rises to an oppressive level, and the room is bathed in a flickering light that seems to pulse with malevolent life, casting dancing shadows that writhe and twist on the walls like tortured spirits. In the entrance stands a creature that defies natural law—its crimson eyes, like burning coals in the darkness, shine with ancient malice despite its small stature. It has large, twisted goat horns protruding from its head, their surface marked with arcane symbols that shift in the unstable light. Its badly burned body bears the evidence of some hellish torment, skin blackened and cracked like ancient leather.

The huge inferno behind it intensifies the eerie scene, casting an apocalyptic glow that bathes everything in hellish orange and crimson. Its smile, a grotesque mockery of mirth, reveals rows of decaying teeth stained with age and corruption, some barely clinging to blackened gums. It limps toward her with unnatural purpose, dragging one twisted leg across the floor with a wet scraping sound. She can see the predatory determination burning in its eyes as she gradually thaws from the paralyzing grip of fear. In a desperate panic, she jumps into the tub, her piercing screams reverberating throughout the bathroom, bouncing off the cold tile walls like a trapped animal's final cry.

As it approaches her, an overwhelming stench of rotting flesh and sulfur burns her nostrils and churns her stomach, forcing her to vomit violently into the porcelain tub again and again until only bitter bile remains. The creature's gnarled fingers—impossibly strong and cold as death—clamp around her ankles like iron manacles, dragging her inexorably toward the hellish inferno that has manifested in her doorway. Despite her desperate attempts to claw at the smooth tub walls, kicking frantically against its iron grip, and her throat-shredding screams echoing off the bathroom tiles, the creature's otherworldly strength remains overwhelming.

Her body convulses and blackens in the supernatural flames, skin blistering and peeling away as the heat consumes her. The bathroom door slams shut behind them with a thunderous finality that shakes the walls, abruptly silencing her agonized screams and leaving only the crackle of ethereal fire. As the lights flicker back to life with an artificial buzz, her room door creaks open with excruciating slowness, revealing only the smell of death and darkness beyond.

That morning, Llia awakens with a start, her dark hair tangled from a restless night. Clumsily, she makes her way to the bathroom, still half-asleep, her bare feet padding against the cold tile floor. She reaches for the brass doorknob and turns it, the sound of the latch clicking as she opens the door echoing in the quiet morning air. Stepping into the frigid room, she feels the icy air nip at her exposed skin, sending a shiver down her spine. The unexpected noise from the hall catches her attention—hushed voices and the scratching of pen on paper. As she approaches the front door, wrapping her arms around herself for warmth, she cautiously peeks into the hallway and sees Detective Moro taking a nurse's statement, his face stern and professional as he jots notes in his worn orange notebook.

"There are eight individuals unaccounted for. All the bathroom doors were locked internally, but there was no one inside?" Moro asks.

"Yes, and another nurse mentioned that every room had vomit in its bathroom," the lead nurse replies as Moro drops his pen with a soft clatter against his notepad, his weathered fingers tensing at the implications of synchronized bathroom incidents across multiple rooms. A shadow of concern crosses his typically stoic features.

"Tell me, were the victims all female?" Moro picks up his pen, his calloused fingers wrapping around the barrel with practiced ease. He braces himself for what he suspects will be a disturbing answer.

"Yes, yes, they were, ranging from ages twenty-five to thirty."

He looks toward Llia's room just as she quickly pops her head back in, her dark hair swishing against the doorframe like a curtain caught in a sudden breeze. The movement, though brief, carries an unmistakable urgency that makes Moro's detective instincts prickle with unease.

Eight girls are missing on my floor, all around my age! Someone was looking for me... Shit! I've got to get out of here.

Llia darts to her closet with frantic energy, yanking open the door and grabbing her worn duffel bag from the floor. Her trembling hands seize whatever clothes are within reach, stuffing them haphazardly inside while her mind races with escape routes. A sharp rap at the door makes her jump, and before she can respond, Detective Moro enters, his eyes deliberately fixed on the floor, his professional courtesy at odds with the urgency of his intrusion.

"Listen, kid, we have to talk. This might sound a bit odd, but are you familiar with what a Yokai is?"

"Yeah, my grandfather shared stories about them when I was a child, and they terrified me. What about them?"

"I know you've heard the buzz about what's going on here. The clues point to the work of a Yokai called Manto. He preys on women while they are in the bathroom. He poses a question involving two colors: red and blue. Choose red, and he will slice the skin off your back and force you to wear it like a cloak. Select blue, and he will strangle you violently, leaving you blue from suffocation. If you choose any other color, he will drag you to hell alive. But you already knew that, didn't you?"

Llia stands frozen by the closet, her fingers trembling against the wooden door frame, unable to move as the reality of the situation sinks in. Detective Moro approaches her with measured steps, his weathered face etched with concern as he places his steady hands on her shoulders to ground her. "Calm down, kid. Everything will be alright."

"You're starting to sound unhinged. I think you've been working too many hours, Moro!"

"I wish that were true, but they exist. I encountered them often when I was a cop in Japan, though they were usually the good ones in disguise. But there are also evil ones who consume people or thrive on their suffering. I've always worried they'd come to the States, and now they have. I need to make a call. There was a questionable incident at your party. Be careful and contact me immediately if you see Reo. Trust me on this, and I promise to come by tomorrow to explain everything in detail. Also, while I was downstairs, Maddix asked me if he could drive you home. I have some matters to finish here first. We can talk more later, and remember to take it easy." Moro states as he exits the room.

Llia closes the door to her room with trembling hands and leans heavily against the solid wood. As she struggles to catch her breath, her chest heaving with each ragged inhale, her mind races through Moro's cryptic warnings. The dim light filtering through the window casts short shadows across the floor, making every corner of the room seem more ominous than before.

Her fingers press against the cool surface of the door, seeking stability as Moro's words settle over her like a heavy shroud.

Okay, there has to be an explanation for all of this. Reo! All of this started happening when I met him. I've got to find him, but first, I need to get the hell out of here.

She makes her way to the bathroom, her hand on the door-knob, then slams the door shut.

"Fuck that. I think I've had enough bathroom encounters for one lifetime. I'll wait till I get home to take a shower." Slowly, she pulls on her clothes as the muscles in her neck and spine continue to throb with pain.

Once she's all packed up and ready to go, she heads to the elevator and hits the call button. Her gaze sweeps the corridor as the doors slide apart, revealing Maddix standing there with a bouquet. She darts forward to embrace him, clutching him desperately. Then she pulls away and playfully smacks his shoulder while the elevator seals shut and carries them downward.

"You beg me to come to that damn party, and you don't even show up? Not even a phone call! We were worried sick about you. I thought the worst when I found out about Char—oh, Maddix, I am so sorry about Charlie. He was such a great guy," Llia takes the flowers from his hand, admiring the vibrant mix of white lilies and pink roses. Tears roll down their faces unbidden, grief and relief mingling, and they hug each other again with the bouquet pressed between them, petals crushed against their trembling bodies. The elevator continues its descent, the soft hum of machinery a stark contrast to their raw emotions.

I'm just so glad you're okay. He must be in shock about Charlie. He's barely hugging me back or saying a word. We're here for you, Maddix.

"I was tied up at the office and couldn't get away. I'm really sorry, Camellia."

Camellia?! Llia tries to hide the shock that must be on her face. He has never called me by my full name before. In fact, no one has since Mom died two years ago...

Something is definitely wrong with him; he seems different, and his hug moments ago was almost nonexistent. Llia figures he must feel terrible about Charlie and the others at the party. "I won't give you a hard time over it. I'm just genuinely relieved you're alright. I'm sorry about Charlie."

"I'm fine, really. Now let me get you home," Maddix says, his voice trailing off as they step out of the elevator and into the bustling lobby. The scent of antiseptic and the hum of conversations fill the air around them. They navigate the maze of hallways, passing by nurses and patients, before finally reaching the cool, dimly lit parking garage. The echoes of their footsteps bounce off the concrete walls as they head toward Maddix's car and make their way to her apartment.

The streetlights cast intermittent shadows across Maddix's face as he drives. Llia clutches the flowers in her lap, her mind racing through Detective Moro's warnings about the Yokai. The silence in the car feels heavy and unnatural compared to their usual easy banter.

Manto targets women in bathrooms. Eight are missing, all my age. And now Maddix is acting strange… Her fingers trace the petals of a lily, remembering how Moro's face had tightened when he mentioned Reo.

She glances at Maddix's hands on the steering wheel—too rigid, too precise. In five years of friendship, he'd never called her Camellia. It felt wrong to hear it come from his lips, as if he'd read it from a script. Even in their most serious moments, it had always been "Llia" or his personal favorite, "Lils."

The facts align in her mind: Charlie is dead, people are missing, bathroom doors are locked, and synchronized vomiting has occurred. Now, Maddix, who should be devastated about Charlie, seems eerily composed. Too composed.

"The traffic's light today," she ventures, watching his reaction carefully.

His response is flat and emotionless. "Yes, the roads are clear."

That's not how Maddix talks. He usually makes some joke about finally catching all the green lights. She presses her back against the seat, the hospital-fresh flowers suddenly feeling like props in an elaborate performance.

Moro's words echo in her mind: "Trust me on this." He had seemed desperate for her to understand about the Yokai and about Reo. But the pieces don't quite fit. She needs more information, more context to make sense of the supernatural threading through what should have been a normal hospital stay.

Several minutes later, they arrive at Llia's apartment building. She hurriedly gets out of the car, her movements still a bit unsteady, and she leans on the passenger door. The cool metal steadies her as a gentle breeze rustles through the nearby trees, carrying with it the faint scent of rain-washed pavement. "Hey, are you coming upstairs? I have to tell you about this guy I met the night of the party and all the wild things that went down."

"I'm still not feeling great. I think I'll head home and rest. You should get some sleep too. I'll catch up with you later, and we can talk then, I promise."

"Yeah, I might just watch some TV or something, but I'll ring you later to see how you're doing. Please pick up when I call." Llia says as Maddix simply nods and drives away.

Alright, something is really off. I mention meeting a guy and he doesn't show any interest? He's been trying to set me up with someone for years, and now he doesn't care?!

Ascending to her third-floor unit, she checks the time—nine o'clock, when her roommates typically aren't around. After locking the door behind her, she wanders into the kitchen. The gleaming wooden flooring catches her attention as she makes herself a cappuccino. Taking a sip, she sighs contentedly, rolling her head back and widening her eyes. Looking downward, she observes the floor's pristine sparkle, as if it had just been installed. Reaching for her phone, she sends a message to the CP squad group chat.

"Hey everyone, I just got home and I'm feeling much better today. Maddix gave me a lift. Rose, the floors look amazing. Thanks a ton for sticking to your promise!" Llia texts.

"Rosie? Cleaned? Yeah right! LOL," Iris replies.

"Oh, be quiet, Iris. I started on my to-do list, and number one was the milk, which you'll find in the fridge. The floor was number ten."

"What number are you currently on in your list now?" Llia asks.

"Uh, number one, unfortunately! I didn't clean the floors," Rose replies.

"We need to talk." The disembodied voice seems to come from the living room. Llia spits out her cappuccino and spins around, drawing her gun. Reo lounges in her father's recliner.

"Reo?! Shit, you scared me! And get out of my dad's chair, I'm the only one who sits there. Wait, what am I saying? What the hell are you doing in my apartment?" She doesn't get too close to him. "Don't you dare move! Actually, forget that, get out of my dad's chair! Sit over there and stay put!" Llia shouts, pressing the power button on her phone three times to send an emergency alert with her location to Moro, who would arrive quickly.

"Before you end up in jail, explain what really happened the other night Reo, if that is your name. Or was that just another lie? And what on earth happened to my floors?" Llia demands, as the polished floor catches the light of the morning sun, blinding her fiery eyes that well up with tears.

"I wasn't untruthful with you. My name is Uchima Reo, and I cleaned your floors. You can learn a lot about someone from their living conditions. The state of the floors here was appalling." Reo states.

Llia's angry eyes narrow further. "Are you asking for a bullet to the face? You showed up to disrespect me and die?! So far, you're succeeding, jerk! How I clean isn't any of your business! And don't dodge the question, what the hell is happening?"

"The people in your life are in serious peril. Those you care about will be gone in a matter of months, along with everyone in this city."

Llia takes a deep breath and lowers herself into her father's chair. "Go on." She looks at Reo with steady eyes, studying his composed features and measured breathing. Despite his earlier criticism of her housekeeping, there's no trace of deception in his stance or expression. The weight of his words hangs heavily in the air between them. She notices his calm demeanor—the kind of unshakeable certainty that comes only from bearing witness to terrible truths—and realizes that he is telling the truth or, at the very least, believes with absolute conviction that what he is saying is true.

I knew there had to be something wrong with him. He was way too attractive, of course he's completely insane!

"I arrived in America a few days before we met. Within hours of stepping off the plane, I caught the unmistakable scent of a Yokai. The trail led me straight to that party."

Wait, I didn't mention anything about Yokai to him, so how did he—

"So, Yokai are real?! There was a person I saw for a split second. Their eyes were glowing." Llia lowers her weapon.

Reo glances toward the shadowy corner of the room. He takes a deep breath and exhales forcefully.

Llia clutches her abdomen as a sudden pain shoots through her.

"Indeed, they're very real and dangerous, and they're after you."

"So, Moro was right... holy shit! Okay, I guess the obvious question would be: why did they attack me? Until today, I didn't even know they existed."

"Like I told you at the bar, you are extraordinary. You are what is known as an earthly deity."

Llia's eyes widen as she raises a single brow, then stares again in disbelief. "Right, of course, I am. Look, I think you might be having a mental breakdown. I'll find you some help, her name is Rose..."

Reo shook his head. This is gonna be harder than I thought. TJ said most Americans are skeptics, but we don't have time for this.

"Most likely, they want to take your powers and abilities," Reo replies.

"Sure they do. Help is on the way, buddy. What kind of medication do you take?"

"Look, there is a story that may help answer your questions. If you will indulge me."

CHAPTER FIVE
EARTHLY DEITY

"About eight hundred years ago, in the village of Fukui (foo-kwee), Japan, there was a beautiful samurai village where a young Yokai Ex named Tatsuo (tat-su-O) encountered what seemed to be a plague. All of the women in the village were dying, while the men were not.

"Wait, I'm sorry...Yokai Ex?"

"Yes, it stands for Yokai Executioner. That's what I am. I guess you would call them monster hunters."

Yep, he's completely lost it. But I'll go along with it and see what happens, Llia thinks.

"Okay...continue."

"When Tatsuo reached the village, the lord presented his daughter to him. Acknowledging Tatsuo's remarkable fighting skills, the lord intended to ask him to protect her. However, since Tatsuo was not a guard, he refused the request. His goal was to execute his duties efficiently and quickly uncover the source of the problem, but the daughter revealed herself unexpectedly. As he looked into her eyes, the world around him faded away. It felt as if he were submerged underwater. Her presence eclipsed everything else; she shone like the sun. His heart, usually hardened, raced, and his hands grew sweaty as he fought the impulse to bask in her brilliance for a moment longer. Each word she spoke resonated in his ears like a sweet melody. He was immediately captivated by everything about her."

"She sounds like a vision," Llia says, narrowing her eyes to read his reactions.

"Indeed, she was. Her father knew of Tatsuo's infamous standing as a fierce warrior. Previous fighters who tried to safeguard the missing women had failed. Desiring Tatsuo to escort his daughter to a far-off place, away from the cursed village, the lord promised Tatsuo substantial riches in return. Little did he know, Tatsuo was already wealthy, yet he declared his readiness to do it for free. Gazing deeply into her eyes, he could see the fear gradually tainting her beauty. Her alluring voice trembled as she whispered her name, Yumi (Yue-Me), meaning perfect beauty. He assured the lord that he would protect his daughter and vanquish the evil tormenting their village. The lord implored Tatsuo to remove her from the village and run away, but Tatsuo saw this as an affront to his honor. He scowled at the lord for even implying that a Yokai Ex should flee from his duty. He grasped the hilt of his sword, but Yumi placed her hand on his."

"Did he kill the lord for insulting his honor? My grandfather always said that even minor offenses could lead a samurai to kill."

"No, he did not. Yumi offered her hand in marriage if he'd spare her father's life for the insult. Tatsuo accepted the offer and stayed in the village to investigate for a while."

Llia was fixated on the tale as it progressed, her brown eyes wide with fascination. She leaned forward in her seat, hanging on every word like a child hearing their favorite bedtime story for the first time.

"It turns out the Umbra was behind everything. They were trying to free a powerful Japanese goddess. The Umbra is a group of powerful Yokai who were once human, except for their leader, Myou. The other three traded their humanity for power and immortality. They were among the greatest warriors ever known, and throughout their history, only one has fallen in combat. They are invincible. I believe the same events that unfolded in that village back then are happening now."

Okay, he's good. That is a really specific story for a psychotic break.

"Wait! What exactly happened to the women in the village? What happened to Yumi and Tatsuo?" Her impatient stare presses into him.

"Well, it all has something to do with the goddess known as—

Moro bursts through the door with his gun drawn, wood splintering around the frame as it slams against the wall. His service weapon, steady in his experienced grip, is aimed directly at Reo's chest. The fluorescent lights overhead catch the gleam of cold steel as the detective's knuckles whiten around the grip.

"Freeze! Don't move!" Moro shouts, until recognition passes across his face. "Uchima Reo?!" With a broad grin, Moro lowers his weapon and strides toward Reo, then dips into a respectful bow.

"Watanabe Moro, it's so good to see you again. It's been years since I've seen you. How are you, my friend?"

Llia's jaw drops. *Wait a minute! What the hell?*

"I'm doing great. I moved to America about thirty-five years ago and became a detective. Wait, if you're here, then..." The color drains from Moro's face.

"What on earth is happening here? Moro, do you know this unstable individual?" Llia asks.

"Reo-sama, please excuse her, her manners are those of a child."

"Well, she hasn't shot me yet, so she has been very hospitable."

"Oh, the day isn't over yet, so I suggest one of you talk now! How do you know each other?" Llia demands.

"Reo-sama is a Yokai Ex. If he is here, then things are worse than I thought."

Just like his story. So that part is true too. Wait, that part is—true?! He looks about twenty-six. Could he be a Yokai too? Moro mentioned there are good ones out there...

Four menacing shadows materialize in the darkest corner of the apartment, their forms writhing and twisting like living ink against the walls. Llia and Moro instinctively draw their weapons, the sharp crack of gunfire echoing through the space as they empty their clips. The bullets whiz harmlessly through the shadowy figures, falling to the floor with metallic tinks. With practiced authority, Reo gestures for them to retreat into the kitchen, his movements swift and deliberate. He positions himself as a human barrier between them and the advancing figures, which began to take shape as demonic ninjas, their ethereal forms rippling with malevolent energy. The temperature in the room seems to drop several degrees as Reo turns his head towards Llia and Moro, his expression grave but determined.

"Do not leave the kitchen. Stay there!" He stands in a deceptively relaxed stance, weight balanced evenly on the balls of his feet, hands loose at his sides—a posture that belies his combat-ready state. The shadow warriors advance with predatory grace, their forms rippling like ink in water, taking measured steps as they spread out in classic flanking formations. Their celestial weapons gleam with an otherworldly sheen as they prepare to strike.

They all attack in unison, and Llia yells for Reo to look out. The shadow warriors move with supernatural speed, their limbs blurring as they unleash a torrent of strikes from all directions. Reo masterfully dodges every single punch and kick that the four Yokai throw, his body flowing like water between their attacks. His movements are precise and economical, each shift of weight and subtle lean allowing him to evade their onslaught by mere millimeters, making their deadly assault look like a poorly choreographed dance.

They are attacking from every angle, how is he dodging all four of them? His weight distribution on his pivot foot is masterful.

With lightning speed, Reo switches to the offensive, firmly gripping two of the Yokai's wrists and delivering a forceful kick to another, all in one seamless motion, his movements like a violent dance. The impact of his kick sends shockwaves through the air as he hurls one shadow warrior into his companion with bone-crushing force, their ghostly bodies crashing through the wall in an explosion of concrete and dust. Without hesitation, he tightens his grip on the remaining Yokai's wrist, twisting with practiced precision until the sickening crack of breaking bone echoes through the room. In one fluid motion, he sweeps the creature's legs, snapping the limb beneath his heel, before delivering a devastating strike to its throat. The sound of vertebrae shattering punctuates the brutal exchange as the Yokai's body goes limp, its supernatural essence dissipating into the shadows from which it came.

Holy shit! That was amazing. How—how is he so fast? I've never seen that form of martial arts before.

Undeterred by their previous defeat, the three remaining adversaries gather their strength, their shadowy forms coalescing with renewed malice. They launch a fresh assault on Reo, moving in perfect synchronization like a well-rehearsed death squad. However, his swift and precise counterattacks flow like the wind—a palm strike crushes one's sternum, an elbow shatters another's jaw, and a devastating knee strike ruptures vital organs. The brutal exchange proves fatal, swiftly ending the confrontation in a matter of seconds. Their lifeless bodies dissolve into wisps of inky black smoke, curling upward before dissipating into nothingness, leaving behind only the acrid stench of sulfur and defeat.

"What just happened? Are we safe?" Llia exclaims.

"They were Yokai assassins, targeting you. They typically attack from the shadows with poison-coated blades. I don't sense any more of them for the moment," Reo replies.

She rests her hand on her forehead and takes a seat in her father's chair. Her rapid breathing steadies after a few moments of contemplation.

"Alright, my sisters—Rose and Iris, who you met at the party—do you think they're at risk of being attacked?" Llia nervously plays with her hands.

"Just to clarify, are they your biological sisters?" Reo questions.

"Iris is Indian-American, Rose is Caucasian, and I am African-American and Japanese, what do you think? No, my dad was not a rolling stone. We're all the only kids in our families and we lived in the same neighborhood growing up. They are my sisters, just not by blood."

So, you are the only deity in the group, the only target, he thinks.

"I don't believe they're in jeopardy. Clearly, you're their focus. However, I'll have my partner, TJ, keep an eye on them for a while to ensure they're safe. He'll also visit later to upgrade your apartment's security and fix the damages here. He plans to incorporate protective sutra spells to ward off evil spirits and Yokai. They won't be able to enter your apartment anymore, but they can still target you outside it. Your friends will be safe with TJ watching over them, although managing all three will be a bit tough. Moro, can you keep an eye on Rose? TJ will take care of Iris."

"Yes, yes, I can do that. I'll put a car on Maddix as well, but Reo-sama, what about Llia?"

"She's armed. She'll be alright," Reo quips.

"Full transparency: I thought you were mentally ill until shadow people burst into my apartment. So, yeah, I'm gonna need your help."

"You've got a major choice ahead. Firearms are useless against Yokai; their hide is too tough for bullets. It'd be like tossing a pebble at a mountain. Train under me like a Yokai Ex. I reviewed your last tournament fight—you're an outstanding combatant. Assist my partner and me in rescuing this city. But before you decide, be aware that the training will take several months in an isolated location. Only those present here will be informed about it."

"Oh, is that everything?" Llia teases.

"We'd need to depart tomorrow. Take the night to think it over and let me know your decision in the morning. I only mentor those I consider deserving, and I believe you are."

"Kid, I can vouch for Reo-sama. He is an honorable man, and his words are true. He rarely takes a student. The Yokai threat is real and we must make haste. They will overrun us in no time. Just think about it, and let's have lunch tomorrow. I can better explain how I know him then. I have to put a tail on Rose and Maddix. I leave her safety to you, Reo-sama; she is precious to me." Moro says with an air of finality, his weathered face etched with concern. They bow deeply to each other in the traditional Japanese manner, a gesture heavy with mutual respect. The detective's footsteps echo through the dimly lit hallway as he leaves the apartment, his silhouette disappearing into the shadows beyond the doorway.

Reo walks to the door and starts to repair it, his practiced hands moving with fluid precision as he examines the splintered wood and torn hinges. The familiar scent of aged oak fills his nostrils as he works, his centuries of experience evident in every measured movement. A faint whisper of spiritual energy still lingers in the air from the earlier confrontation. He knows all too well that in his line of work, a broken door often means far more trouble lies ahead.

This is intense. I have to make sure everyone stays safe. But what about my position at the police station? Moro mentioned I could take as much time off as necessary. I could simply tell the girls I'm visiting my grandparents in Japan for a while. There's a lot to consider here. That fight was amazing; I've never seen anyone move like that before. I wouldn't mind learning those skills.

"Okay, I'll think about it. Moro's like a father to me, I trust his judgement."

Reo finishes securing the last hinge on the damaged door, testing it with a gentle push to ensure it swings smoothly. He turns to face her, reaching into his jacket pocket to withdraw a delicate silver bracelet that catches the dim light. The intricate piece of jewelry features an array of miniature charms—tiny wolves, rabbits, and foxes, each one expertly crafted with remarkable detail. Their metallic forms seem to dance as he holds it out to her, the precious trinket swaying gently in his outstretched hand.

"I understand this is a lot to take in. Put this on and never take it off. It's a Dogu bracelet, the only one of its kind. If you ever need me, I'll come right to you," Reo says as he sinks into the couch and closes his eyes to sleep.

Llia stands there with a range of emotions on her face. "So, you're just going to give me a bracelet and get comfortable in my apartment?" She gently picks up a delicate ceramic vase from her coffee table, her fingers trembling slightly as they wrap around its cool surface. She slowly creeps toward Reo, making no sound across the hardwood floor, each step calculated and precise. She even holds her breath, her chest tight with anticipation, and lifts the vase high over his head, its shadow falling across his peaceful, sleeping face.

If he is some kind of badass, then he should be able to sense what I am about to do!

"That is the path to hell!" Reo says, his eyes still closed.

Llia replaces the vase and heads toward her room.

"And that was the path to heaven. I will be long gone before your friends get back. Get some rest. I will watch over you." Reo smirks and folds his arms. His sharp inhale sends him into a much-needed slumber. Llia closes her room door.

Slumbering, Reo's eyes flutter open to find his beloved spouse nestled beside him in their shared bed. Glancing around frantically, he realizes he's returned to their Japanese residence. His palm presses against his heart as memories and anxiety flood his consciousness.

The inevitable truth haunts him—sleep will steal her away once more when his lids grow heavy. His vacant stare pierces the distance while his spouse observes his troubled demeanor. Attempting to soothe his distress, she rests her delicate fingers upon his torso. The gentle touch breaks his reverie, and he clasps her hand firmly. Shifting to admire his stunning wife's features, his lips curve into a smile. Her heart always flutters at the sight of his grin; it never fails to captivate her. Understanding this effect, he makes every effort to bestow such moments upon her.

She draws near and presses her soft, rosy mouth against his. They melt into a fervent, intimate embrace. Their pulses quicken. The crisp evening air drifts in from the star-filled sky through their partially ajar window. Moonlight streams inside, bathing the chamber in a faint silvery radiance. She nestles against his chest while his fingers glide through her flowing, smooth tresses. Her countenance radiates happiness, wearing a broad grin that inevitably causes him to echo her delight.

Her drowsy voice and drooping eyelids signal she will drift into slumber any moment now. Brushing his lips against her brow, his attention shifts to the magnificent heavens framed by the side window. Taking a shaky inhale, he silently prays the terror won't visit tonight. He tucks one palm beneath his head while darkness descends behind his clenched eyes. A single teardrop escapes as the crushing truth hits him—when his eyes open again, this sweet reverie will vanish. In a tender whisper, he utters his cherished farewell. "I love you, Yumi."

CHAPTER SIX
YOUR MOVE

Detective Moro Watanabe leans back in his chair, rubbing his tired eyes as he studies the security footage for the hundredth time. The murders at Turn Up and the hospital deaths on Llia's floor play across his screen in an endless loop. His notepad is filled with scribbled observations—each victim had died at exactly 9:00 PM.

The screen flickers, and text appears across his monitor:

ACCESS GRANTED

"Damn it, Maddix," Moro mutters, fingers flying across the keyboard. *"This is a secured police network. Hacking is a federal offense."*

The response comes immediately: *Not Maddix. But don't worry; your security needed an upgrade anyway.*

Moro sits up straighter. *"Who is this?"*

Name's TJ. I work with Rio. Just wanted to introduce myself properly.

"The tech specialist?"

That firewall was embarrassingly basic. I fixed it for you, though. Listen, I'm tracking Rose and Iris through their phones. Thought we could help each other out—share intel. Reo speaks highly of your work.

Moro's eyes narrow at the screen. *"I know Reo personally. Why should I trust you?"*

Because we're on the same side, Detective. I am also a Yokai Executioner, and these aren't normal homicides you're dealing with. I'll keep you updated on anything I find regarding our mutual persons of interest. All I ask is that you do the same.

The cursor blinks expectantly. After a long moment, Moro types: *"Fine. But next time, use the phone."*

LOL. Will do. Looking forward to working together, Detective.

The screen returns to normal, leaving Moro staring at the paused footage. He shakes his head, wondering what terrible things were coming to Seattle.

Reo's phone buzzes as he meditates in Llia's apartment. The screen lights up with TJ's name.

"Progress?" Reo keeps his eyes closed, maintaining his centered breathing.

"Got eyes everywhere now—phones, cameras, traffic systems—the works. Otis is processing the data streams as we speak."

"And?"

TJ's keyboard clicks carry through the line. "Those murders at Turn Up and the hospital? Otis found similar patterns dating back months. All victims died at exactly 9 PM. The precision is… unnatural."

Reo opens his eyes, focusing on the city lights beyond his window. "You think it's her?"

"Otis analyzed police records against known Yokai killing patterns. The timing, the methods, the lack of evidence—it all points to Myou. The AI's confidence level is 92%."

"She's marking her territory." Reo's jaw tightens. "Testing boundaries."

"That's not all. Remember that detective I contacted? His investigation turned up some interesting details. These deaths aren't random—they're calculated, like pieces being moved on a board."

"Can Otis predict her next move?"

More typing sounds. "Based on the geographic spread and timing of incidents, Otis places her somewhere in the greater Seattle area. The murders form a pattern—like she's preparing or drawing something."

"Keep monitoring. I want to know the moment Otis detects any new anomalies."

"Already on it. I've set up alerts for anything matching her MO. If she makes a move, we'll know."

Reo paces near the window, watching Seattle's twinkling skyline. "TJ, I need a favor. Can you get a crew to outfit the Olympic Forest cabin as a training ground?"

"The cabin? That's like four hours from Seattle." Keys clack in the background. "Why so far out?"

"Llia's being hunted. If I take her there, whoever's after her will follow, leading them away from the city and innocent people."

"And maybe slow down these killings." TJ's typing pauses. "Buy us some breathing room to figure out what's really going on."

"Exactly. Can you handle it?"

"Already on it. Otis, initiate Cabin Protocol Alpha." More keystrokes follow. "He'll coordinate the setup team and get everything you need: training equipment, security systems—the works. Should be ready within 48 hours."

"Make it 24. We don't have much time."

"Done. I'll have Otis send you the access codes when it's ready." TJ clears his throat. "Just... be careful out there, senpai. If this is who we think it is..."

"I know. Keep monitoring the city. Let me know if anything changes." Reo shifts his weight, uncharacteristically hesitant. "There's one more thing..."

"What is it?" TJ's voice crackles through the phone.

"I need..." Reo runs a hand through his long hair, glancing at his reflection in the window. His traditional clothing stands out starkly against the modern Seattle backdrop. "I could use a haircut. And some new clothes. To blend in better."

TJ's laughter fills the line. "The great Yokai Executioner needs a makeover? Man, I've been waiting years to hear you admit that."

"Are you finished?"

"Almost. Just savoring this moment." TJ's keyboard clicks resume. "Say no more, I'll handle it. After Llia meets with Moro tomorrow, come by Pike Place Market. I know a place that'll help you look less... feudal Japan."

"I don't look feudal."

"Senpai, you're wearing hakama pants in downtown Seattle. Trust me on this one."

Reo glances down at his traditional garments. Perhaps TJ has a point. "Fine. Send me the exact location."

"Already done. Check your watch." A ping confirms the coordinates. "And Reo? This is going to be fun."

"Just make it quick. We have work to do."

"Quick and discreet. Got it. No Instagram posts about your transformation."

Reo ends the call before TJ can make any more jokes at his expense. He turns back to his meditation, trying to ignore the warmth of embarrassment in his cheeks.

The neon sign of Ma's Japanese Restaurant casts a warm glow across the rain-slicked sidewalk. Four college students huddle under the awning, shaking water from their umbrellas.

"Made it just in time," Sarah says, pointing to the 'WAIT LIST' sign being placed in the window.

They squeeze inside the packed restaurant. Red paper lanterns hang from wooden beams, and intricately carved screens divide the dining areas. A koi pond burbles beneath a small bridge near the entrance.

"This place is gorgeous," Mike whispers, running his hand along a painted silk screen. "How have we never been here before?"

The hostess leads them to the last available table. Steam wafts from the kitchen, carrying scents of ginger and garlic that make their mouths water.

"The ramen looks amazing," Jenny says, watching a steaming bowl pass by. She orders the house special, while the others opt for udon and katsu curry.

"Check out those paintings," Tom says, pointing to ukiyo-e prints adorning the walls. "The colors are so vivid."

Their food arrives quickly, presented in elegant ceramic bowls. Jenny inhales deeply over her ramen. "This smells incredible."

At the first bite, their eyes widen. The flavors are intense, beyond anything they'd ever experienced. Without warning, Jenny plunges her face into the ramen, slurping violently. Mike shoves fistfuls of curry into his mouth, rice scattering across the table.

Sarah and Tom crash face-first into their bowls, breaking their noses against the ceramic. Blood mixes with broth as they continued gorging, unable to stop. Their fingers cramp from gripping chopsticks, knuckles white as they shovel food past their bloodied lips.

Around them, other diners remain oblivious, lost in their own violent feasting. The sounds of slurping and crunching fill the air, punctuated by the occasional crack of bone against ceramic.

Shadows writh along the walls, stretching and contracting like living things. The fluorescent lights flicker, casting an unnatural pallor over the scene of mass consumption. Chopsticks clatter against empty bowls as diners scrape desperately for every last morsel, their faces and clothes stained with broth and sauce.

From a back office emerges an elderly Japanese woman, her silk kimono whispering across the floor. A darkness seems to pool at her feet, following her measured steps through the restaurant. Her lips curve into an unsettling smile as she watches her customers feed with animalistic abandon, their movements mechanical and unrelenting.

The bell above the door chimes. A young couple steps in from the rain, shaking water from their coats.

"Hi, we were wondering if you had any tables available?" the woman asks, wringing out her scarf.

The elderly woman glides toward them, her shadow stretching impossibly long behind her. "I am Ma," she says, bowing. Her voice carries an echo as if multiple people are speaking at once. "There is always room for more."

The couple exchange excited glances, oblivious to the sounds of cracking ceramic and splintering chopsticks around them. Ma's smile widens, revealing too many teeth as she gestures for them to follow her into the dimly lit dining room.

CHAPTER SEVEN

THROUGH THE TORII GATE

The following morning, Llia cautiously glances beyond her doorway, spotting Reo restlessly shifting on the sofa. Agony surges through her limbs as she inches toward the living room to retrieve her coat. Each movement brings waves of discomfort that slow her careful progress.

The girls must have let me sleep when they came in yesterday. Did they see Reo on the couch? No, Rose would have woken me up. He must have left and come back. Well, it's time to meet Moro and see what I'm going to do.

With a gentle touch, she closes the apartment door and remains in the hallway. She exhales, pulls out her phone, and texts Moro to meet her at their favorite coffee shop in fifteen minutes. Then she makes her way out of her apartment building. As she passes by the dim alley, a pair of eyes follows her. Reo emerges from the alley and watches as she turns the corner a block away.

He then walks in the opposite direction, pressing several buttons on his watch.

I think she will accept the offer to train with me. I will not take it easy on her. She will endure the same training I put TJ through, the training he refers to as hell on earth.

Reo's phone buzzes. He pulls it from his pocket and glances at the screen, seeing TJ's name flash.

"Everything's set up," TJ's voice crackles through. "Supplies are in place, and the camp's ready for action."

"Good," Reo replies. "I'm on my way to meet you. Need to update my look." He ends the call and changes direction, heading toward the bustling mall.

After several minutes, Reo steps inside the glass doors, the warm air a stark contrast to the chilli breeze outside. The aroma of pretzels and fresh coffee mingles with the faint scent of new clothes.

He spots TJ leaning casually against a pillar near a sneaker store. TJ stands out as a striking African American man with an athletic build and towering frame. His low-cut hair has waves that catch the light, and his physique resembles that of a welterweight boxer—solid but not overly bulky. His mouth stretches into a grin as Reo nears, and he embraces him with the enthusiasm of long-lost friends reunited.

"Looking sharp as always," Reo greets him with a nod.

"Got to maintain the look," TJ responds, showcasing his flawless smile. "Feels like ages since our last in-person meetup. Are you ready for your stateside makeover?"

"It has been ages. And I'm as ready as I'll ever be."

TJ leads Reo through the maze of stores, stopping first at a trendy clothing shop. The racks are filled with jeans, jackets, and shirts in various styles and colors.

"This is your chance to ditch the old-school warrior look," TJ teases, pulling out a pair of dark denim jeans. "Try these on."

Reo takes the items and disappears into the fitting room. Moments later, he emerges looking both hesitant and curious.

"Not bad," TJ assesses, nodding approvingly. "But we need more."

They move from store to store, adding shirts, sneakers, and accessories to their haul. By the time they finish, Reo barely recognizes himself in the mirror—a modern twist on his timeless appearance.

As they walk out of the last store, TJ claps Reo on the back.

"You're ready for anything now," he says.

Reo adjusts his new jacket, feeling both comfortable and strange in his updated look.

"Thanks for this," he says sincerely.

"No problem," TJ replies with a grin. "Now let's get back to work. I have one last thing to give you."

Reo and TJ walk into a barbershop, the familiar hum of clippers and soft banter filling the air. The walls are adorned with posters of various hairstyles, from classic cuts to modern fades. The barbers greet them with nods, and they take their seats in the worn leather chairs.

"Just a trim for me," TJ instructs, settling in comfortably.

Reo glances at himself in the mirror and opts for a more significant change. "Let's make it shorter," he decides, pointing to a photo of a clean, tapered style.

The barbers work quickly and skillfully. In no time, TJ's waves are sharp and defined, while Reo's hair is neatly trimmed and stylish. They pay for their cuts and step back into the bustling street.

Almost immediately, a group of women approaches them. Their laughter and light conversation draw attention, and they seem eager to chat.

"'Seattle freeze' my ass," TJ whispers with a smirk as he pulls out his phone to exchange Instagram information with them.

Reo smiles politely but shakes his head when one of the women hands him her phone. "I'm sorry, but I can't."

She nods understandingly, and the group soon disperses with waves and smiles.

TJ chuckles as they walk toward the parking lot. "You're always so damn polite," he teases.

"It's just how I am," Reo replies with a shrug.

They reach the parking lot where TJ stops in front of a sleek, custom black muscle car. The vehicle gleams under the sunlight, its curves and lines exuding power and elegance.

"Here she is," TJ announces proudly, tossing Reo the keys. "Don't put a scratch on her. She's one of a kind."

Reo catches the keys mid-air and runs his hand along the car's smooth surface. "I'll be careful."

TJ pats the car affectionately. "You better be. I may not be able to take you in a fight, but that doesn't mean I won't try."

Reo slides into the driver's seat, adjusting to the feel of the luxurious interior. The engine roars to life as he turns the key, sending vibrations through his body.

TJ climbs into the passenger seat with a grin. "It's also voice-activated. Now, let's roll."

Reo slams on the accelerator, and the high-performance engine responds with a thunderous growl. G-forces press TJ deep into the supple leather seat as the speedometer needle climbs rapidly. The pristine sports car carves through the empty streets like a bullet, its precision handling making even the sharpest turns feel effortless. The city lights blur past them in streaks of neon and shadow.

Llia arrives at the coffee shop a few minutes late and hobbles toward Moro, who is seated by the window in the rear of the shop. "Oh, you made it, late as always. How do you feel, kid? Have you eaten yet? If not, we can eat at Ma's after this. I don't like the name, but they say it's great."

"No, I'm not all that hungry after the last 48 hours. Tell me everything you know about the Yokai Ex. What did you mean when you said 'it happened before' in the apartment?

And why are you talking to Reo like he's forty-nine years old when he looks twenty-five?" Llia says as she orders a medium Costa cappuccino.

"Woah, slow down, kid. Does this mean you're considering Reo's offer to train with him?"

What's the alternative? Watch the ones I love die? Wait for the world to end?

"You said you would explain things better."

"Okay, fine. The Yokai Executioners are an old order that operates in the shadows; few people know about them. My grandfather told me they were assembled by an earthly deity to help fight against the Orochi dragon from taking his daughters. Over the centuries, they fought all kinds of powerful Yokai, but the most famous of them was a powerful goddess, Penumbra." Moro explains.

"Penumbra is part of a shadow, but I've never heard of her in Japanese lore."

"Yes, in an American dictionary. Thanks to the Yokai Ex, few have heard of her. She was the goddess of the moonless night. Some say she was the daughter of Amaterasu and Tsukuyomi. Out of all the gods of Japan, she was the most dangerous. The story goes that Amaterasu was so angry at her brother that she hid in a cave for thousands of years. When she did this, her daughter reigned supreme, casting the world into complete darkness. Every living thing except the Yokai despised her. The Yokai loved her because they thrived in the darkness. They called this period the *Kokuten*."

"*Kokuten...* the dark spot. What happened to Penumbra?"

"No one really knows. It's a great mystery. She suffered defeat at the hands of the first Yokai Ex member, and then her mother emerged from the cave and brought back the light with her."

"That hardly explains how you ended up knowing about them."

"Yeah, it's something I wish I could forget. My grandfather was a top detective in Japan. This was forty-five years ago. Every night, he would come home, and I would be up waiting for him to hear about his day and all the bad guys he had caught. He would lay out the crime and give me the clues so I could figure it out myself."

"That game sounds familiar," Llia smiles.

"Yeah, he was my hero. Then came the times he came home later and later until one day, he stopped playing the game with me. I waited up one particular night until one in the morning. Then the phone rang. It startled me because no one called that late. So, I answered the phone. 'Moshi, Moshi.' Do you know why we say 'Moshi Moshi' when we answer the phone?"

"Roughly translated, it means 'I'm talking. I'm talking,' right?" Llia replies.

Moro nodded as the past came back to him. "Correct, but it also means so much more."

A young Moro, about fourteen years old, sits in his living room in front of his television. His head drifts back and forth as he struggles to keep his eyes open. There's a note on the coffee table from his parents telling him not to wait up late for his grandpa and that they will be home in the morning. The phone rings and makes him jump. He runs toward the phone with excitement and answers it.

"Moshi, Moshi. Grandpa? When are you coming home?"

"Moshi...

"Grandpa?!" he replies.

"Ha-ha-ha." The low voice laughs and hangs up the phone.

Moro hangs up the phone, and it rings again. He takes several steps away from the phone when the front door slams shut. He quickly turns to see his grandpa sitting on the couch. His pale complexion and shallow breaths are alarming to Moro.

"Grandpa, are you okay? You look sick."

"Yes, I am fine. I just need to rest. Help me to my room."

Moro slowly walks toward his grandpa, who doesn't blink. He extends his hand to help his grandpa to his room. His grandpa grabs Moro's hand and pulls to get up from the couch. His icy hand shocks Moro, who rushes him to the room to get him warm, turning on every light he passes. He removes his grandpa's shoes and helps him to the bed, placing several blankets on him.

"I'm going to fix your dinner. I'll be right back. Try to get warm, Grandpa."

Moro darts off to the kitchen to heat the food his mother left for them. He hears a loud bang in the hall and walks to see that every light he turned on is off. The moans of his ailing grandpa fill the hall. Moro walks to the kitchen drawer and grabs a flashlight. His hands tremble as he takes tiny, cautious steps toward his grandpa, who is now screaming his name.

"MORO, MORO, MMMOOORRROOO!"

He opens the door, and the room falls silent. Moro trembles uncontrollably. He pushes the door open and shines the light toward his grandpa. The flashlight dies as soon as it hits him. Piercing red eyes shine in the pitch-black room.

"Come to me, Moro. I need your help," his raspy voice sounds like a completely different person.

Moro makes his way toward the heavy breathing in the dark room, inching closer to him. *"What is it, Grandpa? What do you need?"*

"I am hungry."

"I'll go get your food." Moro turns to leave the dark room, but a pair of rough, chilly hands grip his neck and squeeze.

"Hungry!"

Moro's face pales, and all vitality seems to seep out of him. A deafening noise, accompanied by a blinding burst of light, fills the room. A man wearing a hoodie with the words "Heho Sho" displayed on the sleeve enters. He swiftly pulls out a magnificent sword, its sharp edge slicing through the air as he decapitates the Yokai that had Moro in its grip. Just before Moro loses consciousness, the gruesome sight of his grandpa's decapitated head fills his vision. His grandpa's complexion is ashen and lifeless, eyes a piercing shade of red, and his teeth sharp and menacingly uneven.

"I woke up in the hospital several days later, surrounded by police officers and my parents. I overheard a few of them talking, saying it was the Yokai Ex that saved me. They said I was lucky. One of them gave me my grandpa's notebook, which contained all of his case notes. When they took my statement, I told them that the voice on the phone only said 'Moshi' once. That's when he explained that spirits can't say it back twice. That's why we say it twice in Japan," Moro said.

"I am so sorry, Moro. He didn't deserve that," Llia said, her hand over her mouth in shock.

"Yeah, but I will finish his work one day. It's all in this note-book. I will figure it out and get some answers."

"That's why you're always looking through it."

Moro nodded. "That's a lovely bracelet. A long time ago in Japan, people would place large Dogu figurines, similar to those, outside their homes. They say if they ever needed help from a supernatural force, they would go to a Dogu and ask for assistance and the Yokai Executioner would show up soon after. It was like their calling card, or like a pager," Moro said as he sipped his coffee and looked at Llia.

"What's a pager?"

"Old people's stuff, don't worry about it. I see you squirming, how do you feel?"

"Surprisingly, I feel great. But I need some advice. What do you think I should do?"

"Your father saved my life. He was more than just my partner; he was like a brother to me. You're like a daughter to me. I just don't want you to get hurt. This opportunity will ensure you have a fighting chance against these dark forces. I don't want you to feel helpless like I did when I faced them. Be careful and remember everything I taught you. If something makes little sense...?"

"Then you make sense of it. I gotcha. And how about calling off the tail I spotted following me two blocks ago? Maybe assign him to watch Maddix instead," Llia said as she stood up to leave.

"I guess I taught you a little too well, huh? It's just an extra security blanket, but okay," Moro said as he sent a text.

"Just keep Rose and Maddix safe. I'm going to do it, I'll train with Reo. But I don't want the others to know about this, they've been through enough already."

"That makes sense. Reo is the absolute best warrior I have ever seen, he's the right guy to train you. And don't worry about work, I will cover for you. Just send me a text every once in a while so I know you're okay. I will respond with a detailed report on Rose and Maddix's activities," Moro said as he paid the bill.

"Well, it's time to go. I need to pack and leave before the girls get back. They will ask too many questions about the situation, and I can't lie, Rose will sniff it out. Thanks for everything, Moro," Llia stood to her feet and they embraced each other.

Moro's eyes became misty. He wiped his eyes and smiled. "Go on, kid, get out of here!"

Wiping her eyes, Llia left the shop and started walking toward her apartment.

She made her way to her apartment building, feeling the warmth of the sun on her skin and the concrete beneath her feet. The rushing wind kissed her with a cool breeze, and the smell of food from nearby restaurants filled the air. The cars that sped past her every other second added to the symphony of the city.

Okay, so the Umbra is targeting me because, apparently, I'm special. They want me so they can free Penumbra, the goddess of the moonless night. Once freed, the Yokai can come out and take over everything again. I can't help but feel there's a critical piece of info I'm missing. Plus, there's the question of Reo's age and strength. Is he a Yokai too? I don't know, but I will figure it out.

Outside her apartment building, people passed by, staring at a marvelous car. A few women approached Reo with eager smiles, some handing him pieces of paper. Llia moved closer and clearly saw why he was getting so much attention.

"Damn... what kind of car is this?"

"This is TJ's custom-built car, the only one in the world. He calls it the Kokuten, the fastest V8 in the world."

"Flashy—impressive—but too flashy." Reo shrugged good-naturedly and waited for her to continue, sensing that wasn't all she had to say.

"I've made my decision... I'll train with you. I need to protect my family and make sense of this. When they finally come for me, I don't want to be helpless. I want to fight."

Reo smiled as he opened the passenger door for her, "Good. Don't bother packing. I have everything you'll need for training. You can call your friends to explain things on the road. Here's the exact spot where we will be training, only give it to Moro to ease any doubts you may have about my intentions, but we have to go now."

"Can I drive?" Llia asked.

Reo nodded and slid into the passenger seat. Llia jumped up and down but forgot about her beat-up body, pain shooting through her and putting an end to her public display. She made her way to the driver's seat. Some girls who had given Reo their numbers looked at Llia and rolled their eyes. She smiled at them and entered the car. While making her adjustments, she marveled at the interior, fully loaded with the latest tech and some things she had never seen before. She didn't see any push start or keyhole.

"Oh, yes, forgive me. Start!" Reo said, bringing the car's engine roaring to life. A crowd gathered along the sidewalk, buzzing with chatter and excitement as they snapped pictures. Llia took one last look at her apartment and put the car in first gear. She sped away from the cheering onlookers and headed out of the city on I-5 S toward the Olympic National Forest. The route appeared on the car's GPS, indicating it would take roughly three hours to reach their destination.

"Just tell the car what you want, and it will do it: make a call, read a message, text a message. Whatever you need, all you have to do is say it. It has an A.I. called Otis, and it is very useful. Everything is going to be fine. Don't worry."

His calm voice assured her he wasn't lying. She could always tell if someone was lying, which is why it troubled her that Maddix had lied to her in the elevator.

He said he was at work and couldn't call. His job would have been the first place Charlie looked, so why did he lie, and where the hell was he?

Three hours flew by, and they arrived at a Shinto shrine called The Ever Green near Olympic Park. Llia parked in the massive parking lot, and Reo exited the car. As he walked to the trunk, it opened automatically. Llia approached and saw it was full of supplies as Reo began to unload. She shifted her gaze and stood in awe of the shrine. It was a large building surrounded by tall walls and featured a magnificent Torii gate in front, leading up a flight of stairs. The entire area was enveloped by beautiful trees.

"Wow, it's still so beautiful. My mom and dad used to bring me here when I was a little girl," Llia exclaimed, her hair dancing in the cool breeze, sending chills up her arms. Reo draped a jacket over her shoulders.

"Yes, it is beautiful. This shrine houses many gods, including Amaterasu, Tsukuyomi, and Susanoo. Have you ever been to the Grand Shrine of Ise in Japan?"

"No, I've always wanted to go. They say it's stunning. I heard that long ago, people from all over Japan would travel to visit that shrine at least once in their lifetime."

"Yes, they did. It is one of the oldest and most famous shrines in Japan. You should definitely visit one day. We need to get moving, it will be dark soon. Our destination is about ten days west of here. When we reach our camp, we will rest for a few days, and then we will train," Reo said, lifting his backpack and heading toward the woods.

"Wait, so we aren't training here? It seems like just food and a tent in here," she said as she gave her backpack a shake, "What about...?"

"The rest of our supplies are already at the camp waiting for us. I have everything you'll need."

"Okay, I will be right there." Llia texted Moro a picture of the shrine and Reo's license plate just in case. She groaned as she lifted her pack and slowly hobbled toward the woods where Reo was waiting for her.

"So, the car and the supplies? Do you and TJ have someone backing you?"

"No, I was born rich, but instead of using the money for personal gain and worldly pleasures, I use it to fund the Yokai Ex."

"Oh, wow, that's great. So, how much are we talking about here? How much are you worth…just out of curiosity?"

"I don't believe in money or materialistic things. To me, it's just a means to an end. If you must know, I am worth about two hundred billion yen."

"WHAT! Holy shi…crap! That's over a billion dollars!"

"Yes, roughly. Llia, it's not good for you to know too much about me. We should stay focused on the mission and try not to ask too many questions about each other," Reo said, speeding up and causing Llia to fall behind.

Is he kidding me? I have to hike ten days with this mountain on my back, and I can't ask questions? Bullshit!

"Tell me about TJ then."

I said me; I didn't say us. Way to go, Reo, he thought.

"Very well, I will tell you something about TJ. He walks a little faster than you do."

"So, he is your student?"

"Not anymore. He's a Yokai Ex now."

"Oh, interesting. Go on."

"He is an expert with the spear, bo staff, and two forms of karate. He is an incredibly smart engineer and the one who created all our weapons and gear, including the AI I mentioned earlier, Otis."

"Impressive. I can't wait to meet him."

"Get through this training and you will."

"How did you guys meet?"

"It was about ten years ago. He attended a robotics engineering school in Japan. I was tracking a Yokai at the school when it attacked TJ, and I stepped in to save him. I recognized he was an extraordinary person and trained him for several years. We've been working together ever since."

"You always seem to show up at the right time, saving people's lives."

If only that were true, he thinks.

They travel through the woods for twelve hours a day: six hours in the morning with a few hours of break around lunch, and another six hours before making camp for the night. Reo cooks their dinner using fresh vegetables from the woods, while Llia gazes at the beautiful night sky, diamonds salted across the dark void. She takes in the cool, fresh air until her lungs are at capacity. Her mind races toward the past as she analyzes everything about the Yokai while eating her soup.

Every morning, Reo makes Llia exercise before she eats breakfast. They bathe in a nearby river that winds deep into the woods. Each night, the crickets, owls, and sounds of the forest serenade her to sleep.

After several days of hiking, they arrive at a campsite with a cabin that has two bedrooms, two bathrooms, a large kitchen, and a fireplace with a couch and coffee table in front of it. It even has a room with a hot tub offering a splendid view of the mountain in the distance.

"I remember this place! The girls and I camped here one summer years ago. They closed it down not long after that because of a string of murders that were never solved. It looks like someone has renovated it recently."

"Yeah, that was me, about ten days ago. I had it furnished and filled with our clothes this morning. I was originally going to use it for TJ and me as a base of operations, but then I met you. If your clothes don't fit, you can blame TJ for that," Reo says as he enters the cabin.

Why in the hell did he bring me all the way out here to the camp, and why didn't we just drive?

"*Shinrin-yoku*," Reo says.

"Forest bathing? What does that mean?"

"It's why we are here. It means taking in the forest through the senses. It puts you in a relaxed state where you will absorb much more knowledge. It's time for a break and some ground rules," Reo sits down on the couch, and Llia tosses her backpack into a distant corner. She notices a beautiful Japanese sword with engraved Tsubaki symbols displayed over the fireplace.

"Are those your swords? They're magnificent!" Llia exclaims.

"Those belong to the most powerful Yokai Executioner ever. I am not worthy to use them, so I keep them close," Reo replies. Llia marvels at the swords as Reo clears his throat.

"The rules are as follows: First, no going out at night. Stay in the cabin after dark, no matter what. Second, during your training, while on the mat, I am not Reo; I am your Sensei. Finally, don't lose sight of why we are here—training and nothing else. Can you follow these rules?"

Let me get this straight: you think you can bring me into this beautiful forest, take me to a gorgeous refurbished cabin with a hot tub, and expect to get lucky? YES!

"Can I follow the rules? Yes, Sensei. Now, can we get some sleep? I'm tired," Llia says.

"Take this time to rest or call your friends. In two days, we will train," Reo says as he enters his room and closes the door. Llia walks around the rustic cabin before lying down on the soft couch. Her eyes become too heavy to keep open, and she drifts off into a deep sleep.

Deep in the woods on the other side of the mountain, a half-eaten deer lies ripped apart. There's a trail of broken trees leading toward their camp.

In the city, Maddix heads toward Ma's, located near the college. Upon entering the restaurant, he moves to the rear, walking past a group of busy co-workers. He notices their familiar faces savoring their meals, indulging in the flavors, and ensuring that not a single scrap is left uneaten. As he enters the manager's expansive office, the absence of windows is immediately noticeable. Seeking warmth, he crosses his arms and rubs them with his hands. His lip trembles as he breathes, and a faint cloud of vapor escapes his mouth, reminiscent of smoke. Behind an old desk sits an elderly woman, her frail figure hunching in her chair. Darkness consumes everything on her side of the room.

"Where did he take the girl?" the old woman asks, her voice sounding weathered by many years. As she moves her decrepit hands, the sound of cracking joints fills the air.

"I don't know, but I'm not doing this anymore! You can kill me or whatever, but you're not going to use me to kill my friends!" Maddix exclaims, turning to walk out but stopping dead in his tracks. He clutches his stomach and slumps over before falling to one knee. Blood surges from his mouth as the old woman rises to her feet.

"I can only imagine how many sleepless nights it took to gather the courage to speak to me in such a way!" the old woman says as she approaches him. As she walks, the darkness of the room seems to cling to her.

"However, I don't have to imagine the penalty for such a dishonor: to look at me directly and speak to me as if you had a choice in the matter, as if you had a life! The intensity of my wrath is overwhelming, and what you're experiencing is just the beginning. I can make this last for five fleeting minutes or for five hundred enduring years! THAT, and only that, is the choice you have, boy! Where is she?!"

Tears well up in Maddix's eyes as he fights to protect the secrecy of Llia's whereabouts. "They're in the forest, at... the old Olympic camp. Please, make it stop! I can't—" He lets out a piercing scream as he crumbles to the ground, writhing in agony. Standing over him, she casts her dark gaze downward. A sinister grin slowly appears on her face, but she quickly conceals it by placing her hand over her mouth.

"This will be the position of all mankind, groveling at my feet, worshiping me as a goddess!" the old woman declares as she opens the door to leave the office.

"Now that that's done, I have customers to greet and a person to find. I'll send someone unforgiving to retrieve the girl and kill Reo!" She walks out.

"Wait, please, I told you where they were. The pain—I can't take it... please!" Maddix yells, his eyes wide, veins bulging, and face beet-red. He curls up in the fetal position.

"Yes, you told me!" she exclaims, her voice filled with exasperation. "And as punishment for your sins, you must endure an additional four minutes. You're mine now!" The door slams shut behind her, swallowing him in the room's darkness. His haunting wails crescendo, filling the room with the sound of his agony.

CHAPTER EIGHT

THIS WILL ALL
END IN TEARS

L lia powers up the computer Reo provided. Having spent twenty-four hours unwinding, she notices an application titled 'Yokai Ex' among the desktop icons. When she double-clicks it, a striking dark-skinned gentleman wearing a hooded sweatshirt materializes on the screen. His radiant, charismatic grin lights up his face.

"Hey, sis, I finally get to meet you. How are you settling in up there?"

"The renowned TJ, I assume. Now I can finally associate a face with the name. It's wonderful to meet you. We arrived a few days ago, and our training starts tomorrow."

"Best of luck with that, you'll need it. I trained under Reo for five years, but it was so grueling that it felt like twenty. Here's my advice: always remember your purpose for being there. It was different for me; I had no one to protect, but you do."

"Reo mentioned how you ended up involved in all this, but he won't say where you came from. What's your background?"

"You mean, how did a black guy end up in Japan and partner with a cursed Japanese guy to hunt down deadly demonic creatures and stop them from destroying the world?"

"I didn't quite mean it that way..."

Laughter booms through the laptop speakers, deep and resonant, and Llia's shocked expression softens into a sheepish smile. She shifts in her seat, the tension in her shoulders visibly easing as the awkward moment passes.

"You're way too easy, sis. You got to lighten up a little."

Reo and TJ are complete opposites, but I see why he adores him. And did he just say Rio is cursed! That would explain alot. Let me see if I can get him to reveal some more intel.

"Why do you keep calling me 'sis'?"

"Oh, because I'm your brother."

"Come again?"

"Not biologically, obviously. We share the same Sensei, so we're siblings in the martial arts community. As for your question, I'm Tobias Daniels Jr., but everyone knows me as TJ. I graduated from Stanford University with honors, earning two master's degrees in engineering. I'm also quite proficient with the spear and knowledgeable in Kuk Sool and Won martial arts. After college, I moved to Japan for a robotics internship and decided to stay."

"Wow, you look so young. You must be a genius!"

"I hate that word, but thank you. It has limitations, and I don't. I've been into books since I could read, and that's where my drive for learning comes from. So, what's your story?"

"I'm not sure why the Umbra are targeting me. The only one I know by name is Myou, and that's only because Reo mentioned it."

"Well, that's the important one to remember. Each night after practice, meet me here, and I'll give you a masterclass on all the Yokai. I'll also show you how our tech functions. I'll train your mind so that you know what to do when you face a level-one Yokai. Run or fight? Spoiler: run. Those creatures have supernatural abilities, it's better to let Reo take care of them."

"Where do the Yokai come from, anyway?" Llia's curiosity glimmers in her eyes, her voice softening as if bracing for an unsettling truth.

TJ's grin fades, replaced by a somber expression. He leans closer to the camera, the shadows from his hood casting eerie patterns on his face. "That's a heavy question, sis. Yokai are ancient, older than humanity itself. They're spirits or demons born from the darkest parts of the human psyche—fear, anger, sorrow."

Llia listens intently, her fingers drumming lightly on the desk.

"They originated in Japan," TJ continues. "Back in the day, people believed that everything had a spirit—trees, rivers, mountains. Some of these spirits were benevolent, others weren't so friendly. Over centuries, negative emotions and dark energy gathered and formed Yokai."

"So they're like... evil beings?"

"Not just evil," TJ clarifies, "Yokai can be mischievous or neutral too. But the ones we're dealing with? They're corrupted beyond redemption, driven by a hunger for chaos and destruction."

"How did they get so powerful?"

"Imagine centuries of resentment and hatred festering in one place," TJ explains. "Yokai feed on these emotions. The more that humanity grew and developed, the more darkness accumulated. That's where Myou comes in."

"Myou..." Llia's voice is barely above a whisper.

"Yeah," TJ nods. "She's not just any Yokai; she's their queen. Myou's power is unmatched because she harnesses curses and darkness itself. She's lived through countless human generations, learning and growing stronger with each passing century."

Llia's mind races with the weight of this revelation, trying to piece together how she fits into this ancient struggle.

"Why would they target someone like me?"

TJ's eyes soften with empathy. "Sometimes, it's not about who you are but what you represent. You might be connected to something bigger than you realize."

The room seems to grow colder as Llia processes his words.

"But remember," TJ says firmly, breaking through her thoughts, "Reo and I—we've got your back. This fight isn't just yours to bear alone."

Llia nods slowly, feeling a mixture of fear and determination. "Thank you for explaining."

"No problem." His smile returns briefly before his expression becomes serious again. "Get some rest; tomorrow's training won't be easy."

Llia nods once more before shutting down the computer. The screen goes dark, but her mind buzzes with newfound knowledge and questions yet to be answered.

What happens when you fight against a curse? It fights back stronger than before! she thought as she settled in to go to sleep.

Llia lies on her bed, staring at the ceiling, the conversation with TJ replaying in her mind, the weight of his words pressing down on her chest.

"Yokai are a curse," she muttered to herself, feeling the chill of realization seep into her bones. She pulled the blanket tighter around her, seeking comfort in its warmth. Her thoughts spiraled, the question gnawing at her consciousness. "What happens when you fight against a curse?"

The room seems to hold its breath waiting for an answer that would never come. She turns on her side, gazing out the window at the moonlit forest. The night is still, yet it feels alive with unseen forces lurking in the shadows.

"Can you stop it?" she whispers, a shiver running down her spine.

The enormity of her situation settles in. She isn't just up against ordinary enemies; these are ancient beings born from humanity's darkest emotions. Her pulse quickens at the thought of facing such malevolent forces.

In the quiet of the night, she could almost hear Myou's mocking laughter, echoing through time and space. How could she, a mere human, stand a chance against something so powerful and insidious? Doubt creeps in, but she pushes it aside, knowing that fear would only feed the Yokai.

Reo's words from their first meeting came back to her: "Strength doesn't come from physical prowess alone; it comes from resilience and determination." She took a deep breath, grounding herself in his wisdom.

She rolls onto her back again and closes her eyes. Sleep seems distant, but she knows she needs rest for tomorrow's training. Her mind continues to churn with questions and fears, but she forces herself to focus on her breathing, finding a semblance of peace in its steady rhythm.

As she drifts closer to sleep, one final thought lingers: no matter how strong the curse fought back, she wouldn't face it alone. Reo and TJ were by her side—her newfound family in this battle against darkness.

With that comforting notion, Llia allows herself to slip into an uneasy slumber, ready to face whatever challenges lay ahead with renewed resolve.

The smell of breakfast acts as her alarm clock. She trips over her own feet, her nose guiding her. After rubbing her eyes and washing her hands and face, she can finally see the meal ahead.

An assortment of food has been carefully prepared for the occasion. Reo placed the different portions on the table in a tidy and orderly fashion. Sausages shaped like octopuses and bowls of soup filled with carrots, vegetables, and noodles were served. Everything in pairs. The table is brightened by their vivid colors and elaborate presentation.

Reo enters the room donning a white T-shirt. "I made breakfast for you," he says with a smile, muscles becoming more defined as he gets closer to the table.

"Wow, it looks so good. I—I mean, let's eat! It smells wonderful. Where are the forks?" They settle themselves at the table. Reo smiles slightly as he takes a pair of Hashi in his hands. A troubled expression crosses Llia's face; it's been a long time since she used Hashi sticks.

"All the forks are in Seattle. We'll use Hashi. I believe they refer to them as chapsticks in America. This is the correct utensil for eating Japanese cuisine. You'll continue using these until your training is finished." He gestures toward the dishes.

Llia covers her mouth and chuckles. "They call them chopsticks here in the States, not chapsticks."

"Oh, my apologies. We have a long day of training ahead of us, and you will need every ounce of your strength. So, please eat up."

Llia gulps and makes numerous attempts to grip the Hashi properly, failing each time. She watches Reo gracefully lift a piece of sausage and eat it with elegance.

She recalls attempting to eat with them as a young girl in Japan. Patience was crucial for mastering the Hashi, a lesson her grandparents imparted many years ago. The memory resurfaces, and before long, most of the food on the table has vanished. The soup was the tastiest; it was so delicious that her slurping brought a smile to Reo's face, revealing perfectly aligned teeth. His dark eyes crinkle at the edges—a genuine expression that transforms his usually stoic features into something warmer and more approachable.

"In Japan, slurping is a sign of appreciation," Reo sets down his Hashi. "It tells the chef the food brings joy to those who eat it."

The morning sun filters through the kitchen window, casting a golden glow across his face. His smile lingers, a rare sight that makes him appear younger than his perpetual twenty-eight years. The curse that keeps him frozen in time couldn't mask the ancient wisdom in his eyes, but in this moment, there is only lightness there.

"Really?" Llia wipes her mouth with a napkin. "I thought it was rude."

"That's the western view." His smile widens, dimples appearing on his cheeks. "But in my culture, the louder the slurp, the better the meal."

The tension in his shoulders melts away as he watches her return to her soup with renewed enthusiasm. It's been centuries since he'd shared a meal like this—simple, unguarded, free from the weight of their responsibilities as Yokai executioners. His smile carries none of the usual sharp edges honed by years of battle, just pure, unfiltered joy at sharing his heritage.

A lock of his black hair falls across his forehead as he leans forward, and for once, he doesn't immediately brush it back into its disciplined place. The morning light catches the subtle bronze undertones in his skin, highlighting the relaxed set of his jaw and the gentle curve of his lips.

"When you finish, I'll handle the cleanup. I've left some training clothes for you on the sofa." On the sofa, the traditional karate Gi layout; the fabric was white with a black belt.

Llia slips into the bathroom, the polished tiles cool beneath her feet. Steam rises as she adjusts the water temperature, laying out her fresh Gi with reverent care on the nearby counter. After a rejuvenating shower that washed away the last traces of sleep, she towels off and methodically dons the crisp white uniform. The sturdy cotton fabric settles comfortably against her skin as she secures the traditional garment, each fold and tie an echo of centuries of martial tradition.

Reo finished tidying the living space by the time she emerges, her movements graceful and purposeful in the pristine white Gi. He gathers his own uniform and toiletries, stepping into the bathroom with quiet efficiency. The door clicks shut behind him, and the soft sounds of running water soon follow as he begins his own morning preparations.

He looks better today than he has in a while. Not as pale and sick-looking. Maybe he just needed some rest.

She steps to the door and peers through the window. The forest outside is enveloped in darkness. Reo had transformed the front yard into a dojo. A large mat, roughly the size of her apartment, covers the ground. She notices several weapon racks bordering the mat, holding both real and wooden practice weapons. Heavy punching bags dangle from a nearby tree. Adjacent to the mat stands a small shrine adorned with a lovely flower arrangement, and a massive medical kit sits beside the weapons.

"I set up the mat while you slept," Reo says as he emerges from the bathroom, his hair still damp from the shower. He moves with a calm, fluid grace, the kind that comes from years of disciplined training. His eyes, sharp and perceptive, scan the transformed yard with a look of satisfaction.

"The flower arrangement. What is that called?"

She turns to see him dressed in an old, traditional-style Gi, entirely black with gold stripes on his belt. Gold Japanese characters are embroidered on his sleeve and pants, reading, "Heho Sho," meaning 'he who is without equal'. She also observes a stunning bracelet adorning his wrist.

"It's an Ikebana. My mother used them as offerings to the gods for a safe training session. Some believe they can even summon them. I'll train your body and spirit to overcome what's coming. If you step through this door, you'll regret the day you ever met me. You might even come to despise me, but you'll become stronger than you ever thought possible. You'll gain the skills to safeguard your loved ones if you make it through this place. Let's get started."

Her unsteady steps follow him out the door with wide eyes, her heart pounding against her ribs like a caged bird. The weight of his words hang heavy in the crisp morning air as she crosses the threshold, knowing this moment marks a point of no return in her journey. Each footfall feels deliberate and significant, as if the very ground beneath her feet acknowledges the gravity of her decision.

No going back now. I have to succeed and protect my family!

When they make it to the worn training mat in the front yard, muscle memory takes over as she recalls the countless hours spent training with her grandfather. The familiar scent of aged wood and incense filled her nostrils, transporting her back to those precious moments. They face each other with measured composure, bodies aligned in perfect symmetry, and bow to one another with practiced grace. Together they pivot, their bare feet whispering against the textured surface, to bow deeply before the ornate shrine where ancestral spirits stand witness to this sacred ritual of respect and dedication.

"Your obvious strength is hand-to-hand combat, so you'll excel in that part of the training. We will start with weapons training since that is your weakest attribute. Based on TJ's data research, it will increase your chances of victory by as much as

sixty percent, especially when faced with multiple opponents. What is your weapon of choice? Please choose now,"
Reo says.

Llia walks purposefully down the long line of assorted
weapons, her eyes scanning each polished blade and carved
handle with careful consideration. Ancient implements of
war gleam under the soft light—spears, axes, and curved
daggers that have tasted battle across centuries. She makes
her way to the end, turning around with fluid grace, and
starts walking again, her footsteps echoing in the reverent
silence. She stops in the middle, drawn by an inexplica-
ble force to one particular weapon. With steady hands, she
reaches out and wrapped her fingers around the hilt of one
of the most famous weapons in the world, the Katana—its
perfectly balanced blade catches the light like liquid silver,
its wrapped handle promising both deadly precision and
profound responsibility.

"Very good. I am the godmaster of that weapon, so you
will benefit..."

"I think you mean sword master. There is no such thing
as a godmaster," Llia says, realizing she's spoken out of turn,
her voice trailing off into an uncomfortable silence. Reo's
intense glare burns a hole through her, his ancient eyes
carrying centuries of martial wisdom and barely contained
irritation. The weight of his stare makes her want to shrink
into herself, to take back her impulsive words that now hang
heavy in the sacred space.

"Is that so? Then you ought to be able to strike me with that weapon while I stand still, eyes shut. I won't budge from this spot. Go ahead and hit me," he says, shutting his eyes.

"What if I hurt you and you end up dead? Just to make a point? That's insane!"

"If you're able to hit me during our sessions, I will tell you everything there is to know about me, TJ, or whatever else you want to know. No more omissions. All you have to do is hit me!"

Determination flashes across her face. Instinct takes over as she charges at him, blade raised beside her face. She strikes with the force of a lumberjack. Reo remains perfectly still. As her weapon descends toward his skull, he snaps it between two fingers of his left hand. He strips the sword from her grip with his right hand and positions it at her neck. His eyes snap open, fixing her with an icy stare.

"If this had been a real battle, you'd be finished. While you're on this mat, keep quiet and listen; absorb! Don't lecture. Don't instruct. And *never* doubt me again!"

He's right. I think I'm leaning toward hating him, but I have to say, that was phenomenal. Okay, Llia, get on your 'A' game. He is the real deal.

"We won't use actual weapons again until you can find some grace in your technique. Now I will explain the point system: eight points is a match; you get two points for a hit from the waist up to the neck and four points for a hit on the head. If you land a hit with the point or blade of your sword to a vital spot, like the jugular, the crown of the head, or the heart, that's eight points and an instant win."

He walks to the weapons rack and picks up two wooden swords. "This is called a bokken; we will use these for now." He gives her one and tells her to mimic his movements. The bokken was a smooth, round piece of wood in the shape of a Japanese Katana. It looks to be about 40 inches long and weighs about a pound and a half.

"I will turn you into a swordsman. You can't leave until you have proven yourself to me. Now, let's begin. First, holding a sword correctly is paramount. If you don't have the proper grip on your weapon, then you will lose it, and then your life." He approaches her and shows her how to hold the wooden sword, forming her hands over the sword hilt. "Like this."

She studies his grip intently, trying to mirror the way his fingers wrap around the wooden hilt, but her movements are clumsy and uncertain. Reo shakes his head with a patient sigh and corrects her form again, his calloused hands adjusting her fingers one by one until they rest in the proper position. The weight of the practice sword feels foreign in her grasp, nothing like the familiar tools she used to wield.

"Place your right hand about an inch below the *Tsuba* (tsu-ba) of the sword, the hand guard. Your knuckles must be facing outward with the flat side of the handle. Your metacarpal, the bone below your thumb, lines up with the sword's handle. Now, your left-hand goes on the bottom of the handle the same way. Make sure you have some distance between your right and left hand. Keep your back straight and put most of your weight on your back foot so you can move faster when you need to."

Ugh, this is so much to remember.

"Spread your feet apart and keep your legs slightly bent to maintain your balance. Always try to keep both hands on your sword at all times! This is a two-handed weapon, not one-handed."

Llia mimics his stance and movements. Reo positions his sword ahead, aiming at her eyes. His right foot is slightly forward, weight in his back foot. Her palms grow sweaty, and her breath comes in uneven gasps.

"The name of this stance is *Seigan no kamae* (saygan no ka-me) or shadow stance. This stance can be used for both attacking and defending. Pointing the sword at your opponent's eyes obscures its length. By concealing the length of your weapon, you can gain an advantage when your opponent tries to attack. This little trick is well-known among certain Umbra members. As an example, they use a 30-inch sword in a 40-inch sheath for faster drawing. Make sure to remember that. Maintain a safe distance when confronting them."

She adjusts her stance into the poses with the clumsy uncertainty of a novice, her legs remaining stiff and unbent where they should flex, her back curved instead of ramrod straight. Her white-knuckled grip on the sword betrays her tension, fingers wrapped incorrectly around the handle like a baseball bat rather than the precise positioning required for proper control. Reo's burning amber eyes track each imperfection with the keen attention of a master, his jaw tightening imperceptibly at the accumulation of basic errors.

"Ready your guard!" Reo calls out, advancing swiftly toward her. She gasps, wide-eyed, as his blade halts against her neck.

Damn, he's fast. I didn't even have time to react.

She retreats and makes a move, only to have him knock the wooden sword from her hand. Her heavy breathing quickens as her stinging hands take punishment from his powerful attack.

"That's Tsumi (Sue-Me)! Now, get your weapon and try it again. Keep a tight grip. Put seventy percent of your weight on your back leg. This will allow you to move faster. Keep a slight bend in your knees, then spread your feet apart."

Llia follows his instructions.

"That looks horrible!" Reo grimaces, shaking his head at her sloppy form. He lunges forward with another lightning-fast strike, his wooden sword whistling through the air. Just like before, the impact sends tremors through Llia's arms, and her practice weapon clatters across the floor for what feels like the hundredth time. Sweat drips down her temple as frustration builds in her chest.

Come on, Llia, just hold on to the damn thing!

"Again!" he yells.

Several hours pass in a blur of pain and determination. Llia's bruises multiply across her skin like dark blooms, painting her arms and legs with various shades of purple and blue. Each mark tells the story of another failed attempt, another harsh lesson learned in the unforgiving training session. Her muscles ache with a deep, persistent throb that reminds her of every movement, every mistake, and every moment she'd pushed beyond her limits.

"You've been saying Tsumi all day! What does that mean, sensei?" Llia asks while standing back up from a knockdown.

"You've never played shogi? It's like chess, except you get to use the pieces you capture. Tsumi in shogi means checkmate."

Maybe I should have chosen option "B" and stayed home. Wait, TJ tried to warn me. He also said to just remember why I'm here. Okay, come on, Llia! I have to do this for my sisters, for Moro and Maddix,

She stands to her feet with renewed determination, her muscles aching in protest as she assumes her fighting stance. She firmly grips the hilt of her weapon, feeling the familiar texture of the wrapped handle against her calloused palms, her knuckles whitening with intensity as she steadies herself for what comes next.

I don't get it. We've been at it non-stop for hours, and I have taken the beating of a lifetime, but strangely I still feel strong. Normally I would have been tired a while ago. Wait... the hike up here, that's why we didn't drive. He conditioned my body for this with the hike. Genius!

"That looks... better." Circling Llia, Reo studies her form. Her posture appears proper following their exhausting eight-hour practice session. He shoves her flank, causing her to topple. "But still not right. Tsumi. Iris is dead! Get up! Spread your feet apart more. Get up and try it again."

She lies in a heap of pain, her gaze fixed on the somber gray clouds that fill the evening sky. *Yep, I definitely should have stayed my ass at home!*

Rising once more, perspiration drips from her forehead and burns her vision. She clenches her jaw and strengthens her hold on her blade, channeling all her remaining energy and concentration.

I see I'm going to have to add some incentive to get her to pull from that inner strength, he thought.

"Your friends are doomed because you lack the strength to save them, and you'll be next! You'll never live up to the hero your father was!" Reo declares.

Llia's heart pounds against her chest so hard that it feels like it will burst, each thunderous beat echoing in her ears like a war drum. Her eyes widen, pupils dilated with rage, as she suddenly feels a swell of hate and anger pour out of her mouth in a primal scream that rips through the tension-filled air. The raw emotion surges through her veins, making her fingers tremble against the grip of her weapon.

"I'm going to end you, you bastard!"

She lunges forward, killing fury in every step. Moisture glistens in her gaze, each drop carrying years of pain. Her blade whistles through the air with crushing force, yet Reo weaves past each strike effortlessly. While she unleashes a barrage of attacks,

Reo makes no move to counter. Frustrated by her inability to land a blow, she hurls the weapon at his head. He deflects the wooden blade with ease before discarding his own. Raising a single palm, he waits as she barrels toward him once more.

Despite her fiercest attempts, she fails to make contact. Using only a single palm, he thwarts every strike. Eventually exhausted, she collapses to the ground. Her lungs heave rapidly as she gasps for breath. A gentle wind sweeps across her heated skin. Reo retrieves his practice blade unhurriedly and positions its tip against her neck.

"You were dead long before my sword ever touched you. One thought to the next is but a fleeting moment, but your actions are eternally etched in time. To anyone else, my harsh words were meaningless. For you, it was your death sentence. You must master your emotions to become the master of your body. Your anger throws off your focus, and you burn through your remaining energy within seconds. That's Tsumi, and that's all for the day." His cold eyes soften for just a second before he leaves her in a heap on the ground.

"Pick yourself up and get off my mat!"

CHAPTER NINE
KNIGHT TAKES PAWN

Days later, back in the city, Iris steps through the door of their apartment, the familiar scent of coffee lingering in the air. She kicks off her shoes and tosses her bag onto the couch, exhaustion weighing on her limbs after a long shift at the hospital.

Her phone buzzes against the counter, slicing through the silence. She glances at it, a smile creeping onto her face when she sees his name flashing on the screen—Hero.

"Hey there," she answers, a playful tone threading through her voice.

"I didn't think you'd pick up," he replies warmly. "Thought you'd be too busy saving lives or something."

"Just finished a double shift. Now I'm just saving myself from collapsing," Iris chuckles, sinking into the plush embrace of her sofa.

"I guess that's a priority," he says. "I was thinking about that night at the bar. You know, when I came to your rescue?"

She can almost hear him smirking through the phone. "Rescue is one way to put it," Iris replies, a lightness in her chest as memories danced in her mind—his quick reflexes as he intervened with that creep and his easy charm afterward.

"Wasn't it fun?" His voice dips lower, teasing yet sincere. "You were really brave to stand up to him like that."

"I was just trying not to panic." Iris shifts on the couch, wrapping herself in a blanket. "And you? You were pretty heroic yourself."

"Only because I couldn't stand by and watch."

Silence hangs for a moment before he speaks again. "Want to grab dinner tomorrow? Just us?"

Her heart races at the invitation. Images of sharing laughter over candlelight flicker through her mind. "I'd love that," she accepts, biting back an eagerness bubbling within her.

"Great! I'll pick you up around seven?"

"Perfect."

"I'll see you then."

The call ends with a click, leaving Iris smiling at nothing in particular. She sinks deeper into the cushions, replaying their conversation in her head while warmth spreads across her cheeks. The world outside fades away until all that remains is anticipation fluttering inside her like restless butterflies.

Suddenly, a soft knock echoes through the apartment.

Iris stretches her legs out on the couch, still wrapped in the soft blanket, when she hears shifting in the hallway. It comes again, persistent and soft.

"Who is it?" she calls out, and Rose peeks her head into the living room, her eyes sparkling with mischief.

"What's up?" Rose asks, stepping into the room with a casual sway. She brushes her crimson hair back and sits across from Iris on the love seat, a sly grin on her face.

Iris sits up, feeling a hint of annoyance wash over her. "Just talking to Hero."

Rose's eyebrows shoot up, curiosity igniting behind her playful facade. "Hero? Is that the guy you were texting about last week? The one you wouldn't stop gushing over?"

"Maybe," Iris replies, trying to downplay it while warmth creeps into her cheeks again.

"C'mon, don't leave me hanging! What's he like?" Rose steps further inside, perching on the arm of the couch, ready for a full briefing.

Iris shrugs, playing coy. "He's just... nice. We've been talking."

"Nah, you're not getting off that easy." Rose leans closer, lowering her voice as if sharing a secret. "You can't drop a name like 'Hero' and expect me not to pry."

Iris rolls her eyes but can't hide her smile. "He helped me out at a bar once. I guess I thought he was cute."

"Cute? You're holding back!" Rose nudges Iris playfully. "Tell me more! Is he tall? Does he have abs?"

"Seriously?" Iris laughs, shaking her head. "You sound like a teenage girl."

Rose throws up her hands in defense. "Guilty as charged! But I need details! Is he coming over? When do I get to meet this mystery guy?"

Just then, Rose's phone buzzes in her pocket. She glances down at it and grimaces before looking back at Iris. "Okay, fine," Rose says with mock resignation, standing up from the couch and stretching dramatically. "But if you don't spill all your secrets soon... well, just know I have my ways of getting information."

Iris chuckles but can feel the weight of Rose's curiosity pressing in around them as they share conspiratorial smiles in the dim light of their living room.

Detective Moro leans against his car, the Seattle rain tapping softly on the windshield like a persistent ghost. The streetlights flicker, casting an eerie glow on the asphalt as he reviews the case file in his hands. Three people had been reported missing in the last week alone. All from different neighborhoods, all vanishing without a trace.

"Hey, Detective." Officer Martinez jogs up, her breath misting in the chilly air. "You find anything yet?"

Moro shakes his head, frustration knotting his stomach. "Just a string of dead ends."

Martinez pulls out her notepad, her brow furrowing with concentration. "We've canvassed their homes and talked to friends and family. No leads on where they might've gone."

"Right." Moro flips through the file again, scanning each face that stares back at him. Each one blurs with a sense of urgency and dread.

"What about the surveillance footage?" she asks.

"Not much," he admits. "Just regular street footage. No suspicious cars or shady characters lurking around."

Moro's mind races back to the last disappearance—Angela Miller, a waitress who'd served him coffee just days before her disappearance. He can still picture her easy smile as she set down his cup.

"Let's go back to that diner," he decides suddenly, straightening up. "Talk to Angela's coworkers again."

"You think they'll know something new?" Martinez follows as he strides toward his car.

"They might not realize what they saw until it's too late," Moro replies, opening the door and sliding into the driver's seat.

The diner buzzes with activity when they arrive—a clatter of dishes and muffled conversations fill the air. A neon sign flickers outside, illuminating the glass windows.

"Let's start with her manager," Moro suggests as they step inside, shaking off rain.

The manager stands behind the counter, wiping down a row of plates. He looks up at their approach and immediately stiffens. "Moro," he greets warily, eyes darting around like he's seeking an escape route.

"We're here about Angela Miller."

The manager hesitates but nods slowly. "What about her?"

"She vanished without a trace," Martinez chimes in. "Any idea who she hung out with outside of work?"

"I—" The manager swallows hard. "She mentioned some friends from school." His gaze shifts to the other side of the diner, where a couple of waitresses are chatting away—one with bright blue hair and another with a nose ring.

"Can you introduce us?" Moro presses gently.

Reluctantly, the manager nods and leads them toward the pair at a booth near the window, tension coiling tight in Moro's gut as they approach.

"Excuse me," he begins when they reach them, catching their attention.

Both women look up, curiosity and apprehension in their eyes.

Moro studies the two women, gauging their expressions. The blue-haired waitress shifts uncomfortably in her seat, glancing at her friend before speaking.

"We all made plans to eat at this new place, Ma's," she tells him, her voice barely above a whisper. "It's by the college."

"Yeah," the other one chimes in, biting her lip. "We thought it would be fun to try something different."

Moro leans closer, encouraging them with his presence. "What happened when you got there?"

The first girl exchanges a quick look with her friend. They hesitate, fear creeping into their features as if someone might overhear.

"It felt... weird," she finally admits, lowering her voice even further. "When we walked in, it was like this cold cloud settled over us. I can't explain it."

"Cold?" Moro prompts, intrigued.

"Like a dark shadow." The other waitress nods vigorously. "We all just wanted to leave right away."

"What did you see?" Martinez asks.

"Nothing strange," the blue-haired girl replies quickly. "But there was this vibe—like something was off about the place."

Moro notes the trembling in their voices and how they glance toward the exit as if expecting someone to come through the door at any moment.

"We left," the first girl continues, wrapping her arms around herself as though warding off an unseen chill. "But our friends wanted to stay. They didn't feel it like we did."

"Didn't feel what?" Moro presses.

"The... heaviness," she whispers, eyes wide with anxiety. "They were fine with staying while we went home."

Martinez catches Moro's gaze. Her concern mirrors his own.

"That was the last time we saw them," the second waitress adds, her voice trembling now. "They texted us later that night saying they were having a good time."

"And then nothing," the first girl finishes, her breath hitching slightly.

"Did anything happen after that? Did they say anything strange?" Moro pushes further.

"No." The blue-haired girl shakes her head fervently. "They just vanished after that."

As silence envelopes them again, Moro's instincts kick in. Something deeper lurks beneath their words; he felt it heavy in the air between them like smoke thickening in a confined space.

Moro leans back, his mind racing. The thread connecting the missing persons tightens in his thoughts like a noose.

"Ma's," he mutters under his breath, jotting down the name. He feels the weight of their fear and knows he has to dig deeper.

Back at the precinct, Moro spreads out the victims' files across his desk, each one a reminder of lives interrupted. He thumbs through Angela's paperwork first—credit card statements and bank transactions paint a chilling picture.

"Martinez," he calls urgently over his shoulder.

She appears at his side almost instantly, a notepad in hand.

"Look at this." He taps a series of transactions on Angela's statement—three visits to Ma's in the weeks leading up to her disappearance.

"Same with the others?" she asks, leaning closer to scrutinize the papers.

He nods, flipping through each file with quick precision. "Here's one from Kyle—a college student." Moro points at another transaction dated just days before he vanished. "And here's Ashley—two visits within that same week."

"Damn," Martinez murmurs as she examines the documents closely. "What are we looking at? A pattern?"

"A disturbing one." Moro feels an electric charge race through him. "It seems all of them had been to Ma's before they disappeared."

Martinez straightens up, her expression turning serious. "So, we need to check it out—talk to anyone who might have seen them there."

"Exactly." Moro shuffles papers, piecing together a timeline in his mind while anxiety pulses in his veins.

"And if something is off?"

"We'll find out what that 'off' is." He gathers his coat and heads for the door, urgency propelling him forward.

Martinez trails closely behind as they make their way out into the drizzling Seattle streets. The restaurant looms as they arrive—a neon sign buzzing faintly above its entrance like an insect caught in a web.

Moro steps inside first, warmth enveloping them like an embrace after the chill outside. A waitress approaches with a polite smile that falters when she recognizes them as officers.

"We're looking for information on some missing persons," he says without preamble. "I need to speak with someone in charge."

The waitress hesitates but nods toward a door marked *Staff Only*. "You'll want Ma, she's the owner of this place."

Moro exchanges glances with Martinez before striding toward the door, ready to unravel whatever secrets lay within Ma's walls, but he halts in his tracks as he catches sight of Maddix sitting at a small table near the office. He looks disoriented, fork suspended above a half-eaten plate. An elderly woman stands behind him, her hands resting on his shoulders, a broad smile spreading across her weathered face.

"Isn't it lovely here?" she coos, her voice laced with warmth and familiarity.

Moro feels a jolt of recognition. "Ma?" he asks, approaching them cautiously.

The woman turns her gaze toward him, eyes twinkling with innocent curiosity. "Oh dear, yes! You must be one of those nice officers everyone talks about." Her tone drips with feigned naivety.

"What can you tell me about the missing people?" Moro presses, keeping his voice steady despite the tension building in his chest.

Her smile never wavers as she shakes her head slowly. "Missing? Oh my, I wouldn't know anything about that. I just run a Japanese restaurant for folks to enjoy their meals."

Moro glances at Maddix again; the young man's gaze remains fixed on his plate, his pupils dilated as if under some trance.

"Maddix," he calls out gently. "You okay?"

He doesn't respond immediately, he simply continues to push the food around on his plate. Finally, he looks up at Moro but offers nothing more than a blank stare—eyes glassy and unfocused.

"Maddix!" Moro leans closer, urgency prickling the back of his mind. "What's going on? You need to talk to me."

He blinks slowly as if trying to shake off a dream but failing to break free from whatever hold keeps him ensnared.

"I'm... fine," Maddix finally murmurs, but there was an unsettling hollowness to his voice.

Ma chuckles softly, brushing her fingers through Maddix's hair as though soothing a child. "Oh dearie, he's just enjoying our special Isshin Boshi soup! Isn't that right?"

Maddix nods mechanically, without conviction.

Moro's heart races. Every instinct is telling him something is terribly wrong. He studies Ma's expression—her rehearsed and carefully crafted smile.

"Why don't you tell me what you know about Angela Miller?" Moro presses harder, staring into Ma's eyes for any flicker of truth.

"Oh my!" she gasps theatrically. "I couldn't possibly help with such things!"

Maddix remains still, locked in an expression that sends chills down Moro's spine—a puppet on strings held by the old woman behind him.

Moro pulls out his orange notebook, flipping through the pages until he finds a blank one. He quickly jots down "Isshin Boshi soup," circling it for emphasis. The name rings a bell, but he needed to confirm it.

"Wait here," he says, glancing at Martinez before focusing on Ma again. "I'll be right back."

He steps away from the table, taking a few strides toward the entrance, where a couple of patrons chat animatedly over their meals. As he thumbs through his notes, an unsettling thought flickers through his mind: Ma might not be just an ordinary restaurant owner. He would need proof before confronting her.

Martinez joins him after a moment, concern etched on her face. "What did you find?"

"Something doesn't sit right." He taps the page with the soup's name. "I'm looking it up."

"What's wrong with it?" she asks, glancing back at Ma and Maddix.

"I'm not sure yet." Moro focuses on his phone, searching for any mention of Isshin Boshi soup and its significance. His heart races as results flooded in—tales of ancient rituals, folklore surrounding Yokai, and stories of beings who preyed on unsuspecting souls.

He looks up sharply as Ma approaches them again, her smile as wide as ever. "I hope you are enjoying your visit! You simply must try my special Isshin Boshi soup—it's complimentary!"

Moro clenches his jaw and exchanges glances with Martinez. The offer hangs in the air like a trap disguised as hospitality.

"No thanks," Moro replies quickly, shaking his head. "We need to get going."

"Are you sure? I promise you won't regret it." Ma leans closer, eyes glimmering with something sinister hidden beneath that cheerful facade.

"Yeah," Martinez adds hastily. "We really should—"

"No," Moro interrupts firmly. He feels the weight of suspicion pressing against him like an iron wall. The last thing they need was to be lulled into complacency. "We'll come back another time."

As they turn to leave, he feels Ma's gaze bore into his back—a predator watching its prey retreating from its den.

Once outside in the damp Seattle air, Moro takes a deep breath and meets Martinez's concerned eyes. "We need to keep an eye on this place," he says decisively. "Something is definitely off about her."

"Agreed," she replies, her expression serious.

They climb into the car without another word, determination etched in every line of their faces as they plot their next move. It may take some time, but they need proof before they can act.

Once I'm sure, I'll tell Reo and Llia about this place, Moro thinks as they drive back to the station.

CHAPTER TEN

THE WHOLE TRUTH

It's been three months since we started this training, and I still can't land a single blow on him!

Llia perches on her mattress, a jolt of discomfort trailing any abrupt movements as she recalls another grueling day of training. Her features expand as she discards her training uniform. Gazing at her reflection, she observes a multitude of contusions.

He went extra hard today. Let's see if I can actually make it to the shower this time.

The room tilts as she stands, her vision swimming as dark spots dance across her field of view. The walls blur and sway like a ship caught in a storm, and before she can catch herself on the dresser, everything fades to black. The last sensation she registers is the cool hardwood floor rushing up to meet her.

The waves lap against the shore, bringing the crisp aroma of frigid waters. Her vision clears as swirling hues solidify. A fresh thermal pool has emerged near the lodge, where Llia finds herself. The lunar orb drifts serenely across the endless dark canvas overhead, surrounded by countless glittering stars. Flickering illumination bathes the scene. As her eyes adjust, she notices suspended lanterns hanging from the branches. The shifting specks of light around her come from luminous insects. The weight lifts from her limbs. Vitality courses through her, her pulse racing and warmth surging through her body. Whether it's the magical atmosphere or the steaming waters that affect her so deeply, she can't tell, but she's too entranced by the ethereal display to notice her unclothed state.

Aromatic blooms and fragrant herbs float on the surface, scattered by Reo across the steaming pool. Though scalding to the touch, the water embraces her flesh without burning. Her injuries have largely faded away. She sinks down until only her head remains above the surface, luxuriating in the sublime temperature as countless invisible fingers seem to knead her muscles while ripples lap melodiously against the shore. A line of blazing beacons marks the trail back toward the cabin. In the distance, flames dance in an outdoor hearth near the water's edge. Her contentment vanishes as she wonders how she arrived at this healing basin. Try as she might, she cannot recall—only the icy stone beneath her, and then nothing but blackness remains in her mind.

Did he? Oh my God! He saw me naked! That pervert! The nerve of him!

She stands to leave, searching for a towel, water cascading down her skin as she rises from the tranquil pool. Her eyes dart anxiously around the dimly lit space, scanning the rocky outcroppings and wooden racks nearby, but finding no sign of any bathing accessories. The cool night air raises goosebumps across her exposed flesh, making her increasingly desperate to cover herself.

"I hope the spring did the trick?" Reo says as he stands behind the spring.

She jumps out of the water and turns, wrapping herself in a huge towel nearby. "What the fuck, Reo?! How dare you, pervert!"

Reo emerges from the darkness, blindfolded.

"So, you expect me to believe that you can't see with a blindfold on, but you can kick my ass with your eyes closed?!"

"You don't need eyes to navigate, you only need to open your other senses," Reo replies. He retrieves some clothes hanging on a nearby branch, then walks directly to Llia and hands them to her. He walks over to a small table, pours a cup of hot tea, and doesn't spill a single drop.

"If you don't believe me, punch me in the face right now."

"I have a better idea," Llia says as she flashes Reo. He stands there quietly.

"Oh shit, you really can't see me! I—I'm so sorry for the pervert thing..."

"There is no need for apologies. Normally, I wouldn't have done such a thing, but I pushed you to your breaking point this time. Now, please, get dressed. Come get warm by the fire in the backyard."

"How long was I out of it?" Llia pats herself dry with an incredibly plush towel while the gentle wind helps her along.

"About twelve hours. I also have a bento box for you to eat by the fire." They make their way to the backyard, following a winding stone path illuminated by traditional paper lanterns swaying gently in the evening breeze. The sweet scent of cherry blossoms mingles with wood smoke from the fire pit ahead, creating an atmosphere both ancient and comforting.

"I am starving."

Besides that, I feel great. That water is amazing... I wonder what's in it? Everything looks so perfect. Did he do all of this for me?

A shiver runs through her as they approach the flames. Taking her place across from Reo, Llia watches him remove his eye covering. Night insects fill the air with their melody while moonlight ripples across the water's surface. A chilly breeze draws them nearer to the warmth, though they maintain their distance from each other. The wood smoke's aroma calms their spirits, stirring memories of their time at the previous campsite when she and the girls were teens. Her gaze fixes on the lunar glow while she enjoys her meal. An owl's call joins nature's symphony—the ambient sounds of wildlife and water lapping at the shore. Their attention drifts over the enchanting landscape until their glances intersect through the flickering flames.

"How has your Yokai testing with TJ been progressing so far?"

Oh wow, I get an actual question this time. I couldn't get him to say anything for weeks!

"The first month was a complete disaster; I failed in every aspect. However, in recent months, I've become better at recognizing their strengths and weaknesses. There are just so many of them, each with their own distinct abilities. I'm getting really good with the tech that TJ developed to combat them. For instance, the watch you're wearing—it tracks your vitals, can inject meds, provides GPS location, functions as a two-way communicator, and even has combat features."

"Good. Once you know your enemy, then the battle can truly begin."

"Yeah, but when does it end? Or how does it end? This must be a very lonely life. Is there no one waiting for you back home? Girlfriend? Wife? Kids?"

Reo looks into her eyes, his expression heavy with unspoken burdens accumulated over centuries of solitude. He interlaces his fingers until the knuckles whiten, a gesture that betrays his inner tension, and rolls his broad shoulders beneath his weathered jacket with the practiced motion of a warrior preparing for combat. His deep inhale fills his chest as he runs a calloused hand through his dark hair, the telltale signs of a warrior flustered by questions that cut too close to ancient wounds. The tension in his jaw reveals carefully guarded emotions threatening to surface.

"I'm sorry. I didn't mean to upset you."

"No, it's okay. There is no one. I have no one."

"I just noticed that beautiful bracelet and thought your girlfriend may have given it to you because you never take it off."

He looks down at the bracelet, its worn metal catching the dancing firelight. His fingers trace the ancient symbols etched into its surface as his eyes fix on the flames, seeing not the crackling fire before him but memories flickering in its amber depths.

"Someone special gave it to me. I can't take it off."

"Did you love her?"

Reo's fingers trace the worn metal of the bracelet, his usual stoic demeanor cracking like ancient pottery. The firelight caught the tears welling in his eyes, though none fell.

"Yes, I loved her. More than life itself. We were married in the spring, under the cherry blossoms." His voice, normally steady as stone, wavers.

The crackling fire fills the silence between his words. His shoulders hunch forward, the weight of the years pressing down on them. "We had five years together. Five perfect years." He touches the bracelet again, his fingertips lingering on the intricate patterns. "Then Myou came. She'd heard of my abilities, how I'd been hunting her kind. The curse she placed on me—this eternal life—wasn't meant as a gift. It was meant as torture. To watch everyone I loved grow old and die while I remained unchanged."

Llia's breath catches in her throat as understanding dawns. The bracelet wasn't just jewelry—it was the last physical connection to a love lost centuries ago.

"I tried everything to break the curse. I searched for cures until..." His voice trails off, the unspoken words hanging heavy in the night air. "Until time did what time does. And I alone remained. Just as I am now. Just as I will always be."

The owl's call pierces the night again, but this time it felt like a lament. Reo straightens his back, collecting himself, though the sadness lingers in his eyes.

"This bracelet is all I have left of her. Not even our home remains—time has claimed everything else. So no, I cannot take it off. I will never take it off."

A flicker of movement catches Llia's eye—something dark and sinister writhing around Reo's wrist. The bracelet seems to pulse with otherworldly energy for just a heartbeat, tendrils of shadow coiling around the metal before vanishing like smoke in the wind. The firelight dims for that brief moment as if the darkness had consumed it.

Wait, what was that? That wasn't normal metal reflecting the flames. That looked like... No, it couldn't be. But I've seen that type of energy before during TJ's training—that's Yokai magic. Dark magic. A curse.

Her fingers tighten around her teacup as her mind races. The pieces started falling into place—the curse, the bracelet he couldn't remove, Myou's involvement. The romantic tale of eternal love took on a more sinister shade.

He thinks it's his last connection to his wife, but what if... what if it's actually the source of his curse? What if Myou used his love as a weapon against him?

Llia keeps her face carefully neutral as Reo continues staring into the flames, lost in his memories. She didn't dare voice her suspicions—not yet. Not without proof. But the seed of doubt had been planted, and she couldn't shake the feeling that the truth about Reo's curse was literally wrapped around his wrist.

The fire crackles, sending sparks dancing into the night sky. Reo's hand absently strokes the bracelet again, and Llia watches intently, but the dark energy remains hidden. Whatever she'd seen, it was keeping its secrets for now.

"Why did you come to America?"

"I was looking for a traitor named Tristian."

"What happened to him?"

"Justice happened!" Noticing the uncomfortable silence, Reo watches as Llia hurriedly shovels her meal into her mouth. He gives a self-conscious cough.

"When I was a boy, my mother and I would travel to the Ise shrine with her Ikebana at least three times a month. She said it would summon Amaterasu, and I could ask her for anything. I remember being so excited every time we went, thinking today was the day, but it never was. My mother was the strongest person I've ever known. She taught me a great deal. One day, she told me, *try and measure your life, and you'll find the margin for errors to be infinite.*"

"That's beautiful. What does it mean?"

"You can strive to be perfect in life, but you will always have flaws. Don't let your flaws define you, or they will design you."

"Designed by flaws?!" Llia asks.

"Yes, there is no future for those who live in past mistakes."

"Your mother was wise."

"And very strong. When she died, I left and became a Yokai executioner. That's when I encountered the Umbra."

"Who are the members of the Umbra?" Llia asks, moving closer to him while eating her food.

"They are malevolent beings that thrive in darkness. Four formidable Yokai, most devoted to Penumbra. Udai (oo-die), the master of the spear, is a Shaolin monk from an ancient order, unmatched in spear combat. Next is Autsetsubae (ott-setsue-bay), or simply Subae, as TJ refers to him. Subae excels in physical prowess and wields dual swords with lethal precision, never having been defeated in battle. Then there's the leader, Myou, the master of psychological manipulation. She is the most dangerous of all, having conquered the other members and transformed them into Yokai. Always ten steps ahead of her adversaries, she devises schemes that lead others to their own downfall." Reo throws a log into the fire.

"I learned a little about her from TJ, and she is scary. Intelligence has always been more powerful than brawn. Wait, you said you were the godmaster of the sword. Do you think you could take Subae in a fight?" Llia inquires, hanging on to every detail.

Reo takes a deep breath, the smoke from the burning fire swirling around him as he ponders his reply. His brow furrows, the dancing flames casting stark shadows on his well-defined face. Llia's question lingers heavily, and Reo understands that his response might carry significant implications.

"In my current state, I wouldn't survive more than a couple of minutes. He's stronger than I am now. His swordsmanship is impeccable, and he never errs."

"Then how will we stop him?"

"Well, TJ suggested I shoot him. But if we were to fight, the winner would become the god of the sword."

She chuckles at his quip and closes the gap between them, then identifies an inconsistency in his story. "Wait, you said four? That was only three, and what exactly is a godmaster?"

"A godmaster is someone without equal in a particular skill, someone who has perfected their martial skill to such a degree that no one else can match them. Some say that if you kill the previous godmaster in single combat, you become the new one."

"So, if you kill them, you take their place?"

"Yes. Yuu was the fourth member, the godmaster of the sword. He was the most famous of them all. His fights ended with a single swing of his sword. He never had to defend while in combat, and he wielded the most powerful sword in creation: a sword called Fudo."

"Fudo means fire god. It can also refer to a state of Zen, where the mind is as sharp as the blade," Llia says as she moves beside him, watching him gaze into the flames. She reads every emotion on his face.

"That's right. I'm impressed."

"When was the last time you visited a shrine?" She asked.

The Yokai in the woods are trying to break the outer seals again! he thinks.

Reo extinguishes the last embers of the dying fire, casting the small cabin into a soft, flickering darkness. He turns to Llia, his expression pensive. "That's it for tonight. You need to rest. We'll continue our preparations tomorrow."

Llia nods silently, recognizing the weight of responsibility in Reo's voice. The Yokai in the woods were stirring once more, and they would need to be at their sharpest to face the challenges ahead. With a deep breath, Reo leads the way inside, Llia following close behind, their footsteps echoing against the wooden walls as they sought the respite of the cabin's interior.

The very next day, Reo and Llia face each other on the training mat, their bare feet gripping the worn canvas surface. The tension from yesterday has melted away, replaced by a focused determination in Llia's eyes—she felt much better after their talk, more centered and ready to learn.

"Let's start today with a little hand-to-hand," he says.

"At least I stand a slim chance of providing a challenge to you in that department," Llia replies as she bows to Reo.

"We'll see," he responds with a bow and shifts into his stance. Llia springs forward, starting with a light, straight punch, then swings a forceful inside kick, which Reo dodges. He retaliates by aiming a blow at her midriff.

"That's a point for me," he grins.

"How do you do that? I didn't roll my shoulder on the punch or shift my weight on the kick!"

"I knew that punch was a feint. You were setting up for the inside kick, which was beautiful, by the way. Slow, but beautiful. You need to learn how to combine your mind, body, and soul. Thinking about your next moves will slow you down, but if your mind and body are in sync, your attacks will be seamless. Combine that with your soul, and your results will be unmatched; your speed, strength, and techniques will double, maybe even triple. Now try again."

Llia takes a moment with her eyes shut to find her focus. She lets the rustling branches and gusting breeze wash over her. A crisp aroma of foliage and evergreens drifts through the air. The melodies of songbirds and gentle ripples from the water soothe her spirit. Energy ignites within her as her eyes flutter open.

Reo grins and assumes his fighting position.

Llia launches herself at Reo, moving twice as fast as before, and delivers a powerful strike that barely grazes past his jawline. The hit would have landed if Reo hadn't parried it away. "Holy crap, I did it. That's the closest I've ever gotten to hitting you!"

"Congrats, but almost doesn't count!"

"W-what, did you just quote Brandy?"

"I'm a fan," Reo says, grinning.

He is just full of surprises! Lovely surprises! Whoa, Llia, back it up.

"Everything okay? You're making your daydreaming face again."

"I don't have a daydreaming face!" Llia responds, slightly flustered.

"Okay, the next point wins the day. If you land this point, I'll tell you a little more about my past tonight."

"You say that every day, and for the past three months, I've failed."

"Well, thank goodness today is a brand-new day. It could be the day!"

Llia concentrates intently, preparing herself for battle. She takes a long, controlled breath in and out. In her mind, she pictures striking Reo successfully.

He rushes at her, but she stays steady. His flawless string of strikes comes quickly, yet she blocks them all. Each successful defense makes her quicker and more powerful until she matches his pace. Their exchanges carry them back and forth across the training floor, trading precise blows. Neither breaks concentration during their fierce sparring match. When Reo evades Llia's arcing kick, he follows with a direct punch from his right hand. Llia avoids his strike by dropping low and connects solidly with her left fist against his side. They separate, stepping away from one another before bowing respectfully.

"You've won the match," Reo remarks while massaging his side.

Llia can't hide her joy as Reo carefully steps off the mat. He grins as he heads into the cabin. Meanwhile, Llia jogs around the mat, singing "We Are the Champions" by Queen.

Stepping into his room, Reo falls to the floor, blood pouring from his mouth. He taps his smartwatch, which dispenses a sedative to ease his symptoms.

"The poison is worsening. Send my vitals to TJ, Otis. I need to sleep or I won't make it." He brushes away his tears and crawls into bed to rest.

TJ's watch buzzed as Reo's vitals flashed across the holographic display. His heart rate dropped dangerously low, toxicity levels spiked into the red zone, and his blood pressure plummeted. The data painted a grim picture.

"Otis, pull up Reo's medical history for the past week." TJ's fingers flew across the translucent screen floating above his wrist.

"Displaying data now. Analysis shows a 47% decline in organ function since the last measurement. The curse is accelerating its spread through his system." Otis's calm voice contrasted with the alarming statistics scrolling past.

TJ paced his lab, past walls lined with ancient scrolls and modern medical equipment. "Increase the dosage of the stabilizing compound by 15%. Add the new enzyme inhibitor I synthesized yesterday."

"Warning: Previous maximum dosage already reached. Increasing medication could result in—"

"Just do it." TJ slammed his fist on the metal workbench. "The standard dose isn't cutting it anymore. We're running out of options."

"Adjusting medication delivery system now. New dosage will take effect in approximately 3 minutes."

TJ collapsed into his chair, rubbing his temples. The curse that kept Reo eternally young was also slowly killing him from the inside out. Each day brought new symptoms, new complications. The medicine bought time, but they needed a permanent solution.

"Otis, send me an alert if his vitals drop below the 60% threshold. And prep the emergency protocols, just in case."

"Understood. Emergency protocols standing by. Shall I inform Miss Llia of the situation?"

"No." TJ watched Reo's heart rate stabilize slightly as the increased medication kicked in. "It's not for me to tell her. If he wants her to know, he'll tell her."

The following evening, after another day of combat training, Llia awaits Reo beside the outdoor fire. The radiant grin she sported upon emerging victorious from her inaugural bout remains etched across her face. Reo strolls outside and settles down next to her.

"Okay, I'm ready to hear it all. Tell me everything you've been keeping from me about yourself, starting from the very beginning," Llia requests.

"I must confess that I did not reveal everything about Tatsuo and Yumi during our prior discussion. Let's begin there. Their love was so profound that they were inseparable. He even taught her self-defense, driven by his concerns over the Yokai pursuing her, and she proved to be an exceptional student. There was a time when they were utterly content. However, one night, they found themselves bathing beneath a waterfall near the village where they first met, the moon high overhead. They reveled in each other's affections until the waters grew chilly. At that point, they decided to return home."

"Sounds like they were newlyweds," Llia commented.

"As they made their way back to the village, Tatsuo and Yumi encountered an elderly woman resting beside a tree, her hands grasping a large black bag of provisions. One of the wheels on her cart had come loose, so the young couple offered to help transport her belongings to town. The older woman expressed deep appreciation for their assistance. In return, she presented them with a special gift—a set of bracelets known as a 'lovers' bond.' The woman explained that if they wore these bracelets, their love would be eternal. She then proceeded to place one on Tatsuo, and he reciprocated by adorning Yumi with the matching piece."

Llia's eyes fly open in surprise, her brow furrowing as she processes the unexpected turn of events. Beside her, Reo methodically stokes the crackling flames, his gaze transfixed by the dancing embers. The flickering light casts a warm glow on the beautiful metal bracelet adorning his wrist, the intricate symbols and carved patterns catching Llia's eye as she studies him intently.

"After I adorned Yumi with the bracelet, the elderly woman's true nature emerged. It was Myou, a shapeshifter. Her aim was to seize Yumi's life energy, shattering Penumbra's seal to liberate herself. She craved my life force to augment her own power. Instantly, my strength waned, and my reflexes slowed as the godmaster Fuu arrived to claim my life. I drew my sword while Myou vanished into the shadowy woods, chuckling."

"You're Tatsuo!" Llia exclaims, covering her mouth with her hand.

"I positioned myself before Yumi when I spotted Fuu. He lurched toward me, intent on attacking. Struggling to wield my sword as the bracelet drained our vitality, I found Fuu toying with me, effortlessly evading each of my strikes and hitting me on the head with the flat of his blade. Eventually, Yumi crumpled to the ground, and I sank to my knees, my head hanging low as I met her gaze, watching the light fade from her eyes."

Llia nervously bounces her knee, fidgeting while she listens to Reo's harrowing tale. "That's... that's awful. I can't imagine how devastating that must have been for you both." She places a gentle hand on his arm, her touch feather-light. "But you're still here, so somehow you must have survived. What happened next?"

Reo's eyes narrow with determination as he recounts the events. Fuu, wielding his blade, confronted him, but Reo quickly rolled forward to evade the attack and create some distance. As Fuu pursued him, Reo turned and thrust his blade into Fuu's throat, the Fudo sword disappearing as Fuu's lifeless body fell to the ground. Reo then gathered Yumi's fragile form, her breathing shallow but still present, and hurried toward the village with her on his back.

Pausing his tale, Reo reaches for another log to add to the fire as Llia's leg trembles with anticipation for the rest of the story.

"What happened? Tell me you made it back safely!" Llia exclaims, her voice laced with evident concern. The flickering firelight casts dancing shadows across her face, etched with worry as she leaned in, eyes wide and searching Reo's expression for any sign of ill news.

"Yes, we reached the village. A contingent of thirty guards came to our aid, but Subae, Fuu's elder sibling, overpowered them with his twin swords. Death was closing in on me, but I managed to summon just enough strength to remove her cursed bracelet. All I could do was shield her with my own body. The guards' screams echoed until they suddenly stopped. I was utterly paralyzed. Yumi kissed me and whispered softly, a smile on her face. Subae drove his sword into us. She was the first to die, and I soon followed—or so I thought." Reo's eyes meet Llia's as the silvery light gently illuminates her face.

Llia's eyes fall to the bracelet on his wrist. "Reo," she begins slowly, "you were able to remove Yumi's bracelet, but yours... it's still on."

Reo looks down at the bracelet, a hint of sadness in his eyes. "Yes, I've tried everything. It won't come off."

A spark of realization flickers in Llia's eyes. "Maybe... maybe the person who put it on has to be the one to take it off. Or," she pauses, choosing her words carefully, "maybe a lover is the only one who can remove it."

Reo's gaze snapped to hers, a mixture of hope and skepticism in his expression. "A lover? But Yumi..."

"Think about it," Llia urges, leaning forward. "If the bracelet symbolizes a 'lovers' bond,' then it makes sense that only someone you love or who loves you could break it. Myou designed it that way to keep you bound, to weaken you."

Reo falls silent, staring into the fire as if searching for answers in the flames. The idea was almost too simple, yet it made a strange kind of sense. His hand subconsciously traces the patterns on the bracelet.

"Maybe you're right," he finally says, his voice low and contemplative. "But how do we test your theory?"

Llia bites her lip, deep in thought. "We need someone who truly cares about you. Someone who loves you enough to try."

Reo's mind flashes through memories of comrades and friends he'd lost over centuries. He sighs heavily. "Love isn't something I can just summon at will."

Llia places a hand on his arm again, her touch steady and reassuring. "We'll figure this out together. You've carried this burden long enough."

The fire crackles between them as they sit in silence, both lost in their thoughts. The night's chill seems to recede slightly with their newfound resolve.

"We'll find a way," Llia whispers, more to herself than to him.

Reo looks at her, gratitude and determination mingling in his gaze. "We will."

They sit together by the fire, sharing a moment of understanding and solidarity. The path ahead remains uncertain, but they know one thing: they won't face it alone.

For now, that was enough.

"What does Myou want?"

It all makes sense now, and I can see why he is so guarded—because of what happened to Yumi. Why he looks so young and acts like he's from another time. But there's still something I'm missing.

"She's looking for earthly deities. They have incredible power. We believe she needs it to free Penumbra, the goddess of the moonless night. Myou's powers come from darkness; her powers will grow and elevate her into godhood. She has been searching for them since her brother, the Orochi dragon, was stopped by Susanoo," Reo says.

"Not the Orochi dragon!"

"Yes, the strongest being to ever live. He was also killing earthly deities to become a god, but he was tricked and killed."

"So, she wants to finish what her brother started. Okay, so how did you survive the attack from Subae?"

"Some mystical monks saved my life, but that's a story for another time. Tomorrow, I want to do another type of training with you. Get some rest, and we will head out first thing."

"Alright, that sounds foreboding. Well… it's getting late. I need to conduct another Yokai test with TJ and then head to bed. I have to wake up early to get beaten up again." Llia laughs softly as she strolls casually to the cabin's entrance. She powers up her laptop to study with TJ. Delving into his history gives her a sense of peace and reassurance.

Reo stayed behind at the lake's edge, staring intensely at the shadowy forest. "Soon, the Yokai will breach the camp's barrier! I believe she'll be prepared. Phase two starts now!" Reo declares as he douses the fire with a bucket of water and heads to his room.

CHAPTER ELEVEN

THE WATERFALL

L lia and Reo trek through the dense forest, the sound of rushing water guiding them to the nearby waterfall. The air thickens with moisture, invigorating Llia's senses as they approach their training ground.

"Focus on the sound," Reo instructs, his voice steady amidst the roar of the cascading water. "Let it drown out everything else."

She nods, narrowing her gaze on the frothy water plunging into the pool below.

Days turn into a rhythm of practice—she wields her blade under Reo's watchful eye, each swing cutting through the humid air.

As they near their final days of training, dark clouds rolled in, smothering the sun. Rain lashes against their faces and fierce winds rattled their makeshift camp.

"Hold on tight!" Reo shouts over the storm as he anchors their tent against gusts that threaten to uproot it.

But nature has other plans. A sudden surge of wind sweeps through like an unseen hand, lifting their tent from its moorings and sending it spiraling into the wilds.

"Great! Now what?" Llia huffs, glancing at Reo as rain drips from her hair.

He surveys their surroundings. "We'll have to share mine for now."

As night falls and temperatures dip, they squeeze into Reo's smaller tent. The fabric clings to them like a second skin as they settle in. Llia shivers slightly despite herself. It isn't just from the cold.

"What are you thinking?" Reo asks quietly, sensing her unease.

"I was thinking about how much we've been through together," she replies softly, warmth creeping into her voice. "You've changed... I've changed."

"Yeah?" He turns to meet her gaze.

She studies him—the way his brow furrows when he concentrates and how his lips curve into a smile that ignites something deep inside her.

As raindrops pelt against the tent and winds howl outside, Llia leans closer. She hesitates for just a moment before pressing her lips to his. The warmth of his body envelopes her, and she feels him respond instantly, no hesitation in his kiss.

Llia melts against him as they lose themselves in each other—passion igniting like a flame in the tempest outside. The world around them fades; only the taste of rain and each other's breath remaining in the confined space.

Reo wraps Llia in his powerful arms, the warmth of his body radiating through the damp fabric of their clothes. Their breaths mingle, filling the small space with a shared pulse. Outside, the storm rages, but inside the tent, time has paused.

Suddenly, the winds subside and the rain lightens to a soft patter. Llia pulls back, her heart racing as she searches Reo's eyes.

"Maybe we should—" he begins, his voice thick with uncertainty.

"No." She interrupts him, her resolve firm. "I wanted this."

He blinks at her, confusion flickering across his face. "You're sure?"

"Absolutely." She smiles, leaning into him again. The air between them buzzes with unspoken words and charged emotions.

Reo's shoulders relax but then tense again, caught in a tug-of-war between desire and caution. "I didn't want to rush things," he says quietly, regret lacing his tone.

"There's no need to apologize," Llia reassures him. "It felt right."

His gaze softens. She can see layers of thought playing behind his eyes—questions that spin around like leaves in a whirlwind.

"Things are complicated," he says after a moment. "With everything going on..."

"I know." She reaches up and brushes her fingers along his jawline, grounding them both amidst the chaos surrounding their lives.

His breath catches for a moment before he leans into her touch, his eyes closing briefly as if savoring the moment. Llia can feel the weight of their reality pressing against them—a world filled with training and danger—but in the tent, they exist in their own bubble.

"Do you think we'll make it?" Llia asks suddenly, pulling back just enough to study his face closely.

He nods slowly but doesn't break eye contact. A moment stretches between them—a breath held tight as they wrestle with what lies ahead while clinging to what they've discovered in their fleeting kiss.

"We should stop before things really heat up," Reo says.

"Yeah, you're right. This may complicate things if we go too far. But after all of this is done?"

"Yes," he replies with smiling eyes.

Moro glances at his phone, the screen glowing in the dim light of his office. He taps TJ's number and waits, the line buzzing in his ear.

"Hello?" TJ's voice is distorted over the speaker.

"It's Moro. I've got some heavy intel on Ma's restaurant," he starts, leaning back in his chair.

"What'd you find?"

"More than we bargained for. The place isn't just a front. It's a den for deadly Yokai."

TJ pauses. "Yokai? You sure?"

"Positive. They're using the food to control people, turning them into zombie-like creatures," Moro explains, his tone grim. "I did some digging—most of the missing persons ate there."

A silence settles over the line before TJ speaks again. "How many people are we talking about?"

"Dozens, maybe more. It's a web of disappearances all linked back to that restaurant."

"Damn." TJ's voice holds a mix of shock and disbelief. "So, what's the plan?"

Moro exhales slowly. "We need to shut it down, but we can't rush in blind. We need to understand their operation fully."

TJ's mind whirs audibly through the phone. "We should get eyes inside first. Any ideas on how to do that without getting caught?"

"I've got a few," Moro replies, hesitation catching his words. "But it'll take precision. We can't afford any mistakes."

"Agreed," TJ responds firmly. "So, who do we trust with this? We need someone who can blend in."

"I'm thinking, Maddix," Moro says after a moment's thought. "He's already in too deep; we can bug him and collect intel."

"Good call. I can hack his phone and turn it into a recording device," TJ acknowledges. "But we'll need a backup plan in case things go south."

"Already working on it," Moro assures him.

"Alright," TJ replies, a note of determination in his voice. "Llia is probably going to kill us when she finds out, but we need to bring these bastards down."

Moro nods to himself, feeling the weight of their task ahead but also the resolve strengthening within him. "We will," he affirms, ending the call and plunging back into his plans with renewed focus.

TJ sits in his dimly lit control room, the glow from his tablet illuminating his face. He taps on Reo's contact and waits for the call to connect. The screen flickers and Reo's image appears sitting cross-legged in his cabin room, eyes closed in meditation.

"Reo, we need to talk," TJ's voice cuts through the quiet.

Reo opens his eyes slowly, focusing on the screen. "What's up?"

"It's about that restaurant," TJ begins. "Moro found out they're not just running a shady business—they're Yokai, and they're building an army."

Reo frowns. "An army?"

"Yeah," TJ continues. "Moro and I suspect they're hiding them underground, right here in Seattle. People are disappearing, and it all leads back to that Ma's restaurant, and there is still no sight of Myou."

Reo absorbs the information, his expression darkening. "This is bad."

"Bad doesn't cover it," TJ says, shaking his head. "We need to hurry with your training with Llia. We're running out of time."

Reo nods. "We'll push harder. We can't afford to waste any more time."

"Exactly," TJ agrees. "The end is coming sooner than we thought. Be ready."

"We will be," Reo promises, determination etched into his features.

TJ ends the call and leans back in his chair, mind racing with strategies and contingency plans. He knew they were up against something formidable, but they have no choice but to fight back with everything they have.

The cabin falls silent again as Reo sits back down to continue meditating, steeling himself for the challenges ahead.

CHAPTER TWELVE
THE DEMON PATH

Months go by, and Llia begins to notice that her training is becoming easier. Her strength, skills, and resilience have significantly improved. Although she still falls short of Reo's expectations, he has started to share more with her each evening. Following their discussions, she would have an hour-long test with TJ. That night, Llia utilized her laptop to reach out to TJ.

"Sup, Sis? How is everything?" TJ asks, his slow speech quickening after a yawn.

"It's good! Yesterday, he started teaching me Heaven's Judgment, the sword style he created. I almost had him; I'm definitely getting close to beating him."

"Okay... Number one, you'll never beat him with a sword in his hand unless he wants you to. But keep that energy! Second, if he's teaching you that technique, you're catching on very quickly."

"Yeah, and I feel a lot stronger and faster since I've been out here."

"That's good. You'll need that confidence when facing the enemy. How is Reo? Has he been sleeping?"

"No, I don't think so. He looks pale sometimes, but at other times he seems fine. I know he's not, though. He's been opening up to me every night. He talks a lot about his mother and his..."

"Sis, remember what I said! It's not a good idea to get too close to him, okay? That makes the job almost impossible! Trust me."

It's a little late for that, she thinks as the memory of the steamy waterfall session pops into her head.

"I've spent months fighting and learning with this man. It would be nearly impossible not to feel something for someone after spending all that time with them, TJ." She softens her speech as she relives some of the long conversations that Reo has shared with her, recalling the vulnerability in his usually stoic expression when he spoke of his past. Those quiet moments by the fire, after training, revealed layers to him she never expected to find.

"I can't even argue with that. I agree it's hard to do. Just be careful." His genuine tone raises her suspicions, causing her to scrutinize his expression and body language for any signs of deceit. The flickering laptop screen makes it harder to discern his true intentions.

"What are you not telling me, TJ?"

"Nothing, I just don't want to see you get hurt."

"You mean like Tatsuo and Yumi?"

"He told you about that?" His voice rises.

"Well, yeah. I told you he's been opening up to me more."

"Llia, it's a moot point. All of this will only end in tears. But lucky for you, I do have some good news. Iris got a job at the hospital as a full-time resident. She works the night shift."

"That's great!"

"Rose is still the same old Rose. She attends her classes and goes on a lot of dates. I looked up her records to get a better understanding of her and Maddix."

"That's impossible."

"Impossible you say? Otis, pull up files for Rose Aday and Maddix Blume. Rose grew up in a broken home. Her mother abandoned her at the tender age of six. Her father was abusive toward her until he left when she was ten years old. Her aunt adopted her, but she was always at work, which only added to her feelings of abandonment. Maddix Blume is a brainy computer software designer by day and a hacker by night. He..."

"What the fuck! How the hell do you know that? They sealed Rose's records, and no one knows about Maddix's side hustle but me and the girls."

"Relax, sis. I have no limits, remember? I do background checks on everyone; it's standard procedure. I then create a data sheet that tracks your behavior, so if you deviate from it, I know something is up!"

"Well, damn, you're very thorough. It suggests that you have been betrayed in the past! Care to tell me about it?"

"He told you about Tristian too?!"

"No, he hinted that something bad happened to him. So, what did he do?"

TJ's face darkens as he leans back in his chair. "Tristian was with us for ten years before Reo arrived in America. The man was a beast—mastered every weapon he touched and could break concrete with his bare hands. He was the closest thing to a brother I ever had."

He rubs his temples, the memory clearly painful. "But power corrupts. The blade we protected housed Penumbra, an ancient goddess. Reo had guarded it for centuries before bringing it here. Tristian…" TJ's jaw clenches. "He made a deal with the yokai. Traded his humanity for power and became one of them just to get his hands on that sword.

"The night Reo landed in San Francisco, we tracked Tristian down. It was the hardest fight of my life, watching my brother try to kill us both. But in the end, two executioners against one traitor—the odds weren't in his favor."

TJ's voice grows quiet. "I weighed his body down myself and dropped him in the bay. Sometimes I still dream about it—the look in his eyes when the blade went through his chest. He wasn't even human anymore, but damn if it didn't hurt like losing family.

"That's why I'm warning you about getting close, Llia. This life we live—it changes people. And not always for the better."

"Shit, that's tough. I'm sorry you guys had to go through that."

And Myou strikes again; I guarantee she was the one who turned Tristian against them.

"Okay, TJ, I have to go. I need to call Moro. He hasn't updated me on Maddix in a while."

"Moro has his hands full searching for all the missing people."

"Missing people?!"

"Well, there has been a wave of missing people. Most of them..."

"Are women?" Llia replies.

"Well, yeah. How did you know that?"

"TJ, Reo's coming. It's way past curfew. I'm supposed to be sleeping! I gotta go, bye!"

"Okay, sis!"

Llia slams the computer shut and pretends to sleep. A trio of knocks sounds before Reo peeks inside. His eyes scan the bedroom, his brow lifts suspiciously, and then he shuts the door and retreats to his quarters. TJ's warning echoes in Llia's mind: *This will all end in tears!*

The following day, she experiences her most successful training session yet. Her movements flowed with newfound grace and precision, each technique executed with deadly accuracy. For the first time since they began, Reo didn't need to shout "Tsumi"—his usual signal for a fatal mistake. The achievement hung in the air like a badge of honor as darkness settled over their camp. That night, after their rigorous training concluded, they settled by the crackling fire, its orange flames casting dancing shadows across their faces. The peaceful moment felt right, and she finally gathered the courage to voice the question that had been gnawing at her thoughts.

"Reo, why don't you ever sleep?" Her eyes widen as she prepares to read his body language.

"Sleep?! How I loathe those tiny slices of death!" He snatches up a branch and prods the fire, warding off the evening's cold air.

"That's Edgar Allan Poe. Do you like his work?" Llia asks, but Reo doesn't respond.

Alright, avoiding my questions again. He's for sure hiding something. Let me try something else.

"Llia Ridley is not the name I was born with. My birth name is Camellia Ridley Sato." Llia says, and Reo becomes intrigued, his eyes flickering with sudden interest. He shifts his position to face her, diverting his attention from the fire. His shoulders tense slightly, betraying a mix of curiosity and wariness at her unexpected revelation.

"Your name is Camellia? *Tsubaki*?" Reo says with a glint in his eye.

"Yes, my grandmother would call me Tsubaki sometimes. It means Camellia in Japanese. I also have trouble sleeping sometimes because of what happened to my mother. Two years ago, she was killed at her shop. At times, I wonder if I could have rescued her or even taken her place if I had been present. The hardest part to accept was my desire to become a detective and solve her case. Moro imparted all his knowledge to me and prepared me to be the best, but…"

"What happened to you?" Reo inquires, hanging on every word she speaks.

"I messed everything up. The day before my exam, Iris and Rose convinced me to join them at the Turn Up, marking one year since my mother's passing. Rose believed it would help me cope with the loss, and for a while, it did. That is until some guys on the dance floor began groping Rose. She told them to knock it off, but they just laughed and continued."

Okay, I know how this is going to end. He thinks.

"I noticed them from the bar and hurried to her side. I told them to leave her alone. I took her hand and attempted to pull her away with me. They blocked my way and began hurling offensive names at me. But that wasn't the real issue; when one of them reached out and grabbed my breast, I snapped. They were no longer just creeps in my mind. They transformed into the ones who killed my mother, and to make a long story short, I broke arms, noses, and bruised a few egos. The guy pressed charges against me. Moro used his clout to keep me out of prison. Plus, having my dad as a heroic cop helped. However, I'm ineligible to serve in law enforcement again. I would have ended up in an institution if it weren't for my CP squad providing me with moral support. I spent the following year just wondering; the police chief agreed to bring me on as a case filer for the police department, but it's merely a desk job that nobody wanted."

"What is a CP squad?"

"Oh yeah, ha-ha... It's something we came up with when we were in junior high. My mom had a beautiful garden that we played in as little girls. She taught us about companion planting—different plants that help each other grow... Get it? Iris, Rose, Camellia."

Reo smiles. "Yes, I am familiar with companion planting, although the rose and the iris aren't the best flowers to plant with the camellia."

"You're telling me! We stay at each other's throats," Llia jokes. Reo's bright smile is delightful, a warm and genuine expression that lights up his face. Llia can't help but notice the way he wets his lips, a subtle gesture that draws her attention as he prepares to speak, hinting at the thoughtfulness and care he puts into his words.

"Back home, I have an enormous garden. It belonged to my mother. Her favorite flower was the camellia, which drove my father crazy." Reo chuckles.

"Really? Why is that?"

"The camellia flower was detested by warriors in Japan, particularly samurai. They interpreted the flower as a weakness because all the petals fell simultaneously instead of individually. I take after my mother in many ways."

Reo shares his fondness for the camellia flower while grabbing another log from behind him. Llia quietly celebrates out of his sight but halts when he faces her to place the log on the fire.

"My dad was a proud and highly skilled warrior, commanding both admiration and fear from everyone. Aware of my resemblance to my mother and younger brother, he chose to exile me, expecting my death. He enrolled me in a school operated by our sworn enemy, and in return, they sent their son to live in my house. This action was a show of respect and a positive step toward achieving peace. I managed to survive and even acquired some advanced sword techniques."

"He put you in harm's way! Your mother must have been devastated. Is that the reason you have trouble sleeping? I notice you seem more sluggish on certain days." *But you still manage to kick my ass.*

"No, but I'll tell you only if I can call you Camellia from now on."

A colossal smile stretches across her face, illuminating her features with infectious joy, and her heart quickens, pounding in her chest like a drum echoing through a quiet forest. The air around them shimmers with the weight of unspoken promises as the moment hangs delicately in the balance, ripe with possibility.

"Okay, deal."

He holds up his bracelet and clears his throat.

"As you figured out a while ago, I am cursed and poisoned. What you don't know is that I relive my wedding night every time I fall asleep, which is why I avoid sleeping. The experience is so intense that it feels like I'm reliving it. Regarding the poison, the longer I stay awake, the closer it gets to my heart. I heal when I sleep, but I can't completely cure myself. It's all tied to the bracelet."

"When you say you relive, you're saying that this isn't just a memory. You're saying that someone is forcing you to relive that moment using a spell?"

"Yes, it is so real that I wake up each day still reaching for her, but she's never there. I have to relive her death every day. I know this is just manipulation to keep me off balance, but sometimes it becomes unbearable. Sometimes I hope to die in battle so that it would all just end, but there is no honor in that, only great shame."

Oh my God! "Myou is evil!"

"Yes, but there is more," Reo says, his hair falling into his eyes as he speaks. He takes a deep breath, filling his lungs with crisp, fresh air, and glances at Llia.

"The monks nurtured me back to health and introduced me to the wonders of their mystical teachings. Their home was nestled deep within the mountains, secluded from the rest of the world. Back then, I was twenty-seven years old, and I spent ten years living with them, absorbing their knowledge and becoming a master of all that they taught me. As long as I stayed there, time had no effect on my age. I even acquired specialized skills, like the power to heal individuals and trade places with objects. But here's the catch: thanks to my curse, all my special skills don't work during a moonless night, and they require a tremendous amount of stamina, which I have very little of nowadays."

"Oh wow, that's a lot to process. I can't even imagine what you felt while you were there. You've just lost your wife and your life. How did you leave that place?"

"They allowed me to leave under one condition: I would take a cursed blade and watch over it for all the days of my life. I agreed. When I left their mystical city and came down from the mountain, eight hundred years had passed since they took me in, but I did not age a day."

"So, the monks made you immortal and gave you a job. That was the blade Penumbra was sealed in, TJ told me?"

"Yes. Thousands of years ago, the first and most powerful Yokai Ex named Renzo sealed Penumbra in a very special, god-like blade. A mortal cannot kill a god, but a mortal with a godly weapon can seal them away forever, and that's what Renzo did, but it cost a life to seal an immortal."

Llia stood with her hand over her mouth, her eyes wide, paralyzed by the revelation.

"The blade that Tristian took from you. Did you get it back?"

"No, Myou has it, and now she almost has everything she needs to free her!"

"So, you must kill Myou to free yourself from the curse that is sapping you of your full strength and abilities. You need to stop the Umbra from unsealing Penumbra, the goddess that will bring destruction, death, and eternal darkness!"

"Yes, and all before the diamond fuji of the new year."

What the hell, that's soon, very soon! Now I won't be able to sleep from now on!

Reo stands to his feet. "I have been doing this job for a long time. I know all the tricks. I learned a long time ago to walk the path of the demon, meaning I killed all my emotions to complete the task. I didn't always make the right decisions, especially if they hindered the mission! People have died, but not because of my failure to act in time, but..."

"Because you chose not to save them! How many people died?" Llia's voice trembles as the weight of the accusation hangs in the air. She sits back in shock, her eyes wide and brimming with disbelief and sorrow. The area seems to close in around them, the tension thickening as Reo's expression remains stoic, yet his eyes hint at deep, buried remorse.

"Too many," he replies, his voice barely above a whisper, as if confessing a dark secret. "I'd lost sight of myself, swallowed whole by the shadow of what happened to me." The weight of his admission hangs heavy in the air, a palpable reminder of the scars etched deep within his soul.

"Reo, I believe we've had enough for tonight. I'm going to sleep while I still can." Llia walks to her room and buries her face in her pillow. His words make her stomach churn.

I can't believe I misjudged him so badly. Oh my God!

Outside, Reo walks around the shore of the lake toward the forest, his wandering eyes searching for an answer to his mind. He uses his watch to make a call. "TJ, report."

"Hello to you too, Senpai. Yes, I'm fine as well. Thanks for asking. You started phase three early, I see! You sound flustered," TJ says.

"I'm sorry, TJ. I just told her the truth, which was more complicated than I thought."

"Wait! Even the thing about her mother?"

"No, that would be too much right now; telling her I ignored your intel that could have possibly saved her mother's life would make things...unfixable."

"What the fuck did you just say?!" Llia's eyes flash with fury as she lets out a piercing scream, her voice echoing through the shadowy forest. Rage boils within her, a tempestuous storm of emotions erupting to the surface as she grapples with the devastating truth Reo just revealed. Her body trembles with the intensity of her anguish, every muscle tense and coiled, ready to lash out at the cruel injustice that had been thrust upon her.

"Oh! Damn! Did she hear you?! Shit, I've got my own problem. Maddix is in trouble. I'll check on it, and you handle yours. Good luck." TJ says before ending the call.

Llia gasps for breath as she bares her teeth and waits for his reply.

"I wanted to tell you, but I..."

"How long have you known that she was my mother?"

"Since...you were in the hospital, TJ pulled your records, and I made the connection."

"You lied to me! TJ seems to be the only one I can trust! He warned me not to get too close to you, and boy, I should've listened. So, TJ gave you information that my mother may have been a target, and what did you do best? Nothing!"

"Yes, but Camellia, it's not that simple; there was an underlying…"

"You know, I came back out here to better understand why you did what you did. How you decide who lives or dies! I tried to rationalize it in my head a hundred times over! That's before I learned I was one of your victims."

"Camellia, listen to me!"

"No! Fuck that! And fuck you! You are not the good guy! You were supposed to hunt the Yokai, not become one!" With a swift motion, she removes her bracelet and hurles it toward his feet, then disappears into the eerie depths of the dark forest, tears flowing freely from her eyes.

"Camellia, wait! Don't go past the barrier!"

Her piercing cries of anguish reverberate through the eerie, shadowy forest, sending a chill down Reo's spine. Without a moment's hesitation, he snatches two gleaming swords from the nearby weapons rack and sprints toward the source of the distressed shrieks, his heart pounding with a mixture of dread and determination.

"Camellia!"

Surveying his surroundings, he finds himself immersed in a domain shrouded in shadow. Moonlight filters weakly through the canopy, casting dim shapes across the landscape. His pulse thunders within, each beat echoing through his skull. Searching desperately, he discovers no footprints or path, her essence vanished completely. Without the bracelet, their spiritual link was broken, preventing him from locating her directly. Sinking to one knee, he presses his palm against the cool soil beneath him. The rhythmic swaying of timber above reaches his senses as gusts stir the foliage. Rising, he draws a deep breath, savoring the crisp, pine-scented atmosphere.

He plunges further into the woods, the noise of rustling leaves and breaking twigs echoing around him. His nostrils fill with a familiar, soothing aroma. As he pushes through the dark underbrush, his hands become sweaty and slippery. The odor of decay fills the air, affirming his deepest fears. With a rapid flick of his blades, he easily cuts through any barrier in his way. His smartwatch shows he has covered three miles in mere minutes before indicating a low battery.

"Otis, share my coordinates with TJ! Instruct him to be ready for a possible extraction." He steps into an open space, and the noise of heavy footsteps approaches. A faint light brightens the area, revealing a haunting scene—red eyes peering from the shadowy forest. The footsteps become more pronounced, and he senses tremors beneath him. A deep, thunderous voice resonates through the clearing, bouncing off the trees.

"You should've never followed me here!" a demonic voice echoes, reverberating through the dense forest. Reo advances with measured steps, his eyes narrowing as he approaches the looming, dark figure. Towering over him, its presence is suffo-cating and malevolent, casting an oppressive aura that seems to darken the very air around them.

"Just give her back to me, and I will let you live, Itto!"

Materializing from the darkness, a colossal demon-like creature steps forth, clutching the motionless Llia draped across his shoulder. His monstrous stature dwarfs Reo completely. Crimson skin stretches across his form, while obsidian eyes bore into his opponent. Twin horns jut from his brow, enhancing the menacing presence of his muscular physique. In his massive fist, he wields a brutal, spiked maul studded with lethal metal barbs.

"I've got all the power now, Reo! I've got the girl, and if my memory serves me right, you were the one on the verge of death the last time we fought! You already look half dead, so how about I tuck you in, and I might let the bitch live? Once I'm done having a good time, of course," Itto chuckles, playfully grabbing Llia's ass as she lay unconscious over his shoulder.

"I do recall that, yes. Additionally, I remember engaging with approximately two hundred of your subordinates before you were willing to confront me. You allow your adversaries to exhaust themselves battling your minions and then effortlessly defeat them," Reo replies.

Itto's face twists into a sinister grin, his lips curling upwards in a malevolent display. The Yokai's eyes glint with a predatory gleam, revealing the twisted machinations of his dark mind. This was a being who reveled in the suffering of others, finding pleasure in the pain he inflicts upon his victims. Reo steels himself, knowing he will need to be on guard against Itto's cunning and ruthlessness.

"You got me, but I won't use that trick now. I want to kill you with my own hands. You're dead meat! I've waited months for you to finally get past that damn barrier. Watch it! Don't take another step. It's obvious why you want her back so badly; she is a sweet piece of ass!"

"Don't touch her! On second thought, I've decided I will kill you after all," Reo's sharp words hit their mark as he reveals his dual blades.

"Give it your best shot, but those little blades won't help you at all." Itto tosses Llia aside. Unconscious, she fell to the ground, the rough texture of the earth scraping against her cheek.

The thug heaves his massive bludgeon with raw power, making it sing through the air like a toppling oak. Reo darts with calculated grace, his form melting away as he dodges sideways. The heavy weapon crashes into the earth, scattering soil and fragments everywhere.

"You're too slow, Itto." Reo's voice is cold and calculating.

"Stand still and fight!" Itto roars, swinging again, but Reo is already gone, darting to the side. The ogre's attacks are powerful but clumsy. Each miss only fuels his rage further.

Reo's twin blades glint like shards of starlight in the dim glow, his movements fluid and precise as he closes the distance. The steel finds its mark along Itto's exposed flank. Dark blood sprays in an arc from the deep wound, painting the ground with cerise droplets. Itto howls in pain, the sound echoing off like a wounded beast, his massive frame stumbling sideways from the force of the strike.

"You're just a pest!" Itto bellows, bringing his club around in a wide arc. Reo ducks under it effortlessly, his movements almost graceful in contrast to Itto's brute strength.

"Fight me properly!" Itto demands, his eyes burning with a fury that seemed to intensify the air around him. Veins bulge on his forehead, and his chest heaves with every breath, the ferocity of his anger almost palpable.

Reo doesn't respond. Instead, he leaps forward, driving one blade into Itto's shoulder. The ogre swings wildly in response, trying to dislodge him, but Reo twists the blade deeper before pulling it out swiftly.

Itto staggers back, clutching his shoulder as blood oozes between his fingers. "You think this will stop me?" He snarles through gritted teeth, swinging again with desperate ferocity.

This time, Reo doesn't dodge; he steps inside the swing and slices upward with both blades. His swords meet flesh and bone with a sickening crunch.

Itto screams, dropping his club as he clutches at his chest where deep gashes marred his red skin. Reo stands before him, calm and composed despite the intensity of the fight.

"I've learned patience over the years," Reo says quietly. "You should've too."

With one final effort, Itto lunges at Reo barehanded. But Reo is faster; he steps aside and brings both blades down on Itto's back in a cross-slash. The creature collapses to his knees with a guttural groan.

Reo watches him fall without pity. He wipes the blood from his blades and sheathes them calmly as Llia stirs on the ground nearby.

"Stay down," Reo warns as Itto tried to rise again. The oni glares at him but lacks the strength to continue.

Llia blinks awake, her eyes finding Reo standing tall over their fallen foe. She struggles to her feet, swaying slightly as she takes in the scene. "Is it over?" she asks softly.

"For now," Reo replies curtly. "We need to move before more show up."

Llia nods shakily and takes a tentative step toward him.

A dark mist creeps through the forest clearing, wrapping around Itto's fallen form. His wounds seal shut as black veins spread across his red skin. He rises to his feet, towering higher than before, his muscles swelling with newfound power.

Reo's breath comes in ragged gasps, the poison in his system burning through his veins. His vision blurs as exhaustion pulls at his limbs.

"What's wrong, Reo? Looking a bit pale." Itto's voice booms deeper than before. He swings his fist, catching Reo in the chest before he can dodge.

The impact sends Reo crashing through a tree trunk. He stumbles to his feet, blood trickling from his mouth. His blades feel heavy in his trembling hands.

"Stop it!" Llia screams as Itto grabs Reo by the throat and slams him into the ground so hard the earth cracks beneath the force.

Reo slashes at Itto's arm, but the blade bounces off harmlessly. The darkness has turned the creature's skin to steel. Itto laughs and kicks Reo across the clearing like a ragdoll.

"Watch closely, girl. See how pathetic your protector really is." Itto stalks toward his crumpled body.

He tries to stand, but his legs give out. The exhaustion and poison had finally caught up to him. His body refuses to respond as Itto's massive fist connects with his jaw, sending him spinning through the air.

"No!" Llia's hands cover her mouth as she watches Itto pummel Reo mercilessly. Each impact echoes through the forest like thunder. Blood sprays across the grass with each brutal strike.

Itto grabs Reo's arm and twists until bones snap. Reo's scream pierces the night air. His other arm hangs limp at his side, both swords lying useless on the ground.

"Still think you're better than me?" Itto drives his knee into Reo's ribs. More cracks follow as Reo slumps to the forest floor, barely conscious.

He lies broken on the ground, his blood seeping into the earth. Through the haze of pain, a thought crystallizes—there was only one way out. The weapon he'd sworn never to use again.

He closes his eyes, focusing past the agony of his shattered bones. Golden light sparks between his trembling fingers as he calls forth the Fudo katana. The legendary blade materializes in his grasp, its edge gleaming with the intensity of sunlight.

Itto's eyes widen at the sight. "That sword—"

Reo lunges forward with his remaining strength. The blade cuts through Itto's steel-like skin as if it were paper. Blazing light erupts from the wound, and Itto's scream turns to ash in his throat as the sword's heat consumes him.

But the victory is short-lived. Dark shapes detach from the shadows—three Yokai assassins in black garb, their red eyes glowing beneath demon masks. They move like smoke, silent and deadly.

Reo's vision blurs. His legs buckle beneath him as he clutches the katana. "Llia," he gasps, extending the sword toward her. "Take it. You have to fight."

She grips the handle, feeling the raw power thrumming through the blade. The Yokai circle closer, curved blades glinting.

"Remember your training," Reo whispers before collapsing.

Llia backs away, drawing the demons from Reo's prone form. They follow, moving in perfect synchronization. Her heart hammers as she recalls Reo's lessons—footwork, blade angles, reading opponents' movements.

The Yokai spread out, forming a triangle around her. Their weapons point at her throat, chest, and back. One wrong move would mean death. Llia tightens her grip on the burning sword, its light casting sharp shadows across the demons' masks.

The Yokai strike as one, their blades whistling through the air. Llia drops low, the sword's golden light trailing an arc as she spins beneath their attacks. The closest demon's blade passes inches from her face, but she's already moving.

Her counter-strike blazes upward, catching the first Yokai across its midsection. The demon mask splits in two, revealing nothing but shadow underneath as the creature dissolves into black mist.

The remaining pair move like mirror images, their synchronized attacks forcing Llia to retreat. Steel rings against steel as she parries their relentless assault. Their curved blades became silver blurs, testing her defenses from multiple angles.

One Yokai feints high while the other strikes low. Llia catches the high attack with Reo's katana, its burning light momentarily blinding the demon. She kicks out at the second attacker, buying herself space to maneuver.

The demons press forward again, but now Llia sees the pattern in their movements. As they attack in unison, she steps between them, letting their blades cross where she had been standing. She fluidly pivots and brings the katana down through the nearest Yokai's shoulder. The demon's form shimmers and bursts apart like smoke in a strong wind.

The final Yokai assassin closes its eyes and absorbs the darkness. When he opens his eyes, they glow red as he lunges at Llia faster than before, its blade a blur of deadly precision. She parries the attack, her katana's golden light sparking against the demon's dark steel. The Yokai presses forward, driving her back with a flurry of strikes.

Reo struggles to rise, his broken body screaming in protest. He watches helplessly as Llia fights for her life. Looking at the treetops above, he sees a black crow made of shadow. He knew

Myou was watching; she was the one who powered up Itto and the last Yokai Llia was now facing. He smashes his fist into the ground and watches on.

The Yokai is relentless, a dance of death honed by centuries of killing. But Llia meets each attack with growing confidence. Reo's training flows through her like instinct. She anticipated the Yokai's feints and counters, her body responding almost before her mind could process the moves.

Their blades lock together, the Yokai's red eyes boring into hers. It hisses, baring jagged teeth behind its mask. Llia holds fast, feeling her katana's power surging up her arms as she thinks of Reo's warning about maintaining one's balance in battle.

With a burst of strength, she shoves the demon back. It stumbles, off-balance for a split second. Llia seizes the opening, her blade flashing in a golden arc.

The Yokai's head tumbles from its shoulders, its body crumpling like a marionette with cut strings. Black mist leaks from the stump of its neck as it dissolves into nothing.

Llia stands over the fading remains, her chest heaving. The Fudo katana's light dims as she lowers it to her side. She turns to Reo, her eyes wide with shock and exhilaration.

Reo meets her gaze, a smile tugging at his bloodied lips. "You did it," he rasps. "You've become a true master."

Llia rushes to his side, carefully helping him to his feet. He leans heavily against her, his broken arm cradled to his chest.

"We need to get you out of here," she says urgently. "Those things could come back any second."

Reo nods weakly. "Lead the way. I'll be right behind you."

Together, they limp into the shadows of the forest, leaving the battleground behind. She releases the blade as it grows hot in her hand, vanishing into the night air like a beam of light from a sunset. As they disappear into the darkness, a pair of red eyes watches from above. The shadow crow perches silently in the branches, observing. After a moment, it spreads its smoky wings and takes flight, vanishing into the starless sky to report what it had witnessed.

Several hours had passed, and the sun would soon be rising. Llia knows she can't carry Reo too far, as their battle wounds were taking their toll. She set him down and gathered wood for a fire so they could rest and prepare for the long journey back to the cabin. Quickly, she builds a shelter around him, facing the fire, and lies down beside him, carefully placing her arms around his shivering body. After a while, he eventually warms up, and his shallow breathing stabilizes. She starts to drift off to sleep with him in her arms, lying next to a roaring fire not far from the dazzling waterfall where they had shared that magical night. The memory begins to quell her anger toward him, and the past six months flood her mind. A warm sensation washes over her as she holds his solid body. This warmth grows into a roaring fire as she inhales his musk and exhales ecstasy. Holding him a little tighter, she realizes her true feelings for him. Llia closes her eyes and falls asleep.

Ma's restaurant hums with the usual chatter and clinking of dishes. Behind the counter, Ma stirs a pot of steaming broth, her eyes occasionally flicking to the darkened corner of the room. A shadow shifts there, indistinct and malevolent.

A sudden rush of wind heralds the arrival of the shadow crow. It swoops into the room and perches on a rafter above Ma's head, its red eyes glowing like embers in the dim light.

"Report," Ma says without looking up from her pot.

The crow's voice emerges deep and raspy. "Itto has failed. Llia has escaped, and Reo still lives."

Ma's hand tightens around the ladle, her knuckles whitening. "Explain."

"Llia's strength has grown considerably," the crow continues, "Reo's training has made her formidable. And he cares for her."

A low growl emanates from the shadow in the corner, its form pulsating with rage. The darkness thickens, roiling like a storm cloud about to break.

"He cares for her?" The words drip with venomous disbelief.

The crow shifts uneasily on its perch. "Yes. He fought with a desperation I have not seen before. His concern for Llia is genuine."

Ma turns to face the shadow, her expression unreadable but her eyes cold and calculating. "What do you wish to do?"

The shadow seethes, its voice a hiss that cuts through the room like a knife. "We cannot allow this bond to strengthen.

Reo must be punished!" The shadow writhes in the corner, a swirling mass of darkness pulsing with intent. "If we can't execute Reo and take the girl," it hisses, "we will bring Llia to us."

Ma's brow furrows as she processes the command. "You want me to summon Maddix?"

"Do it. It is time to bring Llia home."

Ma kneels before the shadow, her expression shifting from annoyance to reverence. "As you command."

With a wave of her hand, she summons the crow from its perch. "Go find Maddix. Bring him here."

The crow nods and vanishes into the shadows, its wings whispering through the air like secrets.

Moments later, Maddix stumbles through the restaurant door, his frame gaunt and trembling. The poison coursing through him leaves dark rings under his eyes and pallor on his cheeks. "What do you want?" he croaks, struggling to stand tall before Ma.

She studies him for a moment, feasting on his weakness. "Call Llia home," she orders, her tone icy.

"No." His voice is barely above a whisper but firm as stone.

"Do you understand what I can do to you?" Her voice rises with fury, and the atmosphere crackled with tension.

Maddix straightens despite himself. "I'd rather die than betray my friends."

Anger flares within Ma like wildfire. She can feel the power surging through her veins—the control she wields over him. She steps closer, her presence looming over him like an eclipse.

"The poison I control in your body is but a fraction of my power," she spits. "You will obey me!"

Maddix staggers back at her words, clutching his stomach as if trying to ward off an unseen blow. "You won't break me," he gasps, his face twisting in pain.

Ma smirks at his defiance; it only fuels her wrath further. He thought he could resist forever? How amusing.

Then an idea flickers in her mind—an alternative solution lay right before her. Why wait for him to call Llia?

With that realization came an overwhelming rush of dark pleasure; she would simply kill him.

"Very well," Ma says sweetly, taking deliberate steps toward him as shadows dance around them both.

Before Maddix can react, she thrusts out her hand, and he doubles over as agony surges through him like wildfire igniting dry grass. A scream tears from his lips—sharp and raw—as he crumples onto the floor in a heap of despair and pain.

"Let's see how long you can endure this," Ma whispers with malicious delight, savoring every second of his suffering as shadows swirl around them like hungry beasts ready to feast on despair.

A few days had passed, and Llia and Reo made it back to the cabin, where they had been recovering. Llia creeps into his room to check on him. His broken arm and bruises have nearly healed. TJ had once told her that if he slept a full night, he could heal major injuries in no time. He also mentioned that getting him to sleep was like pulling a wisdom tooth without anesthetics. She shook him to wake him for dinner.

"Ouch!"

"Oh, shit! I'm sorry, Reo."

"No, I'm okay, just sore."

"You've been out for a few days now. I made dinner; are you hungry?"

"Yes, and I am grateful that you saved my life, Camellia. I cannot express how proud I am of you! You were truly remarkable. Your fighting prowess has reached an impressive level."

"Yeah, well, six months of getting your ass kicked all day every day will do that for you. My body knows what to do without having to think about it now. It's pretty powerful, and it helps to have a brilliant teacher like you."

"Camellia, you are no longer my student. You have killed a Yokai, a level two, no less. We can return to the city now and continue searching for the Umbra. Also, about your mother: I had information about three known attacks by the Yokai that day. They were all traps; they divided my team and defeated us. It's how they died the same day your mother did. It was my fault. I didn't see it in time, and we lost many good people that day.

TJ and I were the only ones who made it out. I understand if you hate me for it."

"Listen, I had a few days to think about that. If I were in your shoes, I don't think I could choose who lives and dies either. You did your best, and, like you said, we both lost a great deal that day. Let's work together to stop this threat and try not to lose anyone else in the process. I forgive you. I also want to know about that amazing sword! When I had it, I could feel the power it gave me. Why don't you always use it? You would be unbeatable!"

"When I first used the Fudo sword, it gave me a significant advantage over my enemies, but I lost myself in its awesome power. Myou's goal is to attain the powers of a god so she can kill them for killing her brother, the Orochi dragon. I imagine she started her thirst for power the same way. I became addicted to the power and completely relied on it more and more. I felt invincible, and in my arrogance, my team was killed. I became a leaf in the clouds, just like Myou," Reo says.

"What does that mean?! A leaf in the clouds?"

"It's when you depend on a power to elevate you above your current status; a status that's not your own. A leaf can only make it to the clouds with the strength of the wind. It will also become lost, as I did. Now, I only use it as a last resort. It's still incomplete; it has an ultimate form, but only a worthy swordsman can achieve it. No one has ever come close to doing so, and it gets hotter the longer you use it; if you don't let it go, the flames will consume you."

"Well, shit! It did feel intoxicating. I understand why you don't use it, though, if it can literally destroy you. Listen, I want to help you and TJ fight those fuckers. I want to join the Yokai Ex!"

Reo locks eyes with Llia. "I don't think it's a good idea. It's much too dangerous. Forgive me for saying this, but you have your whole life ahead of you. You're young and beautiful; you should have a career, start a family, and have a real chance at happiness. TJ and I can't have those things; we will fight until we die."

"Do you want those things? A lover? A family?" Llia asks with bated breath.

"I..." Reo's smartwatch comes online after charging in the sunlight, and the alarm rings. He touches the watch to stop the alarm, and TJ appears on the screen.

"TJ, what is it?"

"I have been trying to reach you for the last few days. It's Maddix. He's in the hospital. I'm sending the remote helicopter to the cabin now. Reo, it's not good. They made their move."

CHAPTER THIRTEEN

THE BISHOP ADVANCES

Several hours later, TJ's fingers fly across the holographic keyboard while Otis processes the intercepted messages from all the hospital employees.

"Otis, how many exits does the hospital have?"

"Four main exits, two emergency exits, and a helipad on the roof, sir. Current occupancy shows three hundred twelve patients and ninety-eight staff members."

TJ pulls up the hospital's network infrastructure. "How long until they reach the hospital?"

"Approximately eighteen minutes. Three dozen Yokai signatures detected moving from the east."

"Hack the Chief of Medicine's phone and send Iris a message giving her the night off." TJ accesses the hospital's emergency systems. "And get me building control."

"Message sent. Building controls accessed."

TJ activates the fire alarm. Red lights flash through the hospital corridors as the evacuation protocol initiates. On his screens, he watches as dots representing people stream toward the exits.

"Sir, Iris has received the message, and her phone's location shows she is at home. Maddix is too critical to be moved due to his unusual illness."

"Okay, we will go to his room. How many are still inside?"

"Ninety-three severely critical patients and forty staff members. Evacuation proceeding at optimal speed."

TJ tracks the helicopter carrying Reo and Llia, still ten minutes out. The Yokai signatures draw closer—fifteen minutes. It would be close.

"Otis, seal all entry points except the main doors. Route everyone to the front."

"Done. Seventy-two patients remaining."

TJ's screens light up with security camera feeds. The parking lot fills with evacuees as ambulances arrive to transport critical patients.

"Fifty-one patients. Staff count: thirty."

The Yokai signatures accelerate.

"Sir, they're moving faster than predicted. New arrival estimate: ten minutes."

"How many inside?"

"Twenty-nine patients, eighteen staff members, and Maddix. Reo and Llia's ETA: five minutes."

TJ's jaw clenches. "Lock down the east wing. Buy us more time."

The dots continue flowing out of the building. Soon, the hospital would be empty before either friend or foe arrived—just as he planned.

The dots halt abruptly on TJ's screen, clustering near the main exit. His fingers hover over the keys, his eyes narrowing at the frozen scene.

"Otis, what's happening with those cameras?"

"All lower floor feeds are offline. Attempting to reconnect... no success."

"Damn it." He pushes away from his desk, grabbing several weapons and sprinting toward the door. "Keep trying. I'm going in."

TJ exits the war horse, entering through the back entrance and slipping into the hospital, his heart pounding in his chest. The corridors echo with his footsteps as he makes his way toward the emergency stairwell. As he climbs, the air grows thicker, an unnatural silence pressing down on him.

He can hear the helicopter's rotors from the roof. The chopper descends slowly, kicking up debris and creating a whirlwind of noise and dust. TJ waits in the stairwell, taking a deep breath as he checks his smartwatch for an update on the cameras that had gone down.

"Sir, the cameras are back online." Otis's voice rings through TJ's earpiece. "You need to see this."

TJ's smartwatch projects the feed, and his blood runs cold. Bodies litter the hospital lobby floor, their limbs twisted at unnatural angles. Deep, precise cuts mar their flesh—the kind that only a master swordsman or spearman could deliver. Blood pools beneath each victim, spreading across the sterile white tiles in dark crimson patterns.

"Count?" TJ's voice comes out hoarse.

"Twenty-seven casualties. The cuts... they match the style of the Umbra assassins we've documented. Clean, methodical, no wasted movement."

TJ scans the footage, studying the precise positioning of each body. "Time of death?"

"Based on blood coagulation and body temperature readings, approximately three minutes ago. Sir, the Yokai signatures are still approaching."

The helicopter's rotors grow louder overhead. TJ presses against the stairwell wall, processing the implications. An Umbra member had beaten both them and the Yokai to the hospital. But why?

"Otis, cross-reference these cutting patterns with our database."

"Already done. They match three previous incidents attributed to Umbra operative codename 'Udai.' Probability of match: 92%."

CHAPTER FOURTEEN
DEAD END

Seconds later, TJ's remote helicopter lands on the rooftop of Evergreen Hospital. Instead of Llia being a nervous wreck, as she had been for the past few months, something has changed; she remains composed and alert. Throughout the entire flight, she stays completely silent. She is not interested in mourning anyone. She's ready for a fight.

Evergreen Hospital, that's where Iris works. She'll be on shift and should have some answers.

They make their way down what seems to be a never-ending flight of stairs from the roof. Llia notices something chilling: there isn't a single sound inside the building, coupled with the smell of death. They see someone standing on the stairs by the third-floor door. A handsome African-American male stands by the exit. He's wearing tactical clothing, as if he's special ops. His haircut is short, and he is clean-shaven. He has brown eyes, full, attractive lips, and gorgeous, pearl-white teeth. He's a little taller than Reo and has the build of a welterweight boxer.

"Hi, sis. Nice to see you in the flesh. I wish it were under better circumstances, though," TJ says as he embraces her.

"Oh my goodness, TJ! It's so good to see you in person, and what handsome flesh it is. Thank you so much for all the pep talks," Llia replies with a huge smile.

"No problem. I know how it is training under this guy, and you are just as beautiful as he—"

"Hump," Reo clears his throat, redirecting their attention. His smile reveals perfect white teeth against his olive skin, warm and magnetic. His eyes soften, making their deep brown hues sparkle like honey.

Llia's heart skips a beat. His smile transforms his stern face. It's like sunlight breaking through dark clouds.

"Oh, yeah. Sorry, Reo, bring it in, man," TJ says, embracing him.

"It's been a long time since we worked side by side on the same mission," Reo says.

"Yes, too long *senpai*. Here, sis, put this watch on your left wrist, place this behind your ear, and follow me. You need to see this for yourself." TJ hands her a small clear dot, a beautiful watch that resembles Reo's, and a custom gun.

Senpai means upperclassman.

"Reo, let me talk to you over here for a second. Listen, I've been monitoring your vitals. They were all over the place. How did you summon the Fudo sword in the state you were in? You reported that you couldn't even stand up! And does she know about the curse and the poison?" TJ asks, looking at Llia and smiling.

"Yes, she does. She's with us now. She is Yokai Ex, so tell her everything later on. To tell you the truth, I don't know how I summoned the sword. Whenever I'm around her, I feel stronger for some reason."

"Interesting. I'll run a test later, and we will find out. Okay, you guys ready?" TJ asks.

"Yes, lead the way, TJ," Reo replies.

"Wait a minute, TJ and I have weapons. Where is your weapon, Reo?" Llia asks as TJ smirks and looks at him for an answer.

He looks at her with pure confidence. "I am the weapon! Let's go."

"You see how he said that with rizz? I taught him that," TJ says as he leads the way.

With cautious steps, they enter the halls, their eyes keenly searching the dark corners. As they pass through the dimly lit rooms, the sound of televisions fills the air. Llia's footsteps echo throughout the empty halls as she searches for signs of life. The sudden vibration of her watch catches her attention, and she checks it immediately. A voice resonates from the depths of her thoughts. "I am the AI system. Call me Otis." Otis notifies her that people are evacuating downstairs and that the floor is clear. A smile spreads across her face.

I didn't even have to ask! It was as if he could read my mind.

"Yes, I use fMRI to read your thoughts and put them into action. Need a flashlight? Just think about it. Need to send a distress call? I can even order a pizza," Otis responds to Llia.

Can anyone else see what's in my mind?

"No, this is forbidden. No one will ever know your inner thoughts, and I will never tell." Otis replies.

Suddenly, the entire hallway is engulfed in darkness. With their guns drawn, they move toward a room at the end of the hall. While Reo takes the lead, TJ covers the rear. Their seamless coordination shows they have collaborated for an extended period. To maintain the element of surprise, they resort to using hand signals. When TJ reaches the door, he points toward the room. Upon entering, Llia hurriedly makes her way to the left side of the dimly lit room, meticulously inspecting each corner while TJ simultaneously focuses his attention on the right side. Upon noticing that the window is open, she examines it, but her search yields no results. The room is not just dark, it is a scene of emptiness and desolation.

This makes no sense. How can there be no one walking around outside? Not even a car driving in the streets?!

"Sis, over here!"

She turns and makes her way to the other side of the dim room.

"His chart says he's critical and won't last through the night! Wait!" TJ looks at Reo. "We've seen this before!"

Reo comes closer and looks at Maddix. "*Isshin Boshi* (is-shin-bo-shi) soup!"

"What the hell is... inch-boy soup?" Llia asks.

"It's pure evil! It attacks from within the body. Anyone who comes in contact with its scent will feel an overwhelming hunger to eat the soup. Once consumed, it feels like you're being stabbed from inside your gut. You rot from the inside out; the pain only stops when you do what the soup's creator wants. If you give in to the spell, you'll turn into a Yokai! The Isshin Boshi soup has corrupted Maddix. No medicine can cure this. I'm so sorry," TJ says as he walks toward the door to keep watch.

Observing the situation closely, she approaches his bed and notices that Maddix appears extremely pale. He seems to have lost around ten pounds. Each inhale and exhale is drawn out, his breathing languid and relaxed. His body is slick with sweat, and he remains motionless.

"I've seen this before. Those guys at the party looked like this! Inch-boy soup! Wait, Charlie told me at the party that Maddix ate at that new place... Ma's. That has to be it! It's a new restaurant, and it's near the college. It would be a good place to corrupt a lot of people. I bet that's where all the missing people also went to eat," Llia says.

Reo looks into Llia's eyes and sees the sorrow reflected in them. TJ glances at Reo and does a double take as he witnesses the intensity in Reo's eyes fade away.

"He did go there a few times while Moro and I were tracking him. I didn't see anything out of the ordinary, though. But Moro says he did, but he couldn't prove it. He also said that the people who went missing were stored underground in Seattle; the way he describes it, it's like she's building an army," TJ says.

Reo flashes back to his conversation with the High Priest Makoto about stopping Myou before she builds an army. "Camellia, I'm going to try something, but I need your help. There is no cure for his condition, but I think you and I can help him!"

"What? How? What do you want me to do?"

"Take Maddix's hand and picture him as he was—healthy," he closes his eyes, placing his hands on Maddix's stomach.

TJ leaves the room for a second to check the halls and get a situation report on the approaching Yokai. His footsteps echo softly in the empty hallway.

A warm feeling swells in Llia, quickening her heart. A surge of overwhelming energy flows through her. In her mind, she imagines a vibrant Maddix being consumed by a brilliant, radiant light. Suddenly, the heavy darkness in the room vanishes. Llia looks at Maddix and notices color restored to his face. His breathing is strong once more, and he appears healthy.

How is this possible?! What did we do? Did Reo do this?

"L-Llia, is that really you?" Maddix's shaky voice is low. He sits up and scans the room.

"Yes, it's me!" She hugs him so tightly it hurts.

"What in the hell happened?"

"Well... it's a long story. Let me get you out of here, and I'll tell you all about it." Llia hugs Maddix again.

TJ walks over to a kneeling Reo and helps him to his feet. He notices Reo's color has changed.

"You can't overdo it, senpai, or else…"

"TJ, I'm fine… That should have wiped me out, but…" Reo looks at Llia's huge smile.

"I guess we find strength in the strangest places, right?"

"Yes… yes, we do."

"Reo, what do you think you're doing? You know you can't fall for her!" TJ whispers.

He inhales softly. "I honestly didn't think I could ever feel…"

Proximity alert! You have twenty-five Yokai approaching fast; the estimated time of arrival is two minutes until they reach your location.

"TJ, the helicopter?" Reo asks.

"No go, it's out of juice. I have the warhorse parked in the back, ready to go!"

"Okay, you and Llia take Maddix to the warhorse, and I will provide a distraction. We'll meet up in the parking lot," Reo says as he runs toward the door.

"Wait!"

He stops in his tracks and turns to the voice in the room.

"Be careful," Llia says as she helps Maddix up.

He smiles and nods, his face disappearing into the shadows as he enters the dark hall. He sprints around the corner and collapses to the ground, blood gushing from his mouth and staining the floor. "Not now!" gasps Reo. With sheer determination, he musters the strength to rise and press on down the hall. The room is clear as Llia, TJ, and Maddix depart. They use their watches to illuminate their path as they walk cautiously through the lengthy corridor.

Llia observes the back, followed by Maddix, while TJ assumes the role of leader. Without warning, he ceases walking and extends his hand. He closes his hand, forming a fist. Llia comes to a halt and glances at her surroundings. She notices the entrance to the stairs.

"Llia, when was the last time Reo slept?" TJ whispers.

"A few hours ago. He slept for about thirty hours or so... is he okay?" Llia points out.

"Yeah, he should be."

Llia speaks softly. "All we have to do is make it to the stairwell, and we are home free!"

"Yeah, except the Yokai assassins have surrounded us!" The surrounding darkness takes shape. Dark figures armed with razor-sharp swords that drip with poison line the halls. Their eyes shine with a sinister glow as they creep toward them. Maddix screams and cowers behind Llia. TJ just smiles as he tosses Llia his katana.

"Llia, Maddix, stay back-to-back and try to keep up. Otis, you get the warhorse ready to intercept us!"

TJ pulls out a beautiful, retractable spear. The Yokai all attack at once, their swords leading the way. Llia prepares herself as she sees the gleam from all fifteen blades heading their way.

TJ performs a spinning motion as he thrusts his spear. With each fallen body, he remains focused and doesn't waste any unnecessary movements. The Yokai retreat slightly as the deceased ones turn into dark smoke.

"Well, are you just going to watch me rack up the kills, sis? They aren't going to kill themselves. Let's see what you've learned from your training!"

As Llia inhales deeply, her eyes grow colder, and she concentrates on steadying her hands. One Yokai after another falls victim to her swift and relentless blade. The sight of a Yokai rushing toward her triggers an adrenaline rush, and she quickly counters with a precise low slash. She then pulls out her gun and shoots around Maddix. Reaching the end of the hall, her eyes catch sight of three Yokai, each holding a bow and arrow. Despite being targeted, she wastes little time fighting back, driving her sword into the throat of a nearby Yokai. Using the impaled Yokai as a shield, Llia raises her gun and aims at her attackers. She forcefully pulls the blade from the lifeless Yokai's throat, splattering its blood across the walls as her attackers fall dead.

"Hell yeah, you are a total badass! Reo has taught you well!" TJ says as Maddix wipes his eyes.

"How long have I been out for? Where the hell did you learn to fight like that?" Maddix asks. TJ looks at Llia with wholehearted approval.

"Welcome to the fight! We have minutes before an army of death gets here! Next stop, stairs." He tosses his spear down the hall. It goes through several Yokai before sticking in the wall. He raises his hand, and the spear soars back into his hand, but not before it kills five more Yokai. He then turns his head toward Llia, brandishing an impressed smile.

"How did you do that?!" Llia asks as she reloads her gun.

"The watches have a powerful magnet in them, but you haven't seen half of what they can do," TJ replies as they enter the stairwell. They continue shooting, slashing, and stabbing—the echoes of gunfire and clashing metal filling the stairwell.

At that moment, on the east side of the hospital, Reo nonchalantly strolls down the hall, his fists drenched in blood, leaving a gruesome path of defeated Yokai in his wake. He comes to a sudden halt, his eyes widening in surprise. Approaching the hospital's west side, he senses a mysterious presence where TJ, Llia, and Maddix are. He picks up a sword from a fallen Yokai and darts toward their location, the weight of the weapon giving him a newfound sense of determination.

Seconds later, TJ, Llia, and Maddix emerge from the stairwell. After several minutes of fighting, they finally reach the first floor, panting and covered in sweat. They are amazed that the coast is clear. Their bodies feel heavy with fatigue. Llia surveys the gloomy, frigid lobby and can't help but notice the eerie stillness of the people lying on the floor. TJ shines his watch on the dark floor, casting a small beam of light in the dim room.

"You must hurry, you are out of time!" Otis exclaims to TJ.

"Shit, hurry! Let's go out the back way... move!"

Standing in silence, Llia gazes at the motionless bodies before her, her mind consumed by a trance. A dim emotion overwhelms her, causing tears to fill her eyes as she seeks comfort in Maddix's embrace. "We were too late! We couldn't save them!"

A man with a golden spear walks through the front entrance, covered in blood. His smile is unsettling, like something out of a horror movie. He is dressed as a Shaolin warrior monk, with vibrant red and gold robes representing his Asian heritage. He is taller than average, with a slender frame and an athletic build. They all sprint out of the hospital's back door and into the safety of a massive armored RV.

"Holy shit! Did you make this? It looks like you have an extremely complex HPC system with a petabyte-scale data lake in this thing!" Maddix asks.

"Yeah... Goose, something's gotta power my AI system. And it's actually a zettabyte hard drive. However, let's save the questions for a safer time without a thousand-year-old Chinese monk trying to kill us!"

"Who is that guy, and where is Reo?" Llia asks.

"That's Udai (oo-die). The deadliest person who has ever wielded a spear. He's the reason why spears are not allowed in the temple."

Udai emerges from the door and aims at the rear window with his spear. With deadly velocity and accuracy, it flies from his hand like a bullet. Bursting out of the second-story window, Reo swings the dark sword and sends the spear crashing into the unforgiving concrete. The sword cracks, and the sharp, metallic sound sings through the air. The sound bursts out the windows of nearby cars, echoing through the streets. TJ grabs a pillow from a box, its cover adorned with a picture of a defiant middle finger. He casually tosses it onto the plush leather couch.

"We can't leave him! We have to go back, now!" Llia says.

"Otis, release the drones and get me a visual! Trust me, sis, I would never leave him behind. Now hang on, we have to get out of here!"

In confusion, Llia places her hands on the top of her head. They watch the events unfold on one of the massive screens, mesmerized by its vivid colors and high-definition display. Udai extends his hand and the spear swiftly lands in his grasp. He aims at an unarmed Reo and releases his spear with a powerful throw, the weapon slicing through the air. Reo's hands instinctively rise as the spear hits its target.

"No!" Llia yells as they watch the monitor captured by TJ's drone.

"What!?" Reo replies as he sits on the couch, his chest heaving. Sweat rains from his pale face. Llia and Maddix do a triple take as the warhorse speeds away toward Llia's apartment.

Udai's spear is six inches into the side of the building, a pillow with a middle finger stuck in the spear. His unsettling smile resurfaces as he witnesses the armored RV rounding the corner—the warhorse races down the busy street. Numerous police cars zoom past them. Maddix and Llia simply gaze at Reo.

When did he? How did he? He told me he could do special things, but—wow!

"How—how did he do that?" Maddix asks.

"He told me he could trade places with objects. He learned it from mystical monks," Llia fills him in.

"Oh, of course he did. What the hell is going on?" Maddix replies.

"Maddix!" A voice slices through the chaos, its familiarity causing his heart to race. He spins around, eyes darting across the room, searching for the source.

"Is that...?" His thoughts spiral back to Ma—the way her voice had danced through his mind when he lay in that hospital bed. Her face swirls in memories, flickering like an old film reel. Shadows of their encounters twist with flashes of pain, her laugh morphing into a sinister echo.

"Maddix?" The voice echoes again, more insistent this time. It tightens around his chest like a vice.

"You okay?" TJ's gaze narrows, suspicion creeping into his features. He shifts closer, scanning Maddix's face for signs of something off.

"I'm fine," Maddix snaps, forcing a smile that feels like plastic stretched over cracks. Inside, his stomach knots tight. Was he really fine? Each moment seems to blur as the memories of Ma's manipulations creep back—her whispers laced with threats and promises tangled together in a web of deceit.

"Your heart's racing," TJ studies him closely. "You sure you're not hiding something?"

"No! I said I'm fine!" Maddix clenches his fists at his sides. The walls feel too close, and shadows lengthen around him. Every sound becomes amplified—the ticking clock, the faint hum of machines—all drowned out by the echo of Ma's call.

Llia exchanges glances with TJ, brows furrowed in concern. She can sense something amiss but doesn't know how deep it runs.

Maddix fights to regain control of his thoughts, pushing down the wave of dread rising within him. What if Ma wasn't gone? What if she still had a hold on him?

"Hey." Llia steps forward, gentle yet firm. "You sure you're alright? We can talk about it."

"No," he says too quickly, shaking his head. "I don't need to talk."

But within him, a storm of uncertainty and apprehension swirls—the ordeals he has faced hang over him like a foreboding shadow. TJ's gaze weighs upon him like an accusatory spotlight.

Maddix clenches his jaw and forces himself to breathe steadily, even as anxiety tightens its grip around him once more.

Reo leans against the plush leather couch, his breath ragged and shallow. Sweat drips from his brow, pooling at his temples. Suddenly, he jerks violently, a spasm coursing through his body like an electric shock.

"Reo!" Llia rushes to his side, panic flaring in her chest.

Maddix hovers close, eyes wide as he watches Reo convulse. "What the hell is happening?"

Otis's mechanical voice crackles from the RV's system, interrupting their rising fear. "Reo's vitals are unstable. His heart rate exceeds safe levels. He exhibits symptoms of both exhaustion and poison exposure."

"Poison? What kind?" Llia asks, her expression shifting to alarm.

"Unknown origin," Otis replies coolly. "I recommend immediate intervention to stabilize his condition."

"What do we do?" Llia grasps Reo's shoulder, shaking him gently as he writhes against the couch.

"Two options are available," Otis continues, unperturbed by the escalating tension. "First option: Administer a high-dosage antidote directly into his bloodstream using the IV port attached to the RV's medical kit. This will counteract any toxins."

Maddix exchanges glances with TJ and Llia. "And the second?"

"Second option: A synthetic energy booster can enhance physical endurance temporarily, but it may cause further strain on his already compromised state."

Llia hesitates, her heart racing. "We don't know what that could do to him!"

"His current state poses a greater risk than potential side effects of either option," Otis states with clinical detachment.

Reo lets out a pained groan, eyes fluttering shut for a moment before snapping open again with wild desperation. He gasps for air, struggling against an invisible weight pressing down on him.

"We need to do something!" Maddix shouts over Reo's cries.

"Okay! Let's go with the antidote!" Llia commands, her voice steady despite the panic clawing at her insides.

Maddix dashes toward the medical kit tucked in a corner of the RV while TJ readies Reo's arm, searching for the IV port hidden beneath layers of sweat-soaked fabric.

Reo convulses again, teeth gritted as if fighting off an unseen enemy within himself.

"Hang on!" TJ urges as he prepares to insert the needle into Reo's vein.

"Do it now!" Llia presses closer to Reo's face, brushing back damp strands of hair from his forehead while Maddix rushes back with the antidote in hand.

In that moment of chaos and urgency, hope hangs precariously in the air—every heartbeat counts as they fight against time itself. His breathing slows down, and he falls into a deep sleep.

"His health is getting worse!" Llia's wide-eyed, soft gaze never leaves him.

"Yeah, each time he uses his abilities, it hastens the poison," TJ says, shifting his eyes toward Maddix.

Llia nods and holds Reo's hand. TJ lowers his eyebrows and looks at Llia.

"Maddix, could you please give us a few minutes alone?" Llia asks.

"Is he going to die?" Her calm, low tone reveals her feelings.

"Yes, the curse will sap his strength one day, and he will die. We've tried everything to cure him, but nothing works."

"It's a form of control. Myou cursed him to dampen his abilities and skills so he wouldn't be a threat to them as they tried to free Penumbra. But the real question is, why not just kill him?" Llia says.

"When did you come up with that assumption? It makes a lot of sense."

"I figured out her plan a few months back. It all made sense after Reo told me the whole story. Myou's powers come from darkness; she is at her strongest during the moonless night. She wants to free Penumbra so her own powers can be limitless in Penumbra's eternal darkness. Myou's strength will equal that of a goddess; with her new-found strength, she will be unstoppable! But I am still at a loss as to why she cursed Reo to dream of his dead wife?"

"Damn, I may know why! She knows Reo needs a tremendous amount of focus to remain calm and not advance the poison in his body, right? That's why he seems cold sometimes. He's in a Zen-like state all the time; he can't get emotional or even strain himself by using his abilities too much. If he does, the poison will make it to his heart and then it's game over. When he sleeps, he heals, which revitalizes him but doesn't cure him—a technique courtesy of the monks," TJ replies.

"Hey, I'm sorry to interrupt. This rig is amazing! It looks like you have a perpetual engine running this thing."

"Yeah, Goose, good eye, but if you don't mind, we are in the middle—"

"Oh, right, sorry, it's just... do you have something to eat in your kitchen? I'm starving," Maddix asks.

"Yeah, check the fridge, use passcode zero one four three. Oh! And Goose, touch nothing in my cabinets, including my Marty Mar bars!"

"You know my name is Maddix, right?"

"I know your social security number too! I don't trust you, so for now, you're it! Hence the name Goose."

"That's fair. Wait, you've got Marty Mar bars?"

"Goose! Don't test me! This RV will kill any non-member of this group, especially anyone who touches my snacks!"

"Point received," Maddix says as he goes into the kitchen.

"Otis, secure and soundproof this room. Park us in the alley next to Llia's apartment. Notify us when we arrive." TJ rolls his eyes in annoyance, and Llia mouths an apology for Maddix.

"Okay, here is something else you should know. I told you about our fight with Myou, but I left out that I saw Reo with his sword to Myou's throat. He hesitated, and Tristian knocked him out. That's how they both escaped. I asked him about it, but he never said a word. It has always puzzled me how you have victory so close, but you hesitated." TJ clicks the keys on the keyboard to pull up all the info about that day for Llia.

"So, she turns Tristian against you guys, as I suspected! That's her weapon of choice: to weaponize the people closest to us."

"That may be. But he made that choice. We lost our entire team that day: twelve people I trained and bled with. They were more than just teammates, they were my family."

"And what about Udai? I saw your face when you realized those people at the hospital were killed by him."

"You saw urgency and nothing else. I can't fight him and protect the two of you. The day our team died, we split up into three teams. Udai killed my team. One of my teammates was a student that I trained; his name was Otis. I'd been training under Reo for ten years at that point, and Otis was my first student. I saw a lot of myself in him, and he was very talented with the spear and short sword. I felt he was strong enough to lead a team of his own, and it cost them their lives. Tristian led us all into traps with his false intel."

"TJ, I am so sorry. What happened to you both was a full-scale attack that you haven't been able to recover from. It happened several years ago, and you haven't even tried to rebuild your team, just like she planned. As for Reo, not killing her when he had the chance tells me that something distracted him, or maybe the poison was messing with him. I'm praying it isn't what I think it may be," Llia's gaze lingers on the resting form of Reo, her brow furrowed with concern.

The usually composed and formidable Yokai executioner appears unusually vulnerable in his repose, the weight of his recent trials etched upon his features. Llia's heart aches to see her friend and comrade-in-arms in such a state, a stark reminder of the high stakes and heavy burdens they all carry in their unending war against the malevolent Umbra.

TJ contemplates the details Llia has presented, acknowledging the accuracy of her assessment. He is astonished by her ability to piece together Myou's entire scheme in a matter of months, a feat they have failed to accomplish over several years of investigation.

There are still several pieces that don't fit. If you were my enemy, Reo, and you were more powerful than I, how would I eliminate you as a threat? Trojan horse?

CHAPTER FIFTEEN
The French Defense

Later that night, Udai stepped into Ma's dimly lit office, the air thick with incense and tension. He bowed, his expression carefully neutral.

"Ma, everything is falling into place," he announced, keeping his voice steady. "The plan you laid out is progressing as intended. Phase two is almost ready."

Ma leaned back in her chair, fingers steepled under her chin. A sly smile danced on her lips. "And the trap?"

"Set and waiting." Udai's heart raced beneath his calm facade, a simmering fury bubbling just below the surface. TJ's shadow loomed over him like a specter he couldn't shake.

"Good," she replied coolly. "But remember, TJ has always made you look weak. The way he escaped you last time? Pathetic."

A flash of anger flickered in Udai's eyes before he masked it with a tight-lipped smile. "That was an anomaly."

"Anomaly or not, it can't happen again," she snapped, leaning forward in her chair. "Summon Autsetsubae. He'll deal with Reo quickly."

Udai clenched his fists, the urge to unleash his frustration battling against the discipline ingrained in him as a former Shaolin monk. "Autsetsubae is good," he replied through gritted teeth, "but I am the greatest spear master who ever lived."

"Then act like it," Ma shot back, her voice sharp as a blade. "We need results tomorrow night to summon Penumbra. If you had killed TJ two years ago instead of letting him escape, this would be over by now. He is a brilliant tactician and engineer."

He nodded slowly, but inside, turmoil churned like a tempest. TJ kept slipping through his grasp, making him look like a fool with his inventions, every encounter only fueled Udai's resentment.

"I'll fetch Autsetsubae."

"Do it now," she ordered, dismissing him with a wave of her hand.

Udai stepped outside and took a deep breath to center himself, yet the anger coiled tighter within him as he moved down the corridor toward the training grounds deep in the basement of the restaurant.

Foolish boy, he thought of TJ as he walked past shadowy figures training in silence, their focus unwavering. *You think you can outrun me forever?! I will make you suffer!*

He reached the designated area and found Autsetsubae honing his skills with dual blades. He tossed a handful of rice into the air and danced effortlessly as steel glinted under flickering torchlight. Every grain of rice was perfectly cut in half before it reached the floor.

Udai opened his mouth to call out, but the scene before him silenced his words. Six elite Yokai assassins materialized from the shadows, their weapons gleaming in the torchlight. Udai knew they were vastly stronger than any other Yokai, except himself and Autsetsubae, and he watched on with great delight.

The elite Yokai guard Myou; they are extremely strong. The last time Reo came close to her, he had to fight one of them and barely won; this will be interesting, Udai thought.

The elite Yokai encircled Autsetsubae, moving with lethal grace. The first assassin lunged forward, blade whistling through the air. Autsetsubae's dual swords flashed—a diagonal slash split the attacker from shoulder to hip. The body hadn't hit the ground before he pivoted, his blades singing through the night air.

Two more assassins struck in unison. Autsetsubae dropped low, his first sword deflecting a thrust while the second carved through a hamstring. He rolled beneath a sweeping blade, came up behind the fourth assassin, and separated head from shoulders in one fluid motion.

The remaining two attacked from opposite sides. Autsetsubae's swords moved like extensions of his arms—parry, thrust, slash. Blood sprayed across the stone floor. One assassin's chest exploded open and the other's throat disappeared in a crimson arc.

Six bodies lay scattered across the training ground. The entire display had lasted mere seconds. Autsetsubae flicked the blood from his blades with two precise motions, then sheathed them at his sides. His breathing hadn't even quickened.

Udai stood, transfixed, his intended words still caught in his throat. The display of masterful swordsmanship left him questioning Ma's assessment of his own abilities. Perhaps she had been right to summon this demon of steel and shadow.

"Autsetsubae," Udai called out sharply.

The dual-wielding fighter turned toward him, curiosity sparking in his gaze.

"It's time," Udai declared, masking his ire behind an impenetrable facade of authority.

As they exchanged knowing glances, determination settled between them—a shared understanding of what lay ahead for Reo and TJ later that night.

CHAPTER SIXTEEN

OUT OF THE
FIRE

An hour later, they arrive at Llia's apartment and park the warhorse in her alleyway. Llia suggests they take the fire escape, just in case the girls are home. Maddix and TJ help Reo up the fire escape to reach Llia's room on the third floor. She knows a secret way to open the window from the outside. They enter her room and gently lay Reo down on her bed so he doesn't wake up.

"Okay, TJ—you stay here with Reo. Maddix and I are going to see if anyone is here."

They peek out from her room and notice Iris fast asleep on the couch, a hefty book resting on her lap. Glancing down the hall, Llia sees no one in sight and proceeds to close the door.

"It looks like Rose is already gone, which is strange because it's only ten o'clock. She usually leaves at eleven, but Iris is here. She's asleep on the couch. I think we should tell them everything; things are getting out of control. It's not safe to keep them in the dark about the Yokai anymore. It didn't help Maddix or all those innocent people at the hospital last night. Myou is changing the rules, and sleepers are no longer safe!" Llia says.

"Agreed. You should do it quickly while I raid your kitchen. I'll be here for moral support. Goose ate all my food," TJ replies, rubbing his stomach.

"Being near death gave me a huge appetite. I'm sorry about that," Maddix adds.

"Really?!" Llia says, pouting as she opens the door. She gestures for TJ to follow as they step into the living room.

Maddix walks into the living room and sits by the immense window overlooking the street in front of the building. He can see the park where they often meet for lunch, although the overcast sky hides its beautiful hue.

"Iris, wake up. I need to talk to you," whispers Llia as Iris stirs. She rubs her eyes and scans the room. "Llia? What the hell?! You said a few months in Japan, not six! When did you get back?"

Her gaze doesn't leave TJ's. She fixes her long hair and wipes her face. Llia glances into the kitchen and sees TJ rummaging through the top cabinet. He grabs a coffee cup from the top shelf and a frying pan from the bottom then takes a dish towel from the drawer by the fridge.

What the hell?! Llia thinks.

"Llia! Are you listening to me?" Iris asks.

"I'm sorry—the guy in our kitchen is TJ, and he's a friend. I know I said I was going to Japan; that was a lie. You're going to need some coffee for this one." She spends the next two hours telling Iris and Maddix everything she knows about the current events. Their wide eyes and intense stares hang in silence as Llia finishes explaining everything about the Yokai.

"I just can't believe it! So the Umbra killed all those people at the Turn Up. And the Umbra is a group of powerful Yokai: Autsetsubae, or Subae for short, the deadliest swordsmen who ever lived; Udai, a deadly Shaolin monk from ancient China; and Myou, who is basically a goddess with an army—Shit! And you said they attacked the hospital—wait, I was supposed to work last night! No, no, no—Lacy! She worked in my place because the boss texted me saying I had the night off, which was weird. She never switches the schedules; I have to call her!" Iris says as she grabs her phone to call her work friends from her room.

"TJ? Isn't it the job of the Yokai Ex to ensure everyone's safety?" Llia asks, her eyebrows furrowing.

"Sis, I never said that. We aren't superheroes; we kill the bad Yokai to keep the balance, and I just follow our protocols. For hundreds of years, the protocol has remained the same—the same protocol that saved your life six months ago at that party. The mission comes first, no matter what!"

"Well, how does Reo feel about all of this?"

"Maddix wasn't attacked. Myou weaponized him this entire time, Reo knew about that months ago. And like I said at the hospital, there was no cure for someone being turned into a pawn like Maddix was. It was Reo's idea to keep that info from you to see what intel we could gain!"

"Wait, what? Reo did that?! Granted, I knew something was up with Maddix, but Reo should have told me!"

"At the time, you weren't Yokai Ex. But yeah, I do agree—you should have been told. But that was Reo's call! And Reo lives by the protocol: no relationships, no friend-ships. The mission comes first!"

"Then, in the last six months, the man I've grown to know isn't real."

"I don't know what happened to you guys up there, but as you said in the warhorse: we are under attack. This is psycho-logical warfare. I can admit that a lot has changed in the past six months. Like in the hospital, the Reo I knew would have left Goose to die there. He would have used that opportunity to lure out the Umbra. Oh, and for your information, I sent Iris the text to stay home, not her boss, and I am devastated about the people who didn't make it. I would never stand by and watch people die. I am not a monster!" TJ exclaims as he walks into the kitchen to cool off.

"TJ, I am sorry. If I've learned anything in these past six months, it's that you're a good man and an even better friend. Please forgive me. I projected my anger, and you don't de-serve that," Llia says as she approaches him.

TJ inhales deeply as he locks eyes with Llia. He pauses, fighting back words. He walks into Llia's room to check on Reo.

Llia lowers her head and sits in her dad's chair. After making her calls, Iris returns to the room, and Maddix looks at Llia, his eyebrows rising as he processes everything TJ just said. Llia's wide eyes harden as she pounds the sofa arm.

"Damn you, Reo! Why?"

"Wait, Llia, before you conclude anything about Reo, don't forget he risked his life to save mine. I heard what you said in that RV about the mind games that the evil bitch plays on you. She made me do some horrible things. The hardest was setting you up at the party—and she made me watch Charlie die! If I hadn't done what she said, if I fought back, I would feel pain like you wouldn't believe. Pain that can't be fought. I tried to resist, and I ended up in the hospital, praying for death to take me. But you guys saved me after all the information I gave her!" Maddix fought back tears, but there wasn't a dry eye in the living room. Llia and Iris hug Maddix, comforting him for several minutes as tears stream down their faces.

"I believe people can change. Before I met Charlie, I was a mess. I thought the worst of him when we dated; I figured, give him some time and he would leave—he would be an asshole. He ended up being the best thing that ever happened to me. In the hospital, you were far more confident and powerful than you used to be. You didn't become that person on your own; Reo helped bring out the best in you, and maybe—just maybe—you did the same for him," Maddix says.

He's right; he has helped me find myself again. Maybe I had the same impact on him, Llia thinks. "Thanks, Maddix, you really are a smart cookie."

"Shit!" Iris exclaims, "Didn't you say that a restaurant called Ma's was an evil place? I just remembered that Rose and her friend are meeting for a late lunch there today! I'll try to call her!"

"I'll go tell TJ so we can go get her," Maddix says.

Llia's palms start to sweat; her heart pounds against her chest, and at that moment, all her ability to think clearly vanishes. Filled with an unexpected surge of energy, she swiftly jumps off the couch and hastily makes her way out the door. She sprints toward the college. Before she can fully concentrate on the time, she catches a glimpse of her watch, but the answer has already sprung into her mind.

"One thirty-four; at your current speed, you will be at your destination in about ten minutes!"

"Thanks, Otis... that's so fucking cool."

"I must advise against your current course of action. Protocol states that you should not enter a hostile environment without backup."

"But Otis, I have a backup. I have you!"

"I'm afraid that where you're going, I won't be able to help you. I'll report your current situation to TJ."

Running through alleyways and cutting through parking lots, she sprints toward her destination. With the stinging wind slamming into her face with each stride, she pushes through the numbing pain. Due to her rigorous training, she experiences improvements in her speed, resilience, and strength. In a matter of minutes, she swiftly reaches the restaurant.

Preparing herself before entering, she takes a moment to steady her breath. She sees that it is an authentic Japanese restaurant filled with the lively sounds of people enjoying their meals. She makes her way through the restaurant.

I know most of the people here: John, Sam, and Beth. There's Thomas and Kay-Kay over there. Most of the people here are supposed to be in class right now. Is everyone skipping at the same time? What's going on?

She moves deeper inside, covering her nose to shield herself from the pungent odor. As she walks through the extensive building, her eyes scan the tables, and she can't help but notice the complete lack of conversation or interaction among the diners. They bury their faces in their plates, devouring their food with loud smacking sounds. She focuses on the dishes in front of them.

Taking several steps backward in alarm, she realizes that no matter where she turns her gaze, the scene remains constant. Everyone is casually slurping creepy critters and centipedes as if they were noodles. They fearlessly ingest rice that has turned putrid, teeming with flies and maggots, devouring it as if it were a delectable sushi roll. Some people look pale and nauseous while eating, almost like zombies.

Llia wipes her forehead, feeling beads of sweat trickle down her face. Deep at the back of the restaurant, she spots Rose's vibrant crimson hair and hurriedly makes her way toward her. A waiter tries to stop her, his voice drowned out by the bustling sounds of the restaurant. He is forcefully knocked to the ground by Llia, landing with a jolt as she runs past him. Rose turns her head to see where all the noise is coming from.

"Llia! You're back! Wow, girl, you look great. Have you been working out? Sit down and join us. Jason and I were just about to eat something! You remember Jason, right?" Rose says.

"Hi Llia, it's been…"

"Yep! Listen to me, you both need to get up and get out of here, now! I have reason to believe this place is poisoning people." Llia whispers. Jason and Rose look around to see everyone still eating.

"They started reservations a few months back; I've waited months to get in here. I'm not leaving until I've eaten," Jason declares.

Okay, honesty didn't work! So, let's go to plan B: the angry man tactic. Piss him off so he'll leave.

"Yeah, yeah—Rose told me you had a shrimp dick; you're a functional idiot, and she's only here because you're good at oral sex and she never have to reciprocate. But, bad news for her: she won't get lucky today. Rose, let's get the fuck out of here now! Jason, you too. Leave, now!"

"Camellia! What the fuck?! You weren't supposed to repeat that!" Rose replies.

"Have you eaten anything from here? Now or ever?!" Llia asks as she leans on the table. Her eyes are wide and burn with anticipation. Her heavy breathing makes it hard to articulate some of her words.

"Llia, you sound insane, but no. This is my first time coming here. The food smells divine. I can't wait to dig in."

"Rose, get up. We have to go now! Jason, why are you still here? Are you a fucking idiot? Get the hell out of here!"

"I'm not leaving, and I don't care what you say. Rose and I...."

"And we just got here, and I am starving," Rose says as the server sets their food on the table.

"Rose, get the fuck up! Right now, we're leaving!"

"Hold on, she said she didn't want to leave, so I suggest you get the hell out of here, Camellia! And Rose told me about your angry man tactics, and they won't work on me!" Jason replies as he stands to his feet and squares up with her.

This guy is very stubborn, and Rose is a snitch.

"If you don't get out of my face right now, I'll use my take-a-ride-in-an-ambulance tactic!"

"Uh, Jason? Sit down. She can and will do it. What the fuck has gotten into you?" Rose asks as Llia grabs her hand, and Rose reaches for her fork. Jason defiantly sits down and continues eating.

"Ouch, you shocked me, Llia. What the...!"

Rose looks down at her plate and lets out a piercing scream upon discovering it is teeming with live centipedes, maggots, and roaches. Llia releases her hand, and Rose jumps up from her seat, startled. Her date gazes at them with a skeptical look, as if they were both losing it. He then takes a big bite of the wriggling mixture of maggots and flies, causing Rose to vomit on the floor. Llia's hand instinctively reaches for her gun, and with a deafening blast, she fires a bullet into the ceiling. Chaos erupts, and people spill into the street in a panic. They flee from the restaurant and stand chatting among themselves as hundreds of people come from the city to join them. An army of sickly-looking people talks loudly outside about what happened. The chatter, combined with the city's symphony, is deafening. The servers remain in the restaurant, blocking the exit.

Llia aims her gun as they walk to leave. The servers' beady eyes watch their every move. The girls abruptly halt as the servers arrange themselves into two parallel lines. A mysterious figure emerges from the shadows and confidently walks toward the girls. She is a stunning Japanese woman who makes Llia feel a little insecure.

"Hi, I'm Ma, and this is my restaurant. Is there a problem with the food, ladies?" Her calm, beautiful smile shines through the tension.

"I'll say! You've got bugs and—"

"What my sister is trying to say is that we're okay, just a minor accident, that's all. I'm afraid my service gun went off. We apologize for the disturbance. The police department will pay for the damages, and we will be on our way," Llia says.

The woman's smile changes. The corners of her mouth lift too far, revealing her black teeth. Her soft eyes become hardened. "I would like to offer you a free meal for your troubles," Ma says.

"Hell no!" Rose yells.

"Um, that won't be necessary, we'll just get out of here," Llia replies.

"I'm afraid I must insist... Camellia!" Ma responds.

Llia looks deeper into the woman's chilling eyes. She raises her gun and aims. "You—you're Myou! This is all your doing!"

"Well, well...I see nothing gets past you. Had I known that you fat Americans ate so much, I would have come here years ago! I now have thousands of pawns to do my will. Oh, how rude of me. How is Reo?"

"You bitch! How dare you, after everything you've done to him!"

"Bitch? The English language is filled with a kaleidoscope of vivid expressions; with one simple adjective, you can maximize your derogatory remark. Your entire life has been devoted to honing your skills as a tribute to your parents' memory: a father who died a hero cop, and a mother who was murdered while working your shift at the store."

Rose looks between the two of them. "Llia? What is she talking about? Do you know her?"

She's trying to mess with my head. Trying to make me angry so I make mistakes. I have to remember the training we did in month four with the waterfall—calm my mind and block out the noise.

"Your brilliance outshines every other police officer in the city, yet they still refuse to accept you into their ranks as a detective. Why is that, Hafu? When I think of all your talents, I imagine the lives you could have saved and the world you could have transformed." Ma slowly walks closer. Llia makes a fist.

Stay calm, Llia. Don't fall for the bait. I have to find a way out of here!

"I see you swimming around in there... looking for answers in your mind. Be careful not to drown, Hafu!"

"What the hell is this old woman talking about, Llia? And what the fuck does 'Hafu' mean?"

Llia glances at Rose and looks at Myou.

Old woman? She can't be over thirty. Wait, can she not see the young, beautiful woman? Is it because Reo said I am an earthly deity?

"Hafu means half-breed. She's using it as an insult. Rose, I need you to describe the old woman to me, please!"

"Okay? She's about 5'5", has ragged old clothes and dull, leathery skin. Her lips are thin and chapped. She has small, beady eyes. Her white, slimy hair is thin, and her teeth look black and rotten. No offense, lady! You should really try some hyaluronic acid for your dry skin."

Interesting, TJ taught me during training that she can shape shift, but her records didn't say she can be two people at once, Llia thinks.

"Get the fuck out of our way, Myou, now! Rose, stay close to me. We are leaving!"

"You are leaving?! I was enjoying our English conversation. Well, okay, if you must go." Myou stands to the side and extends her hand to the door. At that moment, the entire army of pawns also moves, forming an opening outside. Llia and Rose walk past Myou and the servers, who don't move a muscle. Llia keeps her gun pointed at Myou as they approach the door.

"Before you go, Hafu, I just thought you might want the name of the person who killed your mother!" Myou says as Llia stops in her tracks.

She turns around and looks Myou in the eyes. Bullshit, she's lying. I looked for years through her case file, and I haven't found a shred of evidence…

"Give it to me… now!" Llia aims the gun at her head as her strong glare bears down on Myou.

"Llia, please don't do this… Let's just go!" Rose pleads, placing her hand on her shoulder, but Llia ignores her.

I have to know, Rose, I have to. You don't understand. Someone has to pay for what they did to my mother!

"I will tell you who they are, but we will have a good old-fashioned full-contact match. The best of three: if you win, I will give you his name and where you can find him. But if I win, you give yourself to me, and no one else has to get hurt."

"Llia, no—don't do this! This is nuts! Of course, you can kick her ass. She is clearly baiting you!"

Don't, Llia. Remember the waterfall! She thinks as she turns to leave the restaurant.

"Well, clearly, you're not your father's daughter. He gave his life for justice, and you—you want to run from it."

Oh, you are dead!

Llia hands Rose the gun, then raises her fists and narrows her eyes; a sharp pain shooting through her stomach. Myou gets into a fighting stance as well. She smirks, then winks at Llia. Llia looks for a weak point in Myou's perfect form before rushing toward her.

Myou holds up her hand. "Wait, I am not ready."

"Llia, I just want to say this is some freaky shit!" Rose declares as she looks out the door and sees the army of people standing outside in a trance-like state.

Myou removes her high geta shoes. The servers pick them up, and she rushes Llia with a barrage of precision attacks. Llia dodges and blocks as many as possible before receiving a sharp blow to her midsection. Llia staggers backward and clutches her stomach, falling to one knee as she huffs for air.

Something's not right. She's stronger and faster than I am! I can't lay a hand on her. It feels like I'm stuck in the mud. The restaurant! It's this place. She's cheating!

"That's one... Your dad would be really proud! Ha-ha!" Myou laughs.

Llia bares her teeth, her eyebrows furrowing as she leaps toward her, but Myou intercepts her and effortlessly knocks her to the ground with one decisive move.

"That's Tsumi... you stupid bitch!" Myou exclaims, grinning. Trapped air fills Llia's lungs as she stares at Myou's ominous sneer with wide eyes.

"You cheated! Give me the name now!" Llia yells. Rose helps her to her feet.

"No one said it would be a fair fight. Now come with me, or she dies!"

The people on the street rush into the building, their hurried footsteps creating a sense of urgency around the girls. With unsteady hands, Rose tries to aim the gun before she hands the heavy weapon back to Llia, who skillfully aims at Myou and fires six shots. But one by one, the servers jump in front of the bullets as Myou casually walks away.

Llia finds herself in a fierce battle for their lives as a swarm of attackers closes in from the outside. She hurls Rose into a corner and positions herself firmly, ready to defend against the approaching crowd. Unleashing a fury of destruction, she shatters arms, legs, and jaws. But they keep coming, their determination unyielding.

"Kill the redhead, but bring me the other one… I need her alive, for now!" Myou says as she continues walking toward her office at the back of the restaurant.

There are too many of them; I can't—I can't—

Llia becomes overwhelmed by the attackers until the wall next to them explodes. The back of the warhorse pulls in and opens like a cargo plane. Llia and Rose run inside, and then it speeds off, mowing over dozens of Myou's pawns.

Myou exits the restaurant and holds her hand up; the entire crowd stops pursuing them and kneels before her. "Allow it, all is as I will it! I'll end this with one last move!"

"TJ! Thank you so much! You saved our asses back there!" Llia exclaims as she lies on the floor, huffing and puffing, soaked in sweat.

"Yeah, I did. So I saved two people—how many did you save back there?" TJ scoffs.

"Okay, I deserved that one. I see now how she uses innocent people as pawns. She puts the inch-boy soup in the food to make people her slaves. She is on a different level, just like a goddess!" Llia says.

"Anyone going to tell me what the fuck just happened back there? Hi sexy, I'm Rose—wait a minute, haven't I seen you before?"

"No, I don't believe so. Llia, what the hell were you thinking? Do you have any idea how reckless that was? If it weren't for Otis, you would be done for! You should never face a godmaster alone! How many times have we told you that?"

"They were going to turn Rose into a pawn, and I couldn't let that happen. There was no time to waste. If that means giving up my life for my sisters, then so be it!"

"We have to be honest with each other if we're going to be on the same team, okay? You can trust me, right, sis?"

"I can trust you, huh? I've always been very perceptive. Reading people is my thing. Back in the apartment, you knew exactly where everything was in the kitchen. You never asked me where anything was. Care to explain, teammate?"

"Wait! I've seen you before! You're the guy who's dating Iris on the down low! I saw a picture of you two on her phone while

I was snooping! Wait, how do you know him, Llia? Don't tell me he's dating you too!"

"No!" Llia exclaims as she attempts to sit up but remains stuck to the floor from exhaustion. "He's my teacher and my teammate. And what the hell, TJ? Please tell me you didn't do that!"

"I can explain. Don't forget, I just saved your life. I've been wanting to tell you, but I just haven't found the right time. But I guess this is it."

"Start talking!" the girls both reply.

"Okay, okay. About a month after you left to train with Reo, some creep was getting too handsy with Iris at a bar she went to, and I stepped in and broke his nose. She asked me out, and I figured I could protect her better if I kept her closer. Plus, it didn't help that she was the most beautiful woman I had ever seen. I fell for her hard. I tried to break it off, but I'm head over heels in love with her. I could see myself marrying her someday," TJ says as Llia covers her face with her hands.

Rose falls out of her chair, laughing hysterically. "Holy shit! Well, good luck with that one!"

That's why Iris was looking at him in the kitchen; she already knew who he was!

"Rose, be quiet! TJ, this is important. Does Iris know you've been spying on them this whole time?" Llia asks.

"Wait, what do you mean by spying on them?"

"Rose, stop! TJ—please answer the question!"

"No, no, she doesn't know," he says as he puts his hand on top of his head, the weight of the moment sinking in.

"Fuck!" Llia exclaims.

"Well, you better wait until you save her life to tell her that, because she's going to kill you!" Rose says as the room falls silent.

CHAPTER SEVENTEEN
THE FEIGNER

Detective Moro's phone buzzes with urgent news of a shooting at Ma's Restaurant. He arrives at the scene, where red and blue lights paint the night. Half the force had shown up—this wasn't just any disturbance call.

Ma stands outside, trembling, dabbing her eyes with a handkerchief as officers swarm around her.

"It was horrible! That girl, Llia, came in and just started shooting! My customers..." Ma's voice cracks. "Several of them died. I want her arrested immediately!"

Moro's eyes narrow. He had seen enough supernatural beings to recognize the signs—the way shadows seem to bend around her, how his skin prickles when she speaks.

Inside the restaurant, bullet holes pepper the walls, but the pattern was wrong. The trajectories suggest defensive fire, not an attack. Blood spatters tell a different tale than Ma's version.

"Captain," Moro approaches his superior. "Let me bring her in. I know where to find her."

"You sure about this, Sato? This is a multiple homicide."

"The evidence doesn't match the witness statement. Something else happened here." Moro gestures to the crime scene. "Those bullet holes? They're from someone shooting back, not initiating. And look at how the tables were overturned—from the inside out—as if people were taking cover in the center of the room."

The captain studies the scene. "Alright, but I'm sending two units to wait downstairs as backup. Don't take any chances."

Moro nods and heads for his car. He knows Ma is lying—the question is why a Yokai would go to such lengths to frame Llia for murder.

Ma shuffles back inside the restaurant, her frail demeanor transforming as soon as the door closed. She pulls out stacks of takeout boxes from behind the counter.

"Officers, please—you must be hungry after all this work. Let me feed you." Her wrinkled hands distribute boxes of steaming noodles and dumplings. "It's the least I can do for your service."

The police officers hesitate for only a moment before accepting the food. The aroma proves too tempting to resist. They sit in their cruisers, slurping noodles between radio calls.

Ma's thin lips stretch into an unnatural grin, revealing teeth sharper than human teeth should be. She watches through the windows as, one by one, the officers devour every last bite.

The click of her heels echoes through the empty restaurant as she makes her way to her office, where Udai's golden spear gleams in the dim light.

"They've taken the bait." Ma's voice drops an octave, all pretense of the kind restaurant owner gone. "When the poison takes hold, go to Llia's apartment and kill them all. But remember—Llia must live. I need her alive for what comes next."

Udai cracks his knuckles, the sound like breaking branches. "And what about Detective Sato?"

"He's not here. He left before I could serve him." Ma's eyes flash with supernatural fire. "No matter. He'll meet his end soon enough. Now go—prepare the others. When these humans start choking on their own blood, that's your signal to begin."

Moro slams his office door and yanks open his desk drawer. His grandfather's leather-bound journal lies beneath stacks of case files. The worn pages crackle as he flips through decades-old notes.

Blood pounds in his temples. The restaurant scene kept replaying in his mind—those wrong trajectories, Ma's convenient story, the eager way she fed the officers. His fingers trace his grandfather's precise handwriting until he finds the entry he needed.

"March 15, 1985—The pattern becomes clear. She uses food establishments as fronts. Humans consume her cursed meals and then fall under her control. The victims turn violent, giving her the perfect cover for..."

The entry ends in a violent slash of ink. His grandfather had died that night.

Moro grabs his supernatural codex, comparing the entries. Ma's restaurant. The strange customers. The way people seem drawn to eat there despite better options nearby. The missing persons reports that had started six months ago, all within blocks of her establishment.

"Shit." He slams both books shut.

Photos were spread across his desk—surveillance shots from the past months. Ma greeting customers. Ma talking with shadowy figures in alleys. Ma's restaurant at night, windows glowing with an unnatural light.

His phone rings. The captain's voice crackles through.

"Sato, we've got officers down. Some kind of seizures. We all ate at Ma's tonight. Medical's en route, but—" Static cuts through the line.

Moro's hand shakes as he picks up his grandfather's journal again. The final entry stares back at him: "Myou isn't working alone. The Oni serve her. She's building an army, using humans as pawns. I've tracked her for twenty years, but I underestima ted..."

He grabs his gun and badge. Llia wasn't the killer—she was the target. Just like his grandfather had been the target when he got too close to exposing Myou's operation.

History was repeating itself, but this time Moro wouldn't let it end the same way.

CHAPTR EIGHTEEN
RESPITE

After a lengthy debate, TJ, Llia, and Rose finally make their way to Llia's place. With lingering tension among them, each retreat to separate corners of the residence. Meanwhile, in Llia's bedroom, Iris and Maddix tend to Reo's injuries. They enter the living room after hearing the front door close.

"Oh, thank goodness you got them back safely, TJ. Thank you! Reo is stable, and he is going to be fine! Um, did someone die?!" Iris assesses the situation and senses the tension.

"Not yet!" Rose replies.

"Rose, please stay out of it!" Llia interjects.

"She's my sister too! Iris, we know all about you and TJ."

"How did you find out? I said nothing... Rosie! Did you go through my things again?" Iris asks, her shoulders drooping.

"Fine, fine. I went through your cell while you were knocked out. It wasn't intentional. My phone disappeared somewhere in here, and I borrowed yours to locate it. I couldn't help myself when I saw how much time you'd been spending texting and going on about some mysterious savior; I had to investigate. That's when I discovered you were keeping something from all of us."

"Rose!" Iris shouts.

"I'm talking about us—your lifelong friends, not your birth parents—who, believe me, are going to be absolutely livid when they hear about this!" Rose snaps back.

"Iris' parents?! What's she getting at?" TJ demands.

"I can't believe it! You didn't go through my phone because I was using it more, it was because I wasn't paying attention to you!" Iris shouts.

"Oh, calm down, it could've been worse. It's not like I secretly watched you for months or anything. It was totally harmless." She makes eye contact with TJ.

"Classic Rosie! Never taking responsibility! I'm done with you. You've always been self-centered!"

"Iris, stop!"

"No, Llia, I'm exhausted. She needs to understand how I feel! I already have enough on my plate with my parents trying to force me into marrying a stranger, I don't need you invading my privacy under the guise of protecting me. You were quick to remind me months ago that this isn't India; well, we're not even real sisters! Stay out of my life!" A wave of panic suddenly hit Iris. The room goes silent. Iris and Rose lock eyes, both with tears forming.

TJ takes a sharp breath and closes his eyes. "Hold on. Did you just say you're getting married?" Iris grabs his hand and they headed to her room.

Llia approaches a distressed Rose and embraces her. "We're all stressed right now. Let me check on Reo, and then we'll talk about it, okay? I want both of you to stay in the apartment. It's too dangerous to go out."

"You're joking, aren't you? I'm not stepping out of this apartment again unless it's absolutely essential. Maddy, I need you to get me around ten cats, because I ain't leaving this apartment again!" Rose settles beside Maddix and switches on the news. She rests her head on his shoulder as he struggles to hold back his sorrowful tears.

Llia breathes out, her eyes drifting to Maddix's expression. She recognizes that he was lost in thoughts of Charlie, and it requires all her strength to suppress the desire to offer him companionship while she heads to her room.

"Llia! I appreciate you not leaving me. You realize I would do the same for you, don't you?" Rose replied.

"I will always stand by both of you. Regardless of the price, we might not share the same blood, but you both are my family!" Llia grins and stepped into her room.

"Iris, I need you to hear me out. Please have a seat. I'll begin with the unfortunate news." TJ settles on the bed beside Iris. He takes her hand and looks deep into her tear-filled eyes.

"TJ, I'm sorry, I should have told you…

"I've been watching you and Rose for the last six months."

Iris withdraws her hand.

"Wait! It's not what you think."

"Then explain!" Her eyes are a gentle fire, radiating a mix of compassion and anger.

"Alright, I was instructed to protect you all from the Yokai. They prefer you not to know about the Yokai, as they target those who are aware. Before we officially met, I knew your favorite color is green, and that you enjoy a fresh macchiato every morning before work. You're the most passionate person I've ever encountered. Safeguarding you was my primary concern. I recognize that my actions were wrong, and I carry profound guilt in my heart. I deceived you by concealing the truth and lying to you, weaving a complicated web of deceit. But I never meant to fall in love with you. For all of it… I'm truly sorry."

Iris' breath grows more labored, and a chill runs down her arms. She rises and moves toward the door. "So, you knew me before I asked you out because you were watching me?"

"Yes, and I'm not proud of it."

Her eyebrows raise, and she walk back to him, sitting down on the bed again.

"And you're the reason I'm not one of the people who died at the hospital?"

"Yeah, I infiltrated your boss's phone and swapped your shifts. I wasn't certain that anyone would be hurt, but I wasn't going to take that risk." Iris gently strokes his cheek, her fierce gaze softening into one of empathy.

"I love you, Iris, and I get it if you don't share those feelings for me anymore."

"As reprehensible as your actions were, I have strong feelings for you as well. It appears you're not the only one keeping secrets. My engagement is an arranged marriage. My family is everything to me, and my parents adhere to traditional Indian values. I am required to marry someone from the appropriate caste, and they must be Indian." She bows her head while TJ runs his hands along his knees, all emotions fading from their expressions.

"There's no way we can be together, then."

"If I choose you and not him, my parents would cut ties with me permanently. I never meant for this to get so serious. It was supposed to be just casual, but you turned out to be the ideal guy for me. Sweet, caring, funny, and strong."

Frustrated, TJ rushes out of the room and heads outside. Rose and Maddix observe his departure with deep worry. After a lengthy walk, TJ reaches the warhorse and slams his fist against the control room wall.

How could I have missed that? I pride myself on doing a background check on everyone, and I missed what was right in front of my eyes. I need to work and get my mind off this. I'll focus on the info Reo gave me at the hospital about his poison.

Otis cross-referenced Reo's health records from all the times he was with Llia. He noticed a pattern—Reo mentioned he didn't have his usual troubling dreams whenever they were together. Intrigued, Otis began collecting and analyzing the data, determined to uncover the reason behind this phenomenon as rain started to fall outside.

Meanwhile, in the apartment, Llia rests on her bed next to Reo. He breathes gently as he sleeps. She gazes at him and recalls their nights in the forest by the fire, talking for hours after a lengthy day of training and enjoying a lovely meal together. She envisions his delightful smile.

"Reo...Reo! Are you up?" Llia tests the waters, "When I first encountered you, I thought, he's far too good-looking to be so serious. You sort of rubbed me the wrong way." She rests her head on his chest and tunes into his heartbeat, listening to the rain pouring outside.

"Being near you makes me feel more powerful. Just thinking of you makes all my worries and shame dissolve. The reason finally clicked. That time we trekked to the stunning waterfall hidden in the forest comes to mind. We spent a couple of days there, practicing how to block out distractions and concentrate on the present moment. Trying to stay centered when your fury flows like rushing water proved impossible for me. I never managed it once," Llia rambles on, still pressed against his chest while gazing through her window. Reo awakens silently, taking in her words.

"That final evening, the temperature plummeted. While answering nature's call, my shelter got swept away in the wind. You welcomed me into yours, and we huddled together to stay warm. I can still feel how my pulse raced, making it difficult to draw breath. My soul swelled with an emotion I believed had vanished forever. That night held no terrors, anxieties, or dark visions. Since then, whenever my dreams turn dark or fears surface, I picture that moment; it's forever etched in my memory as the time I realized I loved you." Llia's voice trails off as her eyelids drop. Reo's expression softens into a gentle grin as she dozes against him. Drawing her closer with one arm, he drifts back to slumber, their bodies intertwined until well past dawn.

Llia started to stir, which roused Reo.

"Llia?" He questions as she blinks awake. "Did you sleep okay?"

"Yeah, just a bit of a nightmare from earlier today."

"What happened?"

"Myou happened! She's Ma, and she has subjugated half the city by using her restaurant to manipulate them. She nearly captured Rose, but I got there just in time to rescue her." They sit up in bed.

"By yourself?!" Reo asks, narrowing his gaze. Llia grins and scratches her head.

"Well, I had little time to come up with a plan, and you were here dozing off on the job, so..."

"That's not funny; it was irresponsible... Did you confront her? Where was TJ during all of this?"

"It's not his fault. He's the reason Rose and I are still here. He didn't even realize that I was missing. And yes, she kicked my ass. She used psychological tricks on me, and the restaurant was hexed! I felt like I was in—"

"Quicksand! She put a curse on the restaurant." Reo interjects.

"Exactly! She is the most malevolent person I have ever encountered. But something felt off, something Rose mentioned. She saw something."

She saw an old woman, and I saw a young one.

"What did she say?"

"Nothing. It's not important right now. My mind was raging when we fought."

"So, you've forgotten the waterfall training?"

"No, I haven't. I'm just not good at focusing when I'm upset. Wait a minute..." Llia sees Reo's smile. "You were playing sleep earlier?" She buries her face in her pillow.

"Yeah, I was. Iris knows her stuff—those remedies worked wonders. Don't feel ashamed about anything. That evening when I held you and we melted into those intense kisses... that place is my home as well." He moves closer to Llia as she lifts her head from her pillow and catches his gentle gaze.

They're face to face in a stare-down, and she dives into his soft lips without hesitation. Her heart races in her chest like a wild butterfly, and their breathing became faster, more urgent with each passing second. She inhales his intoxicating scent and floats into the stratosphere of elation, losing herself in the moment. Her soft lips complement his perfectly as the two fight in a war of passionate kisses, neither willing to surrender. She runs her hands over his sculpted body, tracing every curve and muscle with trembling fingers.

A loud, jarring bang at the door stops them in their tracks, reality crashing back like a bucket of cold water. TJ opens the door without waiting for a response.

"TJ, what the hell?!"

"Sorry sis, I knocked a few times, but no one answered. A detective, Moro, is here for you, and he says it's urgent!"

"Oh, okay, wait. How long were you standing there? Did you hear anything?"

"No, of course not! Are you accusing me of eavesdropping? I would never do something like that!" TJ smirks as he leaves and shuts the door halfway. "Oh, and sis?"

"Yeah?"

"Tell Reo when he's done hiding in the bathroom, I'd like to go over my findings with him, please."

"Sure thing." She replies with an embarrassed smile before walking to her bathroom, where Reo is hiding. "Yeah, we're busted. TJ needs to talk to you. I don't think I've ever seen you move that fast before."

Reo looks at his complexion in the mirror and sees the hue in his cheeks. "You're right. It has been a long time since I felt like this."

CHAPTER NINETEEN
CHECK

TJ chuckles the entire way as he reaches for and swings open the entryway.

"Welcome, Moro. At last, we come face to face. Make yourself comfortable—Llia should join us shortly."

"Indeed, it's wonderful to finally connect in the real world. I notice your speech pattern has a faint drawl. I'd guess...Mississippi region? Though you've been away for some time, that explains why it fades in and out."

"Wow, impressive. That's remarkable. Now I understand where Llia learned her skills." Their attention drifts to Llia's room as she steps out. TJ passes her a steaming mug of coffee, which helps ease her glare. For quite a while, the investigator jots notes in his pad.

"Well, hello! I didn't know you were back in town, kid. It took you shooting up a restaurant and causing thousands of dollars in damages for me to find out you were here!"

"Okay, Moro, firstly, I am so sorry about that. We have been under attack for the last three days. Maddix was in trouble, and we flew here at a moment's notice. But I have some new information. The owner of Ma's restaurant is an S-class Yokai who wants to become a goddess and get vengeance for the murder of her brother, the Orochi dragon. And yes, the same Orochi dragon that killed multiple earthly deities to increase his own strength. She wants my life and the lives of my friends to free Penumbra, the goddess of darkness, which will send the world back into The Kokuten! (The black spot!) Where Myou's powers will be limitless!"

"Okay, we will start with the police business first, then we will get to that. Our time is limited, and I was sent here to officially arrest you. Your buddy Maddix Blume is nowhere to be found at the hospital. Speaking of which, there were thirty deaths yesterday. There was a report of a black male driving a rather large tank-like RV from the scene of the crime. Do you know anything about that?" Moro asks while documenting his observations.

TJ spat out his drink in the kitchen sink. "S-Sorry, wrong pipe. I'm just going," he says as he leaves the room. He encounters Maddix in the hallway, leaving Rose's room to enter the living room. He shoves him back into her room. "Not now, Goose! She's talking to Moro. There are some things we have to go over, anyway."

Iris leaves the bathroom and walks into the living room. "Oh, hi, Uncle Moro."

"Hello, Iris. I'm afraid I have some terrible news for you as well. Your friend Sarah was involved in the incident at the restaurant, and I am so sorry, but she was killed."

Iris stands frozen in horror. Moro lowers his head, and Llia takes a step toward her. But Moro stops Llia, and Iris dashes out of the apartment in tears.

"Wait! Iris, don't leave the apartment! No! Moro, what the hell? She can't leave the apartment; it's protected with sutras that keep out the Yokai!"

Moro's glaring eyes scan the room as he grips his notepad and takes a sharp breath. "Kid, they have you on surveillance killing people at Ma's restaurant. It was you who shot Sarah. You also seriously injured several others, not to mention disturbing the peace and destruction of private property! I asked to come here so I can warn you and help you get out of here."

"It's Ma! She's making her move...."

"I know. TJ and I have been trading intel. She is a Yokai. I think she is a shapeshifter. This is my fault. I should have done a better job helping you with this Yokai threat. Now they are spreading like wildfire. The entire police force is outside. They are trying to link you with the deaths at the Turn Up and the hospital as well!"

"Ma's trying to corner me, make me look guilty, because I figured out that Ma and Myou are one and the same."

Moro staggers back onto the couch. His eyes fix on the floor. He appears transported to a different time, his gaze wide with terror, his frame trembling. *She was supposed to be just a legend!* Moro's mind races.

"That's impossible... I spent years looking for any trace that she existed. In my grandfather's journal, she was his suspect. She's the one who murdered my grandfather."

"Myou was behind that? You've never told me!," Llia's perched on the edge of the couch, her delicate features creased with concern. "I had no idea Myou was involved in your grandfather's murder," she murmured. "This must be a lot to process." She reaches out and gently places her hand on Moro's trembling arm, offering what comfort she could in this trying moment.

"I tried burying it all away. His unsolved murder haunted me—I let him down. That's why I fled across the ocean. But it seems running from the past is futile."

"I came face to face with her. She's cunning to the core, maybe the most brilliant mind I've encountered. When I attempted to get a read on her, she was like a blank slate."

"Llia! Everyone reveals something, even when they appear inscrutable. The key lies in knowing what to probe for. What did she talk about the most? That usually points to her true motivations."

"Well, she pressed me to surrender, promising no further bloodshed if I complied."

"Now we're getting somewhere. What stopped her from eliminating you and Rose right then and there?"

"Uh, I don't know. She even said we could leave. She told the people who attacked us to capture me and kill Rose. I think it's because… it wasn't the right time."

Moro raises an eyebrow at Llia while she searches for the answer.

"I don't think she wanted Rose to be killed either, because she had her in the restaurant before you even got there. She could have killed her and been done with it. It seems like… It wasn't the right time or place. She needs us at a particular place and time! Okay, now we're getting somewhere. I also think she knows Reo personally. It could be her mind games, but she said some particular things. She knows him on a personal level!"

"My grandfather's notes also reveal another fact that made little sense. Now that I look at it, it makes perfect sense; I can't see how I didn't notice it before. There is a list needed to make an Ikebana offering that seems to summon someone or something. Grandfather's notes say it's called the Moonless Night." Moro shows Llia the notebook.

"Ikebana? Reo mentioned that he and his mother would take them to the shrine. But what do Japanese flower arrangements have to do with this?"

"I'm not an expert on the subject, but you might want to hear this next part. The Moonless Night arrangement comprises three flowers: an Iris, a Rose, and a Camellia."

"Oh my God, it's us! The CP squad! We are the Ikebana flowers! So does she need to kill us all, or just one of us?"

"I don't know, that's what my grandfather died trying to figure out."

"Alright, we'll come back to that later. In the restaurant, Rose said she saw an old woman when she looked at Myou, but I saw a beautiful Japanese woman with raven hair and violet eyes." Llia stood at the window, gazing out at the bustling city streets below.

Suddenly, the door to her room flies open, and Detective Moro Watanabe turns and aims his gun at the ready. A familiar voice fills the room, causing Reo to flex his hand, his eyes burning with intensity.

"Reo?!" Llia remembers Myou's exact words to her in the restaurant. "Tsumi! That's what Reo said to me while we were training. When we first met, he told me a story. In the story, he trained his wife. But Myou is the one who killed Reo's wife! Unless... Oh my God!

"She didn't just kill your wife! She *is* your wife!" Llia proclaims as she places her hand over her mouth.

Reo's misty eyes are downcast, and the color drains from his face.

"That's what she told you when you were about to strike the killing blow all those years ago! She tricked you from the very start. Yumi has always been Myou!" Llia exclaims as she stands to her feet.

"Reo-sama, is this true?"

Reo averts his gaze as TJ storms into the room, his glaring eyes locked on Reo. The air crackles with tension as the powerful

Yokai Executioner's presence fills the dimly lit room. TJ's features are etched with fierce determination, his brow furrowed, and his jaw set in a hard line. Reo can feel the weight of TJ's accusatory stare bearing down on him, the unspoken questions and accusations hanging thick between them. He shifts uncomfortably, unable to meet his partner's intense gaze, the gravity of the situation weighing heavily on his mind.

"How could you not tell me that, Reo?! Why didn't you just kill her when you had the chance? We lost everyone because of you!" TJ's outburst triggers an ominous response from Reo's wristband, as shadowy vapors begin seeping out, reminiscent of that night around the flames. Llia seems to be the only one who can see it.

"TJ, wait, it's not his fault!" Llia interjects, positioning herself between the two men.

"How is that not his fault?! He knows the rule for betrayal, you get the same thing we gave Tristian!" TJ thrusts forward with his weapon, but Llia blocks his advance.

"No! Listen to me! This is what she wants. She wants you to kill each other, and there'll be no one to stop her. Reo is not in control of his emotions. That bracelet is controlling them. I first noticed it at the campsite. I know why she kept you alive, and why she kept all of us alive for that matter. Myou doesn't get her power from darkness like the Moonless Night. Her power comes from the darkness she creates in our hearts!"

The silence in the room grows thick as understanding dawns across their faces. TJ lowers his weapon, his shoulders slumping as the pieces fall into place.

"She orchestrated everything. The attack on our team wasn't random." TJ's voice cracks. "She knew exactly where we'd be that night."

Moro pulls out his grandfather's worn journal, its pages yellow with age. "My grandfather was close to exposing her true identity. The night before his murder, he wrote about finding crucial evidence."

"The fire that killed our team," Reo's voice is barely above a whisper. "She waited until we were all separated. Picked them off one by one."

Llia's mind races through memories of her mother—the mysterious circumstances of her death, the strange symbols found at the scene. Her hand flies to her mouth as realization strikes like lightning.

"My mom," Llia thinks as her hands tremble.

"All this time," TJ paces the room, "we've been playing into her hands. Every move we made, every person we tried to protect—she was ten steps ahead."

"It's called choice architecture. Your choices are already selected long before you make them. She just led you to believe that you made them," Rose interjects.

"She's been orchestrating our pain, feeding off our darkness," Llia's voice is hollow.

The weight of collective grief presses down on the room like a physical force. Decades of manipulation, death, and carefully crafted suffering—all serving to strengthen their ancient enemy.

"I am designed by flaws. Fighting her isn't an option for me. So, I'm placing my faith in you. You have to end her, Camellia! You possess the strength to triumph where I fall short; her abilities can't affect you, which means you're our greatest hope," Reo says as his gentle gaze locks with hers.

"Myou has been executing an eight-hundred-year-old plan, and you figured it out within months. I will also entrust Myou to you. And Senpai: I-I'm so sorry, I didn't think that the damn bracelet may have been affecting you like that! I guess there are some things that my tech can't pick up on." TJ shakes his head vigorously, his expression a mix of frustration and regret. The tech genius's usual confident demeanor falters as the weight of his oversight regarding the bracelet settles heavily in the dimly lit room.

"I'll do it! I will stop Myou." Llia stops dead in her tracks, muscles tensing as an icy chill creeps across her exposed skin like frost spreading over a windowpane. A sharp, twisting pain shoots through her stomach, making her double over and press her palm against her abdomen. The front door looms ahead, shrouded in an unnatural darkness that seems to swallow what little light remains. Through the silence, the unmistakable sound of footsteps grows louder—slow, deliberate steps approaching from the other side, each one making the floorboards creak ominously beneath unseen feet.

"The Umbra! They're here!" Llia exclaims.

"A mere mortal like you stands no chance against divine power! Unless you present yourself at the shrine outside the city by sunrise, your companion's life will be forfeit!" The ethereal voice proclaims.

TJ's chest heaves as Myou's haunting voice echoes through the house, each word dripping with malevolent intent. His eyes dart frantically across the darkened room, searching every shadow and corner for signs of movement. With the practiced efficiency of a trained executioner, he springs into action, muscles coiled tight as he rushes to Iris's room, throwing open the door with such force it rattles in its frame. Finding nothing but empty darkness, he pivots sharply on his heel and charges back into the living room, his footsteps thundering against the hardwood floors as sweat begins to bead on his forehead.

"Where's Iris? Reo? Llia! Where's Iris?!" TJ yells as they stare at the front door. His smartwatch vibrates and he scrambles to get to the window.

"Shit, she's downstairs. They have her. But that ain't all they have! Detective Moro? There is a problem with your guys! Look out the window," TJ says, stepping back in shock and going to the front door, his calloused hand gripping the polished brass handle as his tactical mind races through possible scenarios. The streetlights outside cast long shadows through the window, making the mundane scene feel more ominous with each passing second.

Moro and Llia move to the window, gazing at the crowd gathered below. The assembled mass of uniformed cops and onlookers tilt their heads skyward simultaneously, exposing ashen complexions and lifeless stares.

"Your guys are her guys now!" Llia says.

"Damn it! They've got us boxed in," Moro replies.

"I'll go downstairs and see if the way is clear. TJ, go to Plan B," Reo says, opening the front door and closing it behind him.

"Sis, I have a way out, but I need you to get Rose and Maddix into your room. Be ready to bounce when it's time. We have to get to the shrine before dawn; that's about six hours from now. It takes three hours just to drive to the shrine! We have to save Iris!" TJ franticly types on his watch.

At that moment, Reo's watch lights up as he creeps down the stairs in Llia's apartment building. Otis relays detailed information about TJ's plans and their current position. Reo sees several people lying dead in the hall as he turns the corner. The smell of flowers wafting through the air makes him change direction and head back toward Llia's apartment. He sees an old woman dressed in black standing near Llia's door. They lock eyes as she smiles at him.

"Reo, you look fit. Is Camellia home?"

"The last time I saw you, I swore you were going to die. Nothing has changed since then, Myou!"

"Aw, you're not happy to see me? You're not still sore at me for killing your wife, are you?" Myou says as Reo clenches his fist.

"I know you're Yumi, shapeshifter! You tricked me all those years ago. I let my guard down and allowed myself to be cursed by you!" Reo inches closer to her.

A sinister smile spreads across Myou's face. She peels away her artificial visage, exposing the stunning, youthful countenance beneath. "Ah yes, this appearance! Surely you couldn't harm your beloved spouse."

He launches himself at her with lightning speed. As her obsidian gaze meets his, she deftly sidesteps his attack by the slimmest margin. She backs away toward the stairwell with Reo in pursuit. Meanwhile, Udai steps out from the residence of Tom and Kimberly, just opposite Llia's apartment. He halts in front of Llia's entrance. Unlike Myou, TJ's protective talisman prevents him from crossing the threshold.

"You, boy! Release the offerings, or you all will die this day!" Udai says as the hall fills with Yokai crawling out of the shadows.

"They're everywhere! On every floor and in every room. Reo is chasing something away from here!" TJ says, looking at his watch as it shows him a thermal image of the building.

"She's luring him away from us!" Llia replies.

"Okay, everyone, listen; we are about to have a terrible day. We're surrounded. I have weapons right here in my bag: three sutra guns with sixteen-round clips, three retractable katanas, and two retractable spears. Everyone grab something," TJ says.

"I have a gun already!" Moro replies.

"Detective, that gun will just tickle. Then you will be Bandon flushed!"

"What the hell does that mean?"

"Same thing as knocked the fuck out, but vastly more painful! Now, take one of my guns, and everyone stay away from the windows. Trust nothing you see or hear outside this room. We should be good as long as we stay in here. There is a sutra sticker on the front door, and it keeps all of them out," TJ replies.

"TJ, help me barricade the front door."

"Good idea, Moro. Girls, you stay together; don't leave each other's side! Goose, watch them. That's your job."

"I'm giving you thirty seconds, and these officers will come up and kill all of you! The sutra does not bar them. They are not Yokai," Udai says.

TJ motions for the girls to go into Llia's room and close the door. Llia shakes her head, looking at Rose and Maddix's scared faces, giving TJ a thumbs up.

"TJ...You won't get away from me this time. Two years ago, I wiped out your entire team. Do you think you can stand against me alone? I allowed you to survive on that day. My intention was for the guilt to overwhelm you completely, leaving nothing behind. I'm letting you know I won't hold anything back this time. Before allowing you to die, I will make you experience immense suffering, and I plan to kill Iris first so I can dine on your suffering!"

TJ's spear becomes much lighter as he grips it tightly on the handle. The temperature rises as he visualizes stabbing Udai in the chest.

"You think we can take him?" whispers Moro with his eyes and gun fixed on the door. TJ glances toward Llia's room and looks at Moro. "I plan on finding out. I want you to keep them safe no matter what!"

Moro bows his head as he sees the intense gleam in TJ's eyes. He waves at him to go into the room with the girls and Maddix. Moro makes his way into the room and closes the door. TJ buries his spear into the hardwood floor, raises his smartwatch, and presses the red button on the last screen. "Udai, the only thing you're gonna get today is my spear in your heart...*mutha-fucka*!" he exclaims as the five-second countdown ends.

A loud boom covers the entire building as a thick blanket of smoke fills the air. The girls scream at the top of their lungs as Llia runs to the door and opens it, immediately blinded. She kneels to see if she can see anything, but she can't. Moro pulls her off the floor and back into the room, slamming the door behind them. "Listen, we are gonna be alright," Moro says. Llia knows all too well that isn't true. She comforts Maddix and Rose as her watch beeps.

"Llia! Are you there?"

"Reo?! You're okay?! Where are you? Don't overuse your powers; you know Myou's just provoking you."

"I know. It's all a part of Plan B. I'm downstairs. I have your positions. It's an army of Yokai and pawns converging on you."

"I think TJ is dead!" Llia replies.

"What...? No! He's not. I'm tracking him too. His vitals are normal. He is on the second floor. That loud noise you heard was Plan B, as well. He installed small directional charges in the hallways on every level, just in case we ever got pinned inside the apartment. He used his thermal imaging to see if the building was clear before he used it."

"He is a fucking genius! Okay, what do we do?" Llia asks.

"I can get two of you out of there right now using my trade places ability, but you have to be one of those two. Decide quickly."

"Wait, no, I can't do that. Plus, I just told you not to overdo it. You need to conserve your strength. We all get out of here together, or none of us does. We don't leave anyone behind ever! Promise me!" Llia says.

"Okay, I promise. There is another way, but they may not like it." There is a crash at Llia's bedroom window. A ladder leads directly onto the roof of the warhorse.

"Let's go. Those charges only took out some of the Yokai. The others are coming!" Reo says.

Moro guards the door as the girls argue over who goes first. Rose wins and starts her descent. The people in the street below are full of pawns and normal people. They watch as half of the crowd films it with their phones, while the other half stands in awe. The golden beams slowly crawl from the dark corner of the city. The crowd's roar grows as Rose makes it safely into the warhorse, followed by Maddix.

"Okay, Llia, you're next," Moro says. He aims his gun at the door. The door is full of holes, but the army of footsteps on the other side is still there.

"No, I'm not leaving without you!" Llia replies. The Yokai break the door off its hinges.

"Okay, together then!" Moro says as they dart to the window. He grabs Llia by her belt and tucks his notebook into it before tossing her out of the window onto the ladder. He then turns and empties his clip into the horde of Yokai.

"Moro!" Llia yells as she hangs onto the ladder and waits for him to answer.

The Yokai leap toward her from the window sill, and a beaten Moro shoots the Yokai in the back of the head. He blocks the window with his body as countless Yokai stab him all over. They try to get through the window. His death grip on the window frame holds true.

"Get the hell out of here, kid! I am so proud... to have known... you... I... love you," Moro yells. Tears pour from his painful expression. Blood spews from his mouth as he gives Llia enough time to make it to the warhorse. Seeing this, Moro then lets go and falls to the ground below. His lifeless body lies on the cold ground as the army of pawns tramples him while they approach the warhorse. They speed off before the Yokai can reach them.

"Reo's not here. This thing is driving by itself. Where's Moro?" Rose asks. Llia collapses to the floor. She buries her head in her hands, consumed by rage and sorrow.

No—no! No God—No. Moro, I love you too!

"TJ was right. We can't save them all! I—I wasn't strong enough. I couldn't save him! He was my—my family, and I failed him!" Llia says. Her guttural tone is followed by an avalanche of tears and convulsions. She screams bloody murder as the warhorse speeds away. Rose and Maddix console her as they quickly realize that Moro is dead.

CHAPTER TWENTY
DEATH MARCH

Autumn leaves scatter across the park as Reo pursues Myou through the winding paths. She halts near a stone fountain, her silhouette stark against the dying light. Darkness creeps across the ground like spilled ink, radiating from where she stands.

"My beloved," Myou turns, her crimson lips curving into a smile. "How long has it been since we danced beneath cherry blossoms?"

"Don't." Reo's fingers tighten around his sword.

"Remember our wedding night? The way the moonlight painted shadows across our skin?" She steps closer, her kimono rustling against the grass. "At first, it was merely a ploy to gain your trust. But something changed."

The park fades away as memories flood Reo's mind—stolen kisses in temple gardens, whispered promises under starlit skies, hands intertwined as they walked ancient paths. His grip on the sword loosens.

"Join me again," Myou's voice carries on the wind. "We could rule this new world together, just as we once ruled our own hearts."

For a moment, Reo's eyes soften. The weight of centuries presses against his chest as he remembers the warmth of her embrace and the sound of her laughter.

But then different memories surface—Llia's determined gaze as she trained, her genuine smile when she mastered a new technique, the tender kiss they shared in the rain. She saw him not as a weapon or a means to an end, but as someone worth knowing.

His eyes harden, amber irises blazing with renewed purpose. The sword lifts between them, severing the threads of the past.

"Those memories died with the woman I thought you were," Reo's voice is as cold as winter frost.

Myou's smile vanishes like smoke in the wind. She raises her pale hand, moonlight catching on her blood-red nails. "Very well. Then it is death."

The shadows behind her ripple and part. Autsetsubae emerges, wearing a black mask that resembles a demon. His twin blades catch the dying light. The legendary demon's presence thickens the air, making it feel like trying to breathe underwater. His swords—one black as pitch, one gleaming silver—point at Reo's heart.

"When I take your head, there will be no more doubt." Autsetsubae's voice rumbles like distant thunder. "I alone will be known as the god of the blade."

His face transforms from a sneer to a cold focus as he shifted into his fighting stance. His feet spread wide, blades crossing in front of his chest. The very ground seems to tremble beneath his power.

Reo's hands tightened on his own sword. Even at full strength, facing Autsetsubae would be near suicide. In his current state, weakened and worn from battle, death feels certain. But he lifts his blade anyway. If this was to be his end, he would meet it standing.

"Goodbye, my love." Myou turns away, her elaborate kimono swishing against the grass. A single tear rolls down her cheek, glinting like a diamond before falling to the earth. The droplet hits the ground and sizzles, leaving a small crater of blackened soil.

Myou's form dissolves into the shadows, leaving only the lingering scent of cherry blossoms. Autsetsubae studies Reo's ragged breathing, noting the way his shoulders slump ever so slightly.

"You're exhausted." Autsetsubae sheathes his black blade with deliberate slowness. "It would be beneath me to strike you down like this."

The silver sword twirls in his grip, catching the last rays of sunlight. "I've waited centuries for a worthy opponent. The legends speak of your blade work. Show me."

Reo straightens, his amber eyes locked on his opponent. A slight nod acknowledges the demon's gesture of honor. The weight of his sword feels heavier than usual in his tired hands, but his grip remains steady.

They circle each other, feet sliding across grass slick with evening dew. The park falls silent—no birds, no rustling leaves, as if nature itself holds its breath.

Steel meets steel with a sound like thunder. Sparks fly as their blades dance, each strike precise, each parry perfectly timed. Autsetsubae's silver sword whistles through the air, met by Reo's lightning-fast counters.

Their movements blur into a deadly ballet. Reo's blade traces elegant arcs while Autsetsubae's cuts come like strikes of lightning. The demon's mask gleams with each exchange, his raw power matched by Reo's fluid grace.

Trees splinter in their wake. The stone fountain cracks and crumbles as they weave between its jets of water. Their swords sing a duet of destruction, each clash sending shockwaves through the evening air.

"Yes!" Autsetsubae's laugh booms across the park. "This is what I've waited for!" His silver blade becomes a streak of light as he presses his attack.

Reo meets him strike for strike, his fatigue forgotten in the pure focus of combat. Their swords lock again, their faces inches apart, neither willing to yield.

Steel sings through the air as Reo's blade dances with increasing precision. Each strike flows seamlessly into the next, his movements liquid and deadly. Autsetsubae's single silver sword struggles to match the tempo.

"Your reputation doesn't do you justice," Autsetsubae grunts, parrying a vicious slash that sends him sliding backward.

Reo presses forward, his amber eyes focused with laser intensity. His sword becomes a silver blur, forcing Autsetsubae to give ground. The demon's confident smirk begins to fade as sweat beads on his brow.

Their blades lock again, but this time Reo twists his wrist in a complex motion. The move sends Autsetsubae's guard wide, leaving him exposed for a fraction of a second. That's all Reo needs.

His sword flashes upward in a precise arc. The black mask splits with a sharp crack, the blade's edge leaving a thin red line across the bridge of Autsetsubae's nose. The two halves of the mask fall away, clattering against the stone path.

The face beneath belongs to a Japanese man around fifty, with deep lines etched around cold, calculating eyes. A few strands of gray streak through his black hair, and the fresh cut across his nose has already begun to well with blood.

"First blood is yours," Autsetsubae touches the cut, examining the red on his fingertips. His exposed face twists into a snarl. "Perhaps it's time I stopped holding back."

Reo gives a curt nod, his blade steady despite his growing exhaustion. Autsetsubae's hand moves to rest on the hilt of his sheathed black sword, a predatory gleam in his eyes.

Not willing to let him draw both blades, Reo launches forward in a burst of speed. His sword whistles through the air in a deadly arc, but Autsetsubae deflects it with his silver blade.

Reo leaps backward, putting distance between them before the second sword can find its mark.

But the black sword remains sheathed. Autsetsubae's lips curl into a knowing smile.

"The second blood belongs to me," he says, his voice rich with satisfaction.

A sharp pain blooms along Reo's left side. He presses his hand against it, fingers coming away wet with blood. His amber eyes widen. When had the demon struck? He hadn't seen the black blade leave its scabbard.

"Your reputation precedes you, Reo, but I find myself disappointed." Autsetsubae's voice carries across the battlefield. "My twin demon blade technique has no equal. You noticed the first cut, yes, but did you catch the second? The third?"

Reo's breathing grows labored, sweat beading on his brow. His muscles scream in protest as fresh waves of pain radiate from wounds he never saw coming. A grimace twists his features as he struggles to maintain his stance.

Reo shifts, bringing his father's katana up in a defensive position. Moonlight catches the ancient steel, illuminating an intricate symbol etched into the right side of the blade—a coiled dragon wrapped around a chrysanthemum.

Autsetsubae freezes mid-step, his predatory advance halting as his eyes lock onto the marking. The color drains from his face, recognition sparking in his eyes.

"□□□...□□□..." Autsetsubae's words come in an ancient dialect, one rarely heard outside of historical texts. "□□□□□□□□?"

Reo's eyes widen at the archaic Japanese. His grip tightens on the sword's handle as he responds in kind, the old words feeling strange on his tongue. "□□□□□□□□□□□□□□□□□□□□"

Autsetsubae lowers his blades, his demeanor shifting from murderous to contemplative. "Three hundred years ago, your ancestor Fujiwara no Tadashi showed me mercy when others would have struck me down. He saw honor even in a demon."

The demon warrior slides both swords smoothly into their scabbards. "I will repay that debt today. Your life is yours to keep—but know this is the only time such mercy will be extended." Autsetsubae's hand rests on his sword hilts. "The next time we meet, I will kill you without hesitation. This debt is paid."

"When that day comes, you'll find me a different man." Reo's amber eyes meet the demon's gaze.

A smirk plays across Autsetsubae's weathered face. "I hope so." His form melts into the lengthening shadows, leaving only disturbed grass where he had stood.

Reo's legs buckle. He drops to one knee, chest heaving as the toll of battle catches up to him. Blood trickles from unseen cuts, staining his clothes.

"Reo-sama." Otis's voice crackles through his earpiece. "I have grave news. Detective Moro... he's dead."

The words hit harder than any of Autsetsubae's strikes. "How?"

"He sacrificed himself protecting Llia, Rose, and Maddix during their escape from the Umbra. They're in the Warhorse now, heading toward the shrine outside the city."

Reo's fist clenches against the grass. "Send my car. TJ and I need to catch up to them."

"Your vehicle is en route, but..." Otis pauses. "TJ is still unaccounted for at Llia's apartment. His vitals are normal, but he's not responding to calls."

Fresh adrenaline surges through Reo's exhausted body. He pushes himself to his feet, ignoring the protest of his wounds. "How long until the car arrives?"

"Several minutes at least, given the current chaos throughout the city. The army of Yokai is attacking everywhere."

Reo was already moving, his feet carrying him toward TJ's last known location. "Keep trying to reach him. And Otis... thank you for telling me about Moro. I need to retrieve his body."

The night swallows his running form as he races through the streets, praying he won't be too late to save another friend.

CHAPTER TWENTY ONE
FOR HONOR

Dense fumes encircle TJ as he shoves away the planks covering him and surveys the area. Cries and shrieks echo through the neighborhood, stretching for several blocks.

He stumbles into the open. Flames and haze obscure his face while legions of dark figures and mindless pawns flood the roads, slaughtering those who remain unchanged.

"TJ!" calls a voice he recognizes. His eyes dart across the street and spot Reo.

"Stay where you are! I'm coming!"

A Pawn lunges at TJ, blade in hand, but he remains perfectly still.

"Where've you been dragging your feet?" TJ quips.

Reo dispatches the charging assailant before making his way to TJ's position near the ruins of Llia's complex.

A brief grin passes between them as Otis transmits updates to TJ's mind.

"Damn, they got Moro! They're headed for the Shinto Shrine beyond city limits. The sacred torii gates block out the darkness—it's their best chance at survival. What's our next move, Reo?"

"We have to kill Myou. It's the only way to stop her army and prevent them from freeing Penumbra and bringing back the Kokuten. We are dead if they let her go free. Oh—no. That's Moro's body over there!" Reo exclaims. They walk toward Moro's body, tears beginning to drip from their resolute expressions.

"You died like a warrior, old friend. I swear to watch over Llia in your place. Please forgive me." Reo whispers, crouching to gently shut Moro's eyelids. His mangled form shows signs of a savage assault.

"We keep losing friends and family to these bastards! We have to end this, Reo."

An explosion bursts through the wall, hurling them onto the pavement. A piercing ring fills their heads while debris drifts down and Udai emerges from the haze.

"That doesn't feel so good, now, does it? That's enough with the games, boy. I am going to kill you both! To hell with Myou's plan!" Udai declares.

TJ raises his palm to halt Reo's forward movement. "Stay back—this fight belongs to me! I've got a score to settle. Don't get involved, whatever happens. I'm serious! This has to be my battle—he slaughtered our loved ones, my team! I owe him!"

"I know, and you can take him. You are stronger than you know. You don't need to rely on your tech to beat him. That anger inside you seems like an endless power supply, but I've trained you better than that. It will only consume you like a raging fire until there is nothing left of you. Do this for honor, not for revenge! I'm going to take Moro's body and get him somewhere safe for the time being. He deserves an honorable burial. I leave this to you! I'll return with the car, and we'll head to the shrine together," Reo says.

TJ lifts his hand toward Reo, bumping fists and exchanging a knowing grin and a slight head bow. Reo strides past Udai, who remains completely indifferent to his presence. He gathers Moro's remains and departs with them.

TJ looks down at his watch, staring at it for what seems like an eternity. The light in his eyes shines before he turns to face Udai. His hands tremble with rage as he thinks of the friends from his past that Udai helped kill.

"You called me a boy earlier; I'm going to have to beat some respect into you! Otis... give me full power!"

Udai charges forward, gripping his luminous dragon spear with determination burning in his gaze. He spins the weapon with such velocity that it transforms into a shimmering streak of gold. He drives the powerful blade straight for TJ's chest with lightning quickness. TJ raises his right forearm defensively, as though wielding an invisible barrier, and Udai's strike halts mere centimeters from his smartwatch. The force of the impact demolishes the structure looming behind TJ. He flashes an arrogant grin while withdrawing his weapon.

Udai's jaw drops, and his gaze widens in disbelief. He pulls back before lunging forward once more. The two warriors trade blows in a dazzling exhibition of martial prowess, though Udai clearly outmatches TJ in all aspects of their duel.

Every thrust of Udai's weapon unleashes a shockwave that topples structures. His strikes shatter the pavement, leaving craters in their wake. TJ's only defense lies in his watch's electromagnetic capabilities; the advanced tech enables him to counter Udai's overwhelming speed and strength. Despite this, TJ fails to find any weakness in his opponent's stance, frustrated by Udai's exceptional equilibrium and agile reflexes. He realizes he must create an opportunity himself.

TJ forms a V with his fingers, triggering his watch to pulse and chirp. The enemy's weapon hurtles toward his torso with blinding speed, three times faster than before. A piercing mechanical shriek momentarily overwhelms the urban chaos.

The weapon spirals away as Udai stares at his trembling palms, desperately trying to restore sensation to his quivering fingers.

Seizing the opening, TJ launches into action. His boot slams into Udai's sternum with brutal force, and then he hurls his retractable spear at his stumbling adversary.

Scarlet vapor tints the hazy darkness above. Udai drops to his knees, head bowed as he extracts the massive sixty-four-ounce blade from his wounded shoulder. Blood spreads across the asphalt while frigid precipitation continues to drench the metropolis.

"It seems you're still using your technology to evade my assaults. You lack the skills to stand before me as a man, so you are a boy in my eyes! Do you think such toys can defeat me? I am a warrior devoted to the teachings of the Shaolin temple. I have dedicated my entire existence to the mastery of the spear, with nothing to aid me in a fight. The fact that you do such things is revolting and shameful! You are nothing more than a leaf in the clouds! And I am a typhoon!" Udai exclaims.

Glancing at his smartwatch, TJ's face drains of color. A nervous gulp escapes his throat. He reaches out, and his spear flies back into his waiting palm. Shifting into a guarded stance, the cocky grin that once adorned TJ's face vanishes, replaced by an expression of mounting desperation.

With a bowed head, Udai whispers sacred words. His wounds cease their crimson flow as he rises. The chanted verse grows in volume while he extends his arm toward his weapon, embedded in an automobile a football field away. Like a streak of golden electricity, the spear hurtles to his waiting fingers. A deafening crack echoes as his fist closes around the shaft. The impact's force halts the downpour above them, creating a fifteen-second pocket of suspended droplets. His face lifts, revealing eyes that burn with lethal intent.

The rain serenades the city, washing away the blood. TJ holds his spear toward Udai. His blade trembles in the rain as he glances at his smartwatch and sees a timer counting down his remaining power.

"TJ, you only have thirty seconds left!" Otis says.

"Thanks, Otis, but I can clearly see that! Go into silent mode... now!" He looks up at Udai, but he is gone. TJ's gaze darts in every direction without spotting his target. Triple pulses from his smartwatch send tremors through his wrist, and he lifts his weapon skyward to guard himself.

The luminous blade slices through his spear, carving a diagonal gash across his torso. TJ staggers backward before Udai's savage kick hammers into his gut, launching him through glass panes several yards away. His device throbs twice against his skin as he writhes in anguish. Crimson liquid collects beneath him while he stares through the shattered opening.

"Good... nothing is broken. Now I just need to get him into position and..."

Icy droplets trickle down his spine as the downpour intensifies. A pair of rapid pulses from his smartwatch alerts him, and he whirls around to find Udai looming behind him.

Scrambling aside, TJ springs upright, yet Udai closes the distance and unleashes a brutal thrust kick that crashes into his sternum, propelling him through the entrance and out into the drenching storm.

"Yep! That hurt!" TJ whispers. He begins to wheeze, struggling to regain his bearings.

Crumpled and battered, he marinates in blood pools of his own making. With cautious movements, he extends trembling fingers toward the severed spearhead. A sustained buzz from his smartwatch coincides with his weapon tumbling across the earth in his direction. Gripping the shaft, he levels the point at the shadowy figure of Udai prowling ever closer.

"Otis! Now! Activate the Divine weapon!" TJ shouts as he throws his spear toward him.

Udai's eyes widen as he takes a defensive stance. His golden spear easily knocks TJ's spear blade down.

TJ raises an eyebrow, glaring at the sky as he falls to his hands and knees. He looks at the wet, crimson concrete and glances at his watch. Time's up. The warhorse is out of range and unable to execute the Divine weapon.

His pulse races wildly beneath his ribs. Fighting for breath, he chokes as his windpipe tightens and lifts his gaze to find Udai advancing. Though a faint grin plays across his mouth, rage blazes in his stare.

TJ reaches for his spear but hears a faint buzzing sound before his watch abruptly powers off and goes silent.

Ultimately, he surrenders, sensing anger mounting as his attempts prove futile. Crouched on the frigid, soaked pavement, he feels the chill penetrating his garments while his thoughts drift to Reo, Llia, and Iris.

A soothing radiance envelops his frame, drawing a gentle curve to his lips as his eyelids fall closed.

Recollections of cherished moments with Iris flood his mind, echoing with the melody of her laughter and the lingering warmth of her presence.

"I know you think standing against me alone was courageous and honorable, but in hindsight, it was foolish. All these years of running from me after I killed your team of Yokai Ex. Clearly, not all Yokai Ex are equal. You are just a parody of Reo. You have been a thorn lodged just beneath the skin. I've been digging you out for years! It was only now that I realized I should have just cut the entire finger off!" Udai declares.

Towering above him, he lifts his weapon skyward, targeting the nape of TJ's neck for a swift execution. His bladed staff plunges downward through the rainfall toward its destination.

"I love you, Iris." TJ whispers.

A thunderous crack echoes from afar. TJ opens his eyelids to see Reo reaching out from within his ebony sports car.

"Iris is waiting. Let's go get her!" Reo says.

Standing up, TJ spots Udai sprawled on the pavement in the distance. Mustering his energy, he pulls himself into the vehicle.

Udai gets up as Reo steps on the gas. The engine roars as the car hits Udai again. They head toward the shrine just outside the city. Everywhere they pass is in a panic. An army of Yokai and pawns has covered the entire city in flames and blood.

Reo glances at TJ's lacerated body, assessing his wounds. Turning back to focus on driving, he notices TJ's breathing becoming increasingly shallow and his consciousness fading. Time is running out. Once they clear the city limits, Reo steers onto the shoulder and stops. He reaches over, pressing his palm against TJ and shutting his eyes in concentration. Though Llia's cautionary words about restraint echo in his mind, he refuses to let another life slip away, determined to keep his vow.

A brilliant glow envelops TJ. Reo watches anxiously for any sign of response. But before he can check TJ's condition, blood sprays from his own mouth as he slumps forward onto the wheel. Darkness claims his sight.

The city's orange glow paints apocalyptic shadows across the empty highway. Smoke billows into the night sky, turning Seattle's skyline into a hellscape of flame and destruction. Inside the sports car, both men lie motionless—Reo slumped over the steering wheel, TJ sprawled across the passenger seat.

Red eyes flicker between the trees, multiplying by the second. Leaves rustle as dark shapes creep closer to the vulnerable vehicle.

A soft blue glow emanates from TJ's powered-down smartwatch. Circuits hum to life as Otis initiates his emergency protocols. The car's hood splits open with a mechanical whir, revealing twin-mounted gun turrets that swivel toward the encroaching threat.

"Engaging Protector Protocol Alpha," Otis's computerized voice announces through the car's speakers. "Primary objective: preserve life functions of Administrator TJ and Allied Unit Reo."

The red eyes pause their advance. Low growls echo from the treeline as more shapes gather in the darkness.

A rhythmic chopping sound cuts through the night air. TJ's modified military helicopter appears over the burning city, banking hard toward their position. Steel cables with electromagnetic hooks dangle beneath its belly as it approaches.

The turrets track the movement in the woods, barrels gleaming in the fire's reflected light. Whatever creatures lurk there hold back, wary of the automated defenses.

The helicopter positions itself directly overhead. Its hooks descend toward the car's reinforced frame, designed specifically for aerial extraction. With precise movements, they lock into place with metallic clanks.

"Securing vehicle for transport," Otis announces. "Maintaining weapons coverage until elevation is achieved."

The cables go taut. The car's suspension creaks as it lifts slowly off the asphalt, turrets still trained on the woods where red eyes watch their escape.

Three and a half hours have passed, and the warhorse stops just short of the Shinto shrine. Llia has made Otis stop along the way to the shrine, saving all the people they could carry in the armored SUV.

"Llia, there's a tree blocking the path to the shrine. It's about one hundred and ten yards away from our current location. The protocol would be to enter the shrine; any evil Yokai cannot pass the torii gates," Otis says.

"I have confirmed via Reo's smartwatch that he is alive, but his vitals are critical. TJ's status is the same; his smartwatch died while fighting Udai one-on-one."

"Otis, give me an update on their current location," Llia asks.

"They are en route via—Alert! Enemies are approaching rapidly; they will be here in ten minutes. Suggested action: enter the shrine immediately. Torrent guns are now active, but they require an operator. Maddix is allowed by TJ to be the operator. TJ listed him as the newest member of the Yokai Ex, control room technician."

Maddix grips the controls of the torrent guns, his hands trembling. "TJ pulled me aside the other night to talk about this potential moment; we were in Rose's room. The look in his eyes—I'd never seen him so serious."

His mind flashed back to the apartment, the weight of TJ's hand on his shoulder. The room smelled of Rose's jasmine perfume, creating an odd contrast to the gravity of their conversation.

"He said he and Reo needed someone they could trust in the control room—someone who understood what was at stake." Maddix's voice cracks. "After what happened to Charlie... I couldn't just stand by anymore. Not when I could help protect everyone."

The memory of Charlie's broken body haunted him—the way they'd found him, cold and lifeless at the Turn Up Party.

"I didn't hesitate when TJ asked. He showed me the tech and explained what everything does."

Llia watches him take command of the weapons system with surprising confidence. His fingers fly over the controls as he spoke.

"The training started that same night. TJ said we didn't have time to waste. He mentioned something big was coming, and they needed every advantage they could get." Maddix's eyes remain fixed on the monitors. "I promised myself I wouldn't let anyone else die. Not Iris, not Rose, not you. Not if I could help stop it."

The system hums to life under his touch, with defensive grids lighting up across the screens.

"Okay, everyone, head toward the shrine! I know it sounds weird but wash your hands before passing through the torii gates!" Llia yells, manually opening the doors.

The women and children exit first, followed by the men. Maddix hugs Llia and whispers, "For Charlie and Moro!" She tears up and nods in agreement.

Peering into the shadowy forest, Rose notices multiple sets of glowing pink eyes gazing in their direction. The foliage shifts, while snapping limbs and crackling undergrowth signal something approaching. The group of men shouts Llia's name as they sprint toward the shrine's entrance.

Llia exits the warhorse with her gun at the ready. The door closes behind her. She immediately speaks to Maddix through her smartwatch.

"Hey, don't you dare die on me! Stay inside the warhorse."

"Llia, don't worry about me. I've got this. Otis taught me while you slept. I owe you for my part in all this, even if I was under Myou's control. I want you to know that I'm sorry for everything, and I love you; you have always been an excellent friend to me. Now get your ass to the shrine. I will hold them off for as long as I can."

A shadowy presence materializes at Llia's back. A frigid gust sweeps past her neck, bringing with it a rancid stench that sends chills down her spine. As she pivots, she finds herself face-to-face with a lethal Yokai killer. Above, a sinister ebony blade hangs suspended for an instant before plunging downward. Crimson droplets paint a horrific pattern across the earth.

The entire top half of the assassin's body is gone. A massive gun on the warhorse is smoking as it turns toward the woods.

"I told you, Llia, I'll be fine. Now run, they are here!" Maddix yells.

Every gun on the warhorse fires toward the dark woods. Massive trunks topple as Maddix slaughters countless Yokai. The overwhelming roar of gunfire drowns out Llia's thoughts completely. The explosive volley shreds multiple lines of forest that encircle the vast concrete expanse.

Mechanical sounds reverberate across the concrete, intensifying. A dense, murky veil attempts to conceal the devastation from the gleam of approaching lights.

The shadowy barrier dissolves, revealing heaps of mangled corpses and splintered timber scattered along the perimeter of the vacant lot.

"Maddix, we eliminated approximately one hundred and forty-three Yokai, but I am detecting more heading toward this location. The torrents have exhausted all ammunition. We won't be able to stop the force that's headed toward us now. They have Oni with them. The Oni are large, ogre-like creatures with superior strength compared to the Yokai assassin. They can destroy the armor of the warhorse," Otis says.

Gazing through the panes, he witnesses the gory devastation that litters the forest. Rivers of blood seep into the earth, tainting the atmosphere. The approaching thunder of Oni footsteps resonates within his bones.

"Otis, is it possible for them to enter the shrine?"

"No, the Yokai and Oni cannot pass the torii gates. There is no record of any Yokai or Oni ever entering a shrine."

"Okay, great, I just have to hold them off until someone comes to save our asses. Well, since I'm probably going to die anyway..."

Maddix walks into the kitchen and looks into the cabinet. He sees several boxes filled with Marty Mar bars. He takes a few and sits in the master control seat. Unwrapping the first bar, he glances at the screen, revealing the enemies closing in on their location.

"What's that sound? Is that a helicopter?" Maddix asks.

CHAPTER TWENTY TWO

A LEAF IN THE CLOUDS

Moonlight carves harsh shadows across the cliff face as Myou's silhouette looms ominously against the night sky. Her kimono ripples in the cold wind while she gazes down at the shrine grounds below, where the lights of emergency vehicles paint everything in alternating red and blue.

Udai materializes to her left, his massive frame dwarfing her delicate form. Autsetsubae appears moments later on her right, completing their triangle formation at the cliff's edge.

"Tell me, Udai," Myou's voice drips with honeyed poison. "Did you eliminate our troublesome executioner as planned?"

Udai's shoulders tense. Sweat beads on his forehead despite the chill. "My lady, I... I regret to inform you that TJ managed to escape."

Myou's head turns with predatory slowness. Her eyes, usually a warm amber, blaze crimson as they fix on Udai. The raw fury in her gaze sends violent tremors through his body, and his legs give out as he collapses to his knees.

"Please, my lady! Forgive my failure!" Udai presses his forehead to the ground. "He was more resourceful than we anticipated. I swear I will not fail you again!"

The temperature around them plummets. Frost crystallizes across the rocks at their feet. Myou's rage radiates in invisible waves that make the air itself feel heavy and toxic.

Autsetsubae drops to his knees beside Udai, his armor clattering against the rocky ground. "My lady, I too have failed. Reo lives. He proved far more formidable than—"

The air crackles with dark energy. A void-black cloud erupts around Myou, her pristine kimono whipping in an otherworldly wind. For a split second, her carefully maintained human form slips. Through the darkness, something ancient and terrible emerges—a mass of writhing shadows with countless crimson eyes, each burning with the intensity of dying stars. Her true form towers over them, a horror that predates human civilization itself.

Udai and Autsetsubae press their faces into the frost-covered earth, their bodies wracked with tremors. The primal terror that grips them goes far beyond mere fear—it is the instinctive recognition of an apex predator, a being so far above them in the natural order that their very souls scream to flee.

The darkness recedes as quickly as it manifested. Myou's human form solidifies once more, though her eyes retain their blood-red glow. When she speaks, her voice carries echoes of countless screaming souls.

"You disappoint me deeply," she says, her words frosting the air. "I have given you power beyond mortal comprehension, yet you cannot eliminate two simple humans?"

She glides forward, her feet barely touching the ground. "Tonight, you will return to face these executioners. And when the sun rises tomorrow, either they will be dead—" She pauses, letting her gaze bore into each of them. "Or you will be."

Neither warrior dares to move or speak as frost creeps up their armor, the bitter cold biting into their skin.

"Your incompetence disappoints me," she whispers, each word sharp as a blade.

Myou's delicate hand rises towards the dense forest, her fingers spreading like a conductor before her orchestra of destruction. At her gesture, shadows writhe between the trees, taking solid form. Hundreds of lesser Yokai emerge—twisted creatures with too many limbs, faces frozen in eternal screams, and bodies that defy natural law.

The forest floor trembles under their advance. Ancient pines crash down as the horde surges forward, their collective hunger a palpable force. Claws scrape bark, fangs glint in the moonlight, and red eyes pierce the darkness like burning coals.

Below, the shrine's paper lanterns cast warm pools of light across the courtyard. A lone figure hurries up the stone steps—Llia, her dark hair swaying as she disappears through the shrine's massive doors, completely unaware of the death stare upon her from the cliff above.

Myou's painted lips curve into a cruel smile. Her fingers curl into a fist, and the army of Yokai halt, awaiting her command. The air grows thick with anticipation.

"It ends tonight," she whispers, her voice carrying ancient malice. "The earthly deity's power will be mine. Finally, after millennia of waiting, I will ascend." Her eyes blaze brighter, reflecting her consuming ambition. "I will become a goddess."

The words hang in the frozen air like a death sentence. Her army of pawns tense, ready to descend upon the shrine at her command.

CHAPTER TWENTY THREE
CASTLING

"We deeply apologize for crowding your shrine like this," Rose says to the priestess.

"It's alright. There's ample space, food, and water for everyone. You're welcome to stay as long as necessary, but we request that the shrines remain undisturbed, as they are holy," the priestess responds.

"Thank you for your kindness," Llia says, looking around the traditional Shinto shrine that has become their temporary sanctuary.

The shrine is divided into four distinct rooms, each connected by sliding wooden doors adorned with rice paper panels. The main hall (haiden) is the largest, featuring tatami mats and simple wooden benches where most of the refugees have gathered. Incense burns quietly in the corners, its gentle smoke curling toward the high ceiling with exposed wooden beams.

To the left is the shrine's storage room (azekura), now serving as a makeshift pantry and supply area, stocked with emergency provisions and bottled water. The right wing contains the prayer room (honden), which remains largely untouched as per the priestess's request, its altar and sacred objects carefully preserved despite the crisis.

The back room has been converted into a sleeping area, with borrowed futons and blankets arranged in neat rows. Notably, the shrine's main entrance has been retrofitted with a modern addition: a heavy, reinforced steel door—an incongruous but necessary security measure that stands in stark contrast to the shrine's traditional architecture.

"We reinforced the entrance last year," the priestess explains, noticing Rose's gaze on the steel door. "Times change, and sometimes even holy places need practical protection."

Llia and Rose gaze at the altars from afar, their eyes drawn to the vibrant array of flowers that frame the sacred space. The blossoms, in a stunning palette of reds, yellows, and purples, sway gently in the breeze, their delicate petals catching the light and casting colorful reflections on the ground. The air is filled with their sweet, intoxicating fragrance, creating an atmosphere of serene beauty that contrasts with the tension of their mission.

"That flower arrangement is incredible. What are they called?" Rose asks.

"Ah, it's known as Ikebana. It's an old Japanese practice. People often bring their Ikebana to shrines to pray for departed loved ones, pay homage to the deities, or for various other reasons," the priestess explains. Llia fixates on the response, finally addressing the lingering query in her mind. "What else can we use them for? To summon a god?"

"Well, uh... yes, some think they can call forth a deity," the priestess responds, lifting her eyebrows.

"Have you heard of Penumbra?"

"Legend says she is the offspring of the moon and sun. It's thought that she had mighty followers, such as the Orochi dragon." The priestess lowers her head and departs.

"The Orochi dragon? What the fu... I mean, what is that?" Rose asks.

"Absolute destruction, an unstoppable force of sheer demise. He was so powerful that it took the cunning of two gods to defeat him." Llia settles on a nearby bench, piecing it all together after the priestess gave her some new information.

Alright, they aim to resurrect Penumbra so Myou can ascend to godhood in the encompassing darkness since that's where her power is supreme. Tristian secured the sword containing Penumbra. But before anything else, they need to eliminate us to revive Penumbra... Hold on! The priestess mentioned individuals bringing this Ikebana to the shrine—Oh no!

"Please let Iris be safe!" Rose exclaims.

"Rose! It's not about killing us! She needs all of us in the shrine together! That's how Penumbra is summoned! She made sure we couldn't go anywhere but here, it's all been a trick! Everything that's happened, even my mother's death, made me overly protective. I'll do anything for my family, and she knew that. She's been one step ahead of us all along!"

"If that were the case, why didn't she simply abduct us and bring us here from the restaurant? She had ample opportunity."

"Choice! That's why she's been playing these games; she needed us to choose to come here. I don't think it works if we're forced. She's been orchestrating this meticulously for over eight hundred years. Rose, I'm not sure we can defeat her! Wait, do you hear that? It sounds like a helicopter," Llia remarks as she glances at the enormous shrine door.

"Reo! You'll be okay. Just hold on!" TJ shouts as the helicopter sets the car down near the warhorse. He lifts him toward the doors as they swing open, revealing a table that extends from the wall. A cabinet stocked with vials and syringes pops open.

"Otis, update me on Reo's condition and provide guidance!" as he hurriedly gathers syringes and vials. Maddix jumps from the control seat and assists TJ in placing Reo on the examination table.

"Analyzing, drawing blood sample... finished. His blood toxicity is erratic due to extreme stress. Consequently, there are no medical remedies for his state; he will succumb within the next ten minutes."

"I thought he regenerates when he is resting?!" Maddix says.

"He does, but not during a moonless night or if he pushes himself too far. There must be some way to help him!" TJ exclaims. He recalls Reo's words in the hospital, *"We draw strength from the most unexpected places."*

"That's it! Otis, bring up Reo's vital statistics when he's near Llia!"

"Hold on... The data indicates a noticeable improvement in his vitals when he's close to Llia. We've found the answer; take him to Llia."

"What are the odds of that happening? Maddix, I need you to take Reo to Llia. I understand there are many Yokai outside, but I promise you you'll get there safely. I won't let any of those bastards get near you. Do you believe me?!" TJ offers his hand.

"I think that's the first time you didn't call me Goose," Maddix replies as he shakes his hand.

"Alright, I trust you now. There's no need to use that nickname anymore."

"Honestly, it's kind of grown on me."

"Very well then, Goose it is. Now help me save my friend."

TJ quickly grabs a fully charged watch, an arsenal of weapons, and a variety of guns. He dons the custom-made armored vest before guiding them through the total darkness. They navigate through the carnage. The ground trembles with the approach of the advancing army. They reach the center of the parking lot. TJ's nose catches an intriguing scent, prompting him to stop suddenly. He turns his gaze toward a nearby cliff that overlooks the entire area. His astonishment grows as he spots Iris handcuffed in front of the daunting leaders of the Umbra: Myou, Udai, and Subae. The godmasters of the Umbra.

"Goose, keep going. I have to get Iris back!"

"TJ, that's suicide! They will kill you both. She wants you to act irrationally. Don't make that mistake. Don't play her game!"

"Risking my life is part of the mission, Goose, and even if it wasn't, I love her! That whole army won't be enough to stop me from rescuing her. Now GO! Inform Llia of what has to be done; tell her to search within herself and bring Reo back, just like she did for you in the hospital!"

Hundreds of Yokai emerge from the tree line, trailed by four enormous Oni wielding studded clubs as thick as tree trunks. Their thunderous footsteps seem to shake the earth itself. Maddix races away in terror with Reo on his shoulders. He washes his hands, splashes water on Reo, and passes through the torii gates. Ascending the tall stairs, he glances back at the top, taking in the sight of the entire deathly army flooding the parking lot. His heart races and his palms grow clammy. He steps into the shrine. Llia and Rose observe the crowd surging past the gate. Llia stands up and catches a glimpse of Maddix lying on the ground.

"Rose! It's Maddix!" Llia exclaims. She runs through the crowd of people.

"Maddix, are you okay?"

"Reo... he's over there, and he needs you! TJ says only you can save him. Search within yourself! Quick, he's not going to make it!" Maddix pants, struggling to breathe. Llia pushes through the crowd and spots a man examining Reo's vitals, his head shaking in dismay.

Llia's breath catches in her throat. She tries to scream his name, but no sound emerges. She rushes to his side, collapses to her knees, and rests her head on his frigid chest. His pallid skin feels like ice. Desperately, she shakes him and begins administering chest compressions.

"Please, Reo, you have to wake up. Come on! Open your eyes! We need you! Please. *I* need you," Llia shouts, her voice breaking.

Rose places a comforting hand on her shoulder. "Llia, I'm so sorry."

Llia kisses Reo and leans in to whisper. "I'm so sorry. I never got to tell you that I love you." She removes his cursed bracelet, cool to the touch, and flings it aside.

They rise, with Rose wrapping an arm around Llia, and they head toward the bench. The crowd erupts in chaos, and Llia swiftly turns to see Reo's eyes open. He rolls over and expels black smoke. His breathing stabilizes, his pallor transforms back to a beautiful olive hue, and his amber eyes shine brightly.

"I think I overdid it," Reo jokes, smiling to hide his grimace.

Llia grins, wrapping herself in his arms. She squeezes him so tightly that she stows him away in her heart and drowns his pain in her love.

"Llia, you did it. The curse is gone. I feel stronger and faster than I ever have! But I'm not completely healed, the poison is still leaving my body."

"That's great, but how?!"

"Both you and TJ have extraordinary abilities, more than you realize. Where is TJ now?!"

"Outside, TJ is battling a horde to reach Iris. Myou and two others have her. One wields a golden spear and the other has two swords. He mentioned his name was...."

"Subae! Thanks for helping save my life Maddix, and welcome to the Yokai Ex. Your task is to protect these people in the garden area. Subae is the most skilled among the Umbra members. I faced him earlier."

"What happened? Can you defeat him?" Maddix inquires.

"No, his dual sword technique is far superior."

"What about using the Fudo sword? That might level the playing field," Llia suggests.

"Perhaps, but there's only one way to know for sure."

"I sense a change in you. You can handle this, Reo."

"I'll give it everything I have."

Reo grips his wrist where the cursed bracelet once bound him. The absence of its weight is palpable, a phantom reminder of its oppressive hold. His eyes, now unshackled, gleam with a new intensity, radiating strength and an unyielding confidence that had long been buried. The garden around him, bathed in the soft glow of twilight, reflects the dawn of this newfound resolve.

"The toxin hasn't fully dissipated. My body feels somewhat heavy, but there's no pain. I haven't felt this way since before Yumi," Reo muses.

"Good, because TJ needs your help. Those creatures that were coming after us are huge, and there are hundreds of them!" Maddix says.

"Okay. No one steps outside, regardless of what you hear. Llia, hold this." Reo extends his hand, materializes a stunning sword seemingly from nowhere, and passes it to Llia. A collective gasp echoes around them.

"How did you do that?! Oh-wow, I can't accept this. This is the beautiful sword from the cabin. You said it belongs to the most powerful Yokai Ex." Llia says.

"Yes, it did. It belonged to my mother. I told you I took after her."

"Your mother was a Yokai Ex?! I am honored. I will take it and defeat Myou."

"I believe you will. I'll assist TJ. Don't let Myou manipulate your rage; remember the waterfall! Tune out the distractions and concentrate on the present." Reo heads toward the doors.

"Hold on, Reo. I…"

Reo turns back and pulls Llia into a close embrace, their lips meeting in a fervent kiss. "I love you too, Camellia." Reo then hurries toward TJ.

Llia's face lights up, her eyes sparkling with joy as an uncontrollable smile spreads across her lips.

CHAPTER TWENTY FOUR

The Yokai Ex

Reo steps out of the shrine onto the wooden deck, the ancient boards creaking beneath his feet. His smartwatch buzzes against his wrist, Otis's familiar interface lighting up the screen.

"Visual update incoming, Reo-sama," Otis's digital voice announces.

A holographic display projects from his watch, showing aerial footage of Seattle's skyline. Smoke billows from the downtown core, thick black plumes obscuring the Space Needle. Orange flames lick at skyscrapers, their windows shattering from the intense heat.

"No!" Reo breathes, watching National Guard tanks roll through the streets, firing at massive shadowy figures that bounded between buildings. The creatures' inhuman shrieks pierced through the video feed.

Sirens wailed in the distance, their mournful cries reaching him even from miles away. On his watch's screen, helicopters circle downtown, spotlights cutting through the smoke as they attempted to track the faster-moving Yokai.

"Casualty count?" Reo asks, his jaw clenched.

"Unknown at this time. The National Guard has established a perimeter around downtown, but they're losing ground rapidly. The Yokai army appears to number in the hundreds."

The feed switches to street level, showing soldiers firing desperately at a hulking oni as it tears through a military barricade like paper. Citizens flee in terror as more dark shapes emerge from the smoke.

"They're not even trying to hide anymore," Reo mutters, watching the brazen attack unfold. "Myou must be confident she's close to finding what she's looking for."

Reo's fist tightens as his watch feed cuts out. Through the smoky haze, he catches movement on the cliff face looming above—dark silhouettes against the blood-red sky. His enhanced vision picks out Myou's elegant form, her kimono rippling in the eerie wind. Beside her stands Udai and Autsetsubae, their features twisted with anticipation. Between them kneels Iris, her wrists bound in glowing chains.

His heart stops when he spots TJ far below, a lone figure before the ancient torii gate. The sacred red arch stands as the last barrier between the Yokai army and the Shrine. A thousand pairs of eyes gleam in the darkness—oni, tengu, and worse creatures that had no name in any human tongue. Their massive forms fill the parking lot, a writhing mass of shadows and teeth.

Yet TJ doesn't flinch. His spear glints as he twirls it with practiced ease, taking up a defensive stance. The army's advance slows to a crawl as they size up this solitary warrior who dares to stand against their might.

"What are you doing, old friend?" Reo whispers, torn between racing to help and confronting Myou. The weight of the world's fate presses down on his shoulders. If he fails to stop the Umbra tonight, there would be no tomorrow for humanity.

TJ's voice carries across the battlefield, clear and strong: "None shall pass while I draw breath!"

The army's response is a bone-chilling roar that shatters windows for blocks around. Still, TJ holds his ground, spear at the ready, defending the gate as if he commands an army of thousands rather than standing alone.

Pride and fear war in Reo's chest as he watches his former student face impossible odds. But he knows TJ's tactical mind—this was no suicide mission, but part of a larger strategy. The question was whether either of them would survive to see it through.

CHAPTER TWENTY FIVE

MOYAMOYA

A minute later, the fearsome Yokai army charges at TJ while the Umbra leaders observe cautiously from their lookout. A dark wave of destruction sweeps over the edge of the parking lot.

TJ hurls two spears as far as possible to the left and right of the army, taking down two Yokai. He then drives the last spear into the ground in front of him and steps back a few paces.

"I heard you could use some assistance?" a recognizable voice calls out, prompting TJ to turn.

Reo stands next to the torii gates. TJ raises his fist with a broad grin, and Reo mirrors the gesture.

Facing the monstrous advancing army, TJ lifts both hands. "I was really hoping to save this for the Umbra. No matter, Otis... activate the Divine weapon!"

The top of the warhorse splits open, unveiling numerous eight-foot spears. They shoot into the night sky, reaching a thousand feet in altitude. As they fall, they resemble shooting stars tracing the heavens. A second propulsion activates, and Reo gazes in amazement as they plunge into the Yokai army, the clanging of metal resonating through the air.

The spears fell just inside the perimeter of the other spears he threw earlier; he used them to set the kill radius. Ingenious!

TJ stands before the formidable line of spears, their razor-sharp points gleaming in the faint light, ruthlessly impaling every Yokai in the parking lot. His broad grin falters as he spots Udai in the distance. His eyes narrow, and in an instant, his smile vanishes. Reo glances toward the Umbra, his gaze fixing on Iris, and then he nods at TJ in accord.

"Alright, I don't have all night! Udai! I challenge you, one-on-one! I have an ass-whooping with your name all over it, muthafucka!" TJ exclaims, handling his last retractable spear.

Udai grins and takes a step forward, but Myou stops him with an outstretched hand.

"This time, it's either him or you!" Myou declares.

"Udai! Get down here now!" TJ shouts, removing his smartwatch and throwing it aside.

Udai springs several yards into the air, landing in front of TJ. With a nod, Reo swaps places with Iris using his trade places technique. She now stands by the torii gates while Reo positions himself beside Myou and Subae.

TJ jogs toward Iris, his spear twirling with deadly precision. The chains around her wrists shatter with a single strike of his spear, falling to the ground in pieces. He pulls her into his arms, her body trembling against his chest.

"Listen, I need to tell you something." His voice drops low, meant only for her. "I don't care what your parents think about us. Never have, never will."

Iris's eyes widen as his calloused hand cups her face.

"I love you. Always have. Whatever you decide about us, that won't change. But I had to say it, just in case—"

She grabs his shirt, crushing her lips against his. The kiss tastes of salt and desperation as tears stream down her face. Her fingers dig into his shoulders, trying to hold him there, to keep him safe. "Please," she begs between kisses. "Come with me to the shrine. Don't do this."

TJ gently breaks her grip, stepping back with a sad smile. "You know I can't."

Udai's growl echoes across the parking lot, but TJ keeps his eyes on Iris. He turns sideways, giving her one last look.

"Get to the shrine. Now." His voice leaves no room for argument as he strides toward his waiting opponent, each step measured and deliberate.

TJ shouts, "Iris, get inside!"

"Okay. And Tobias? Kick his ASS!" Iris yells. She heads up the stairs, her lip trembling and her eyes filled with tears as she turns to go inside.

"Abandoned your tech to die like a true warrior. I won't go easy this time!" Udai declares, brandishing his magnificent golden spear.

"Neither will I!"

At the edge of the cliff, Myou says, "Reo Uchima. Hello, husband. I've been expecting you. It looks like the curse has been lifted. I assume she discovered her true nature. Unfortunately, you're still predictable."

Reo stands nearby, puzzled by her words.

Udai lunges at TJ, who swiftly accumulates a series of minor injuries within seconds. All TJ can do is continue to move and attempt to fend off the unyielding assault.

Reo observes closely, recognizing that Udai's methods are impeccable. He can't spot a single error in his actions. Such exactness befits a godmaster. He and the Umbra reach a standstill to watch TJ's battle against Udai.

Llia and the others step outside and recoil at the gruesome scene in the parking lot. Iris stands by the steps, watching TJ struggle for his life. Llia rushes over to Iris and wraps an arm around her. As she touches Iris, Llia senses something ominous and warm. She looks behind and notices a corrupted sutra on Iris's shirt. Glancing toward the torii gates at the foot of the stairs, she realizes that Iris has brought it through. The grounds are no longer secure; the Yokai can now infiltrate the shrine.

"We need to leave immediately!" Llia shouts. She tears off the sutra, grips Iris's arm, and heads up the steps.

"Reo! Assist TJ. He's in trouble!" Iris calls out.

Reo moves to aid TJ, but Subae blocks his path with his sword. He stretches out his hand to summon the Fudo sword for protection, but nothing happens.

"You can't aid him. This is an official challenge! Let's test your pupil's abilities," Subae declares. He positions himself before Reo, clad in traditional samurai garb, his face concealed by another Demon mask.

"I'm heading into the shrine. Take your time ending him. This is goodbye, husband. You've fulfilled your role," Myou remarks as she leisurely strides toward the torii gates.

TJ and Udai's battle rages on. Crimson welts crisscross TJ's flesh. His chest heaves with labored breaths while perspiration trickles down his brow, and his composure begins to crack.

His fingers lose their grip on the spear's shaft as sweat and gore make it treacherous to hold. A throbbing gash across his body saps his strength as he fights to keep his footing steady.

The demon monk shows no mercy in his attack. TJ finds no reprieve between strikes, as his opponent maintains complete silence. Gripping the aureate weapon with fierce determination, Udai unleashes a fresh barrage, demonstrating uncanny accuracy while pirouetting and whirling—each lunge and rotation leaving scarlet trails in their wake. Not one of TJ's counters finds its mark.

In a blur of motion, the demon monk pivots and delivers a crushing roundhouse, hurling TJ backward as his weapon spirals away on its own trajectory. Panic scatters through his thoughts as he crashes down, far from where his spear now lies.

Taking his time, Udai strolls toward him, savoring every step of his approach.

TJ remains sprawled on the ground. His gaze drifts toward the sanctuary, where he spots Myou positioned before the vermilion archway.

"The rest is in your hands now, sis!" TJ thinks as he reclines onto his back, eyes fixed on the ebony heavens. He registers the growing thud of unhurried footfalls heralding his end. Each step resonates with failure, a rhythm signaling his doom. Above him looms Udai, his menacing stare bearing down with crushing weight.

"You didn't rely on any of your gadgets this time. Perhaps you understand the concept of honor after all! Even though your people could never genuinely comprehend it, given how you lived your lives ensnared by technology. You clutch at life as though it's yours to monopolize, yet you accomplish nothing but selfish acts with it. You may not have lived honorably, but at least you can die with honor!" He lifts his spear high above TJ.

TJ shuts his eyes and takes a deep breath. His worried look fades away, replaced by a serene expression. He can hear the wind rustling through the trees, and Iris's presence suddenly blots out all the night's noises.

"Tobias, get up! Stand up now and kick his ass!"

Udai thrusts his spear toward TJ's chest, but TJ catches the blade between his palms as if in prayer. Myou shifts her gaze toward them, giving TJ a scornful look.

"Another earthly deity! I must hurry!" Myou thinks as she passes beneath the sacred archway, a thunderous crack echoing across the sky.

Though straining with every ounce of strength, Udai fails to drive the weapon forward. After a final powerful struggle, TJ guides the spearhead down to the earth near his temple. Using tremendous power, he slams both feet into Udai's face. Blood streams from the demon monk's nostrils as he stumbles back.

With a kip-up, TJ lunges to reclaim his weapon. Udai summons his own spear and barrels forward, but TJ snatches up his spear and hurtles back toward his opponent to create separation.

As Udai executes multiple twirling strikes and jabs, TJ mirrors each movement perfectly, managing to deflect and return Udai's offensive maneuvers.

"Ah! How... how did you manage to counter all my attacks? Wait... No! You don't deserve such power! You are an earthly deity too. We believed it was only the girl!" Udai exclaims, launching another assault.

Mirroring each technique with deadly accuracy, TJ matches and deflects every attack in rapid succession.

Painful lacerations burn across Udai's flesh, covering him from head to toe. His respiratory rate accelerates beyond its previous pace. The weapon in his grip grows increasingly unstable as his fingers tremble.

"This cannot be! You don't deserve such ability!" Lunging forward with his weapon, Udai screams.

TJ responds instantly, deflecting and stabbing his spear through his torso.

His gaze shifts to a dark scarlet as his eyes widen in shock. Crimson liquid cascades from his gaping mouth.

"You speak of honor, but you don't understand its meaning! That was for my team, you bastard!" TJ shouts, tears flowing down his face. In one swift move, he pulls the spear from Udai's chest and watches his assailant collapse. A vivid red mist surrounds the disintegrating body until it vanishes completely.

TJ's gaze falls upon the luminous weapon lying on the ground. Its brilliant sheen bathes the area in a mesmerizing light. As he studies the golden shaft, a gentle warmth washes over him. Releasing his grip, he drops his own spear and extends a shaking palm toward the gleaming armament. The mild warmth explodes into searing heat as the weapon leaps into TJ's waiting hand. Though his wounds remain open, the flow of blood stops the instant his fingers close around the shaft.

"I've become the godmaster of the spear! Holy crap! I did it," TJ exclaims. He attempts to move toward the shrine but drops to his knees. His body feels weighed down and sluggish, and his vision becomes blurry. Just before hitting the ground, he hears the distant clash of swords and sees Myou slowly entering the shrine doors.

CHAPTER TWENTY SIX

TSUMI

The moment Myou steps into the sacred building, Autsetsubae turns his gaze toward Reo. With a swift move, he uses his father's katana, deflecting Suebay's obsidian blade with a sharp clang. He held it before him, a barrier against Reo's attempts to help TJ.

"Impressive! So, you enlisted all the earthly deities you encountered. That was a smart tactic, yet you failed to gather enough to change your fate! Be aware that my presence on the battlefield signals that the war's end is near. Nevertheless, you should be proud to confront me twice in one-on-one combat, as no one else has achieved this."

Subae sheathes a single weapon and shifts into a fighting position. Reo skillfully wields his father's blade to parry the flurry of attacks Subae launched. He had no choice but to back away while deflecting the onslaught, the remnants of the curse continuing to weaken him as his body struggled to purge it.

"Your skills have vastly improved in strength and speed; however, you remain no competition for me, Reo!"

Reo acknowledges the truth in Subae's words—he couldn't match his opponent's prowess. Yet with just one weapon in play, his odds improve considerably. Reo launches his offensive, but Subae deftly dodges and blocks the barrage of strikes and stabs. Caught off guard, he finds himself unable to mount any counterattacks against Reo.

Their blades clash with a musical ring as they slice through the frigid darkness. Reo displays superior technique compared to Subae, forcing him to retreat to avoid a deadly blow. Neither warrior advances and Subae remained untouched, not a drop of perspiration appearing on his brow.

Reo's garments are shredded in several places, a long slanting gash stretching across his torso.

"You're quite adept with just one sword. This time, you actually forced me to fall back. No one has ever managed that before. I haven't had to defend myself in over a thousand years!" Subae remarks.

"I'm not naive enough to believe I can match you. I understand you're a much more skilled swordsman with two blades, so why haven't you wielded them both?!" Reo adopts his defensive posture.

Subae smiles and pulls out his second blade, which is slightly shorter than his main sword. "I wanted to see if I could defeat the godmaster of the single blade on his own ground again. But now, it looks like your end has come, Uchima Reo!" He launches an attack with both swords, each strike finding its mark.

Reo can't defend against both weapons at once, leaving him exposed to every blow. Subae's shorter sword cuts deeper than before, and Reo drops to one knee. He circles him like a vulture, savoring the moment. Reo's body is covered in bloody wounds, and his limbs grow heavier. The scent of pine trees drifts on the chilly breeze.

"You seem to be in bad shape, Reo! Perhaps you should lie down and rest!" Both of Subae's swords are coated in blood. He shakes them off and aims them at Reo's back.

Reo tries to parry both weapons, but his sword shatters. Subae quickly finishes the battle in only four strikes. Blood pools around Reo's injured body.

"Too bad. It appears your student gave me false hope that our fight would be as glorious as his! I hoped to get a real challenge from you, but I see the poison has left you weakened. With your death, I will become the god of the blade!" Subae positions himself behind Reo to cut off his head.

Reo closes his eyes, dwelling on TJ's valiant struggle against an invincible opponent. His mind drifts to countless sparring sessions where he had mercilessly defeated Llia. Yet she never stayed down. Reo's thoughts turn to the fallen Yokai Ex warriors of the past. Deep within, an inferno ignites, causing the ambient temperature to soar from freezing to scorching. Determination wells up from the depths of Reo's soul as he rises, clutching at an invisible sword.

"How?! You as well!" Subae cries out.

Blood oozing from Reo's injuries seals shut. The atmosphere vibrates around them, making it difficult to inhale. Reo raises the Fudo blade in his grasp.

Subae retreats a few paces as he beholds the splendid weapon. "At last, our magnificent duel commences!" Subae declares, positioning himself with a wide grin.

"This is where it concludes."

Steel sings as their weapons meet in combat. The exceptional balance of Reo's sword allows him to match Subae's twin-blade assault. Their masterful exchange continues in perfect equilibrium until Reo's edge finds purchase, leaving a thin slice across his opponent's face.

Subae's fingers brush the wound while his eyes blaze with malevolent fury. He shifts his posture, launching into an unconventional offensive pattern where each weapon follows its own trajectory.

Reo adapts by narrowing his profile, successfully deflecting one blade while dodging the other. This strategy serves him well for three exchanges, but on the fourth pass, Subae's strike connects.

Reo withdraws a pace to regain his composure. *I didn't even notice that blow. He wasn't anywhere close to me; how did he manage that?!*

"It's known as a shadow strike, in case you were trying to understand what occurred. The shadow of my weapon can slice you, thanks to the gleam of your sword. Now you see why I never lose!" Subae declares. He regains his footing and edges closer to Reo.

As he contemplates his next move, Reo retreats from his opponent. Battling against shadows seems impossible. He has exhausted his options and finds himself at a loss. His strategic planning halts abruptly when Subae's weapons slice into him. Though each laceration heals itself, the process steadily drains Reo's energy reserves.

"As long as a shadow exists, no one can defeat me, and your sword creates the finest shadows!" Subae chuckles.

Reo grips his sword handle firmly as he exhales sharply. The image of a waterfall pops into his head. He remembers to control his mind and his breath. As he does, the temperature drops again, and the blazing beauty of the sword fades. Reo stretches his sword hand out as if quenching it into the moment. His blade dissolves into a dazzling sparkle of celestial light. Drawing in a deep breath, he shuts his eyes and probes the murky depths of his soul. There, he discovers the guilt he concealed about his feelings for Yumi. His bitterness at being deceived by her schemes has eaten away at him for so long. Now, as he releases those feelings, a powerful wave of energy courses through his body.

Twin swords dart at Reo's neck and torso as Subae launches his attack. The warriors cross paths in a blur of motion. Blood Mists through the air, and when Subae glances behind him, he witnesses the damage dealt to his opponent.

"No!" Subae yells.

Reo spins around to confront Subae. Having overcome his inner shadows, he can now tap into the full might of the Fudo sword. The weapon has reached its ultimate form, radiating power far beyond its previous state.

"Let's finish this in true godmaster fashion, in one stroke!" A lethal glare flashes across Subae's face as he inclines his head. He retreats several paces, then hurls himself toward Reo.

At maximum velocity, the pair launch forward, their shimmering weapons thrust ahead of them.

Their blades collide with a thunderous ring that reverberates through the temple grounds as they streak past one another. A crimson trail seeps across the earth. They whirl to face off, both desperate to glimpse the battle's result.

Though no injuries mar his form, Subae's weapon drips scarlet for a second time.

Crimson seeps between Reo's fingers as he grasps the right side of his torso. Unlike before, the gash refuses to mend—possibly a consequence of the blade's transformation. Grimacing, he braces against his injury, fighting to maintain his balance.

"It seems it's settled then... The one true god of the blade. It was truly magnificent!" Subae declares.

"Yes... The fight is finished!" Reo responds, blood spurting from his mouth in a violent spray, staining his chin and the front of his robes with dark, viscous droplets. About to collapse, he staggers forward, his breath ragged, but he thrusts his sword into the ground, using it as a crutch to keep himself upright, the metallic tang of blood staining his knuckles. With gritted teeth and a determined set to his jaw, he used the last ounce of his strength to remain standing, his body trembling.

Subae bows with an almost theatrical flourish, and in that instant, his head slides cleanly from his shoulders, tumbling through the air in a graceful arc before hitting the ground with a wet thud. His neck spurts a cerise fountain, creating a grisly, bloody shower around him. His prized blades slip from lifeless fingers, one weapon bisected with surgical precision—the steel surfaces reflecting the carnage like dark mirrors as they clatter against the blood-slicked earth. The once-proud warrior's headless body remains frozen in its final gesture of respect before crumpling to its knees.

Reo's labored breathing echoes through the blood-soaked clearing as he bows deeply to Autsetsubae's fallen form. The legendary warrior's body begins to shimmer, breaking apart into glittering particles that drift skyward like diamond dust caught in a breeze. His magnificent broken silver blade follows, dissolving into nothingness.

Only the short black blade remains, its obsidian surface drinking in what little light filters through the trees. Reo's trembling fingers wrap around its handle. Power surges through his arm, racing through his veins like liquid fire. The weapon pulses with an otherworldly energy that resonates with something deep within his soul.

Ancient knowledge floods his mind—centuries of sword techniques, forgotten forms, and deadly arts previously known only to the gods themselves. His wounds knit shut as divine energy courses through him. The blade has chosen him as its new master, bestowing upon him the mantle of the god of the blade.

The short sword grows warm in his grip, its edge catching the light with an almost sentient gleam. Reo feels its power merge with his own, transforming him into something more than human but less than divine—a perfect fusion of mortal skill and godlike ability.

Reo pivots to face the forest, watching the branches thrash in unnatural motion. He sprints with desperate speed in TJ's direction. His friend lies motionless on the ground as the last assault of demons and their minions advances. His eyes dart to the sanctuary.

As he arrives at TJ's side, he sees his friend breathing but drained of strength. A sudden agony pierces his stomach and draws his gaze upward. His body shakes as shock washes over him. The heavens stand empty, devoid of starlight. The Oni's words from within the bamboo grove echoed in his mind. *The stars will fade from the sky, and the mountain will rise and devour the lands and its people.*

The final wave of the mighty Yokai army storms toward the temple. Standing his ground, Reo clutches his splendid swords with determination, walking forward to meet them. He senses a presence advancing behind him.

"Well done, godmaster of the spear," Reo grins.

"You did it, senpai! You beat the best sword master who ever lived. And you have his short sword, too. I can feel the power surging from you."

"And I can sense the change in you as well."

"Senpai, leave this army to me. I stopped them once, I can do it again. Get your revenge on Myou!"

"I've let go of all my revenge. I'm leaving the rest to Camellia. She's like you; she has more strength than she realizes. Besides, you're almost at your limit too. Let's face this together, brother," Reo declares. He stands before the enormous Yokai army, swords in hand.

"They don't have a prayer!" TJ replies, stretching his hand toward his golden spear, which glints ominously under the darkened sky. The spear, imbued with ancient power, obediently soars into his grip, sending a small jolt of energy coursing through his veins. He feels the familiar, electrifying hum of its power—a reassuring reminder of their bond. Side by side, their resolve unshaken, they face the approaching horde of a few hundred Yokai—twisted, malevolent creatures of the night—surging forward to attack, their grotesque forms casting elongated shadows in the dim light. The air buzzes with anticipation of the impending clash, the scent of earth and blood mingling in a heady mix. Reo and TJ's muscles tense in unison, ready to confront the onslaught together as brothers in arms.

Moments later, inside the dimly lit shrine where shadows dance across ancient wooden beams and the sweet scent of burning incense fills the air, paper lanterns sway gently in the draft, casting an ethereal glow over worn tatami mats and weathered stone statues that have stood guard for centuries.

"Iris, are you alright?" Llia inquires, recognizing a familiar expression in her eyes and sensing that something is amiss.

"She—she's coming! That old witch is coming!" Iris exclaims.

"Take the people to the garden at the back of the shrine and stay there! Lock yourselves in, and don't come out no matter what!"

"Absolutely not! We're not abandoning you! If you're staying! I'm STAYING too." Rose declares.

"And that goes for me TOO." Maddix responds.

Myou saunters through the inner shrine gate with predatory grace, her silk kimono rustling like dead leaves in autumn. Spotting them arguing, her blood-red lips curve into an unsettling smile—the kind that makes the hairs on the back of Llia's neck stand up and her stomach churn with nausea. The ancient yokai's presence seems to dim the very air around her as if darkness itself bends to her will.

"Now, to bring my goddess home and ascend to godhood," Myou hisses, fixing them with her cold stare while chanting phrases in archaic Japanese. From her side, she draws forth an obsidian-black blade.

That must be the blade that Tristian took! The one with Penumbra sealed in it! Llia thinks.

She holds up her sword with trembling hands, the steel catching what little light remains in the shadow-drenched air. Myou glares at her with ancient, calculating eyes—windows to centuries of malice that seem to pierce straight through to her soul. For just a fraction of a second, the Yokai's perfect porcelain features twist into something inhuman, revealing glimpses of the monster beneath the beautiful facade.

"I won't let you hurt them! I know you needed all of us to choose to come here! But to bring her back, you need a sacrifice. You won't get it!" Llia says.

Myou's melodic voice fills the air with honeyed words, each syllable dripping with calculated intent. As she speaks, an unsettling transformation ripples across her weapon—the obsidian darkness enveloping the blade begins to dissipate like smoke in a breeze, revealing ordinary steel beneath. The metamorphosis spreads from hilt to tip until the sword appears completely mundane, though no less deadly in her expert grip.

"I'll concede that you possess intelligence—definitely more than the men in your faction—but your emotions obscure your judgment, preventing you from recognizing what lies directly before you. That's why you will never triumph over me. I merely required you to remain exactly where you are; no offering is necessary. I sowed the deception of a sacrifice, fully aware that you would go to any lengths—even walk straight into my trap to rescue them. The seal has been shattered; Penumbra is unleashed! Once I eliminate you, I will immerse myself in the darkness and ascend to become the most formidable goddess ever!"

"You just said you didn't need a sacrifice! Why kill us?" Rose replies.

"I don't. Killing the Hafu is personal! She is the descendant of the earthly deity that escaped my brother, the Orochi dragon, all those years ago. I spent an eternity searching for you to exact my revenge for what your family did to him! And after I kill you, I will raise him from his slumber," Myou declares.

"You are delusional, the Orochi dragon was killed by two gods and chopped into pieces!"

"He was the most powerful being ever to roam the earth, Hafu! He cannot be killed, he can only be—"

"Imprisoned! They imprisoned him! That's why they severed his heads and tails in the legend. I've always wondered why they would go to such lengths," Llia responds.

"So the pieces won't be combined with his body, which I've found. Mount Ryugatake is the Orochi dragon, and once I claim your head, I will present it to him. There will be nowhere to run or hide. The mountain will rise, and everyone will die!"

"Everyone, leave now! I will finish you off before that happens!" Llia assumes a fighting position. Maddix seizes Rose and drags her from the chamber, with Iris trailing behind. Myou sneers at Llia when she spots her weapon.

"He gave you his mother's sword! He must really love you." Myou's fury radiates from her like an ominous storm cloud, darkening the air around her. With a swift, fluid motion, she unsheathes another blade, its polished steel glinting menacingly in the dim light. The weapon seems to hum with sinister energy, ready to slice through the tension crackling in the chamber.

"Yes, he did, and I know exactly where to put it. Now; let's end this!"

"A goddess doesn't sully her hands with Hafu blood!" Myou declares, passing her blade to a single Yokai killer—one of a trio that materializes from the darkness behind her. "Bring me her head!"

Llia raises her blade with lethal precision, her stance a perfect balance of tension and calm as she stands motionless like carved stone. Her trained eye catches every subtle tell in the way the Yokai grip their weapons—the slight tremor in one's hands, another's too-wide stance, the third's eager lean forward. In that crystalline moment of assessment, she maps out their demise. They surge forward as one, their blades whistling through the air, but Llia moves like lightning. One graceful pivot, a horizontal slash, and a finishing thrust—three economical movements that leave the Yokai crumpling to the ground in a heap of dark ichor and broken forms.

"You little bitch! This room isn't big enough for two deities!" Myou hurtles toward Llia with dizzying velocity, her sword poised in its scabbard.

Llia raises her weapon and barely dodges the short sword that flashes from Myou's elongated scabbard. Myou unleashes a flurry of attacks, but Llia parries each attempt. Their deadly dance carries them in sweeping arcs across the chamber. Neither fighter can seize control, though Llia's longer blade gives her the upper hand. She lands several slashing wounds on Myou. Recognizing her tactical weakness, Myou binds their blades together while maintaining crucial space, preventing Llia from exploiting her weapon's length to deliver a fatal strike.

"Reo dreams of me at night. He could never have feelings for a Hafu like you!" Myou twists the pommel of her weapon, extracting a concealed dagger. She plunges the tiny blade into Llia's sword arm, forcing her fingers to slacken. With explosive force, Myou's heel smashes into Llia's midsection, launching her backward while her weapon spins away.

Gasping and writhing on the floor, Llia clutches her gut. Her pulse hammers wildly as she yanks the miniature knife from her flesh. Blood gushes from her injury and she clamps down on it while rising unsteadily, her face contorted in pain.

Myou discards her weapon and beckons Llia forward with a taunting gesture.

She is treacherous. Staying focused is essential. I can manage this! TJ and Reo, where are you two? I hope you're safe. Come on, Llia, stay sharp! It's important to have faith in them!

"I'm sure your parents would be very proud of what you've become—a Hafu whore!" Myou says as Llia rushes her.

Myou blocks all of Llia's attacks, easily avoiding her punches and kicks.

She's testing my limits! Llia thinks as Myou punches her in the mouth.

"Every time you have a thought, your face takes on a constipated expression. I find it revolting!" Myou's assault on Llia persists, connecting with brutal strikes and blows.

Each impact drains more strength and speed from Llia's body and raising her wounded limb grows increasingly difficult.

Myou savors the moment, methodically pursuing her backpedaling opponent. "All this can end now. Just give yourself to me, and I will spare them all: Reo, TJ, Iris, Maddix, and Rose. You can save them right now; just stop fighting and give yourself to me."

Llia stops abruptly, overwhelmed by intense agony. Myou's words resonate in her mind like a powerful shockwave, bringing her to the painful understanding that since her mother's passing, it has fallen upon her to rescue everyone because she failed to save her mother.

"You had my mother killed! Didn't you? To make me overprotective and force me to give in to this very moment. You designed every situation leading up to this!"

"Like I said, you are the smartest in the group! I kept my word in the restaurant; I brought you face to face with the one who killed your mother—me!" Myou smiles.

The shadow that had been trapped within Llia's heart disappears, leaving her with a newfound strength she has never experienced before. The darkness that weighed on her soul as an anchor of guilt melts away, replaced by a surge of raw power coursing through her veins like lightning. For the first time since her mother's death, she feels truly unburdened, as if invisible chains have been shattered, leaving her spirit free to soar.

"Good! How about the best three out of four?!" Llia shouts. The grin vanishes from Myou's face, giving way to annoyance as she realizes that her confession has only given Llia strength. They clash once more, with Llia unleashing a barrage of brutal strikes.

"You can't defeat me! You don't even have a weapon!" Myou exclaims, taken aback by Llia's sudden fervor.

"I am the weapon!" Llia retorts, charging at her.

Myou responds with a blow to Llia's injured arm, causing her to writhe and exposing her to a crushing strike.

Llia collapses to the ground in a disoriented state, experiencing intense pain. Myou approaches to retrieve her sword, standing above Llia as she breathes heavily.

"Earlier, you laid out my eight-hundred-year-old plans with great accuracy, but you can't seem to figure out that you are no match for me. Killing you will bring me great satisfaction! Oh, and don't worry about Reo, I will take great care of him. I know what he likes," Myou mocks while raising her sword high above her head, the polished steel gleaming with malevolent purpose in the dim light.

Several shots crack through the air like thunder, the bullets finding their mark. Myou jerks backward, her face contorting in surprise and pain as she loses her grip. The blade tumbles from her fingers, clattering against the ground mere inches from

Llia's head. She whirls around, her elegant features twisted with rage, to find the source of the attack.

Rose stands unsteadily in the doorway, her small hands white-knuckled around a smoking pistol, the acrid scent of gunpowder filling the air. With inhuman speed, Myou launches herself toward Rose like a dark arrow, but Rose's finger squeezes the trigger again and again, the sound of each shot echoing off the walls with devastating precision. The bullets tear through Myou, her graceful movement faltering mid-stride. She crumples to the ground with almost theatrical finality, her elaborate kimono pooling around her like spilled ink on the cold floor, her body finally still.

Rose rushes forward, her breath still ragged from the confrontation, and gently helps Llia to her feet. The younger woman sways unsteadily, clearly weakened from her ordeal, as Rose carefully positions Llia's trembling arm around her shoulders for support. Together, they move with halting steps toward the garden entrance of the shrine, leaving behind the heavy stillness of death that now permeates the once-sacred space. The lantern casts long shadows through the ornate wooden pillars as they make their escape, their footsteps echoing softly against the ancient stone floor.

"Are you alright? You let the old lady kick your ass again?" Rose remarks as they walk by Myou's lifeless form.

"Ouch! Don't make me laugh! I thought I told you to stay in the garden with everyone else?!"

"What, and abandon my sister?! No chance in hell. You risked everything to save me. CP squad baby!"

Myou rises to her feet with serpentine grace, her silk kimono rustling as she retrieves her ornate dagger from the polished floor. She stalks the girls with predatory focus, her footsteps silent as death itself, taking aim at Llia's exposed back. Her crimson-painted lips curl into a cruel smile as she raises the blade, muscles coiling like a viper preparing to strike, calculating the perfect angle for a fatal blow.

But Rose catches the whisper of her furious advance yet Myou descends on them before they can react. Rose thrusts Llia aside, and the dagger plunges into her own torso. Myou yanks the weapon free from Rose's flesh and charges at Llia.

"Rose, no!" Llia shouts, her voice raw with desperation and fury. Her eyes dart frantically around until they lock onto her sword lying just a foot away, its polished steel catching the shrine's dancing light. With adrenaline flowing, she lunges for the weapon with inhuman speed, her fingers closing around the familiar grip as if drawn by magnetic force.

In one fluid motion, she snatches up the blade and executes a perfect combat roll toward Myou, raising the sword high above her head with deadly intent. The Yokai matriarch halts her advance, caught off guard by the girl's explosive counterattack. Before she can react, Llia's razor-sharp blade cleaves through the air and finds its mark with devastating precision. Maroon arterial spray erupts from Myou's severed throat, painting the shrine walls in macabre patterns.

Even as her lifeblood gushes forth, that haunting, knowing smile spreads across Myou's face one final time. As Llia wrenches her blade free with a sickening sound, Myou's lips form a silent word, her dark eyes gleaming with malevolent promise. Her form begins to waver and distort, collapsing in on itself as her body transforms into a churning cloud of blood-red smoke that dissipates into nothingness, leaving only the metallic scent of blood hanging in the air.

Llia runs to Rose, who is lying in a puddle of blood. "Reo! I need you, Reo!" Llia exclaims. She desperately tries to stop the bleeding, placing her hands on Rose and closing her eyes, but she doesn't feel the same spark she did with Maddix and Reo. Iris and Maddix enter the room after hearing Llia's cry.

"Looks like we're even now. Well, on the bright side, I won't have to clean the floors anymore," Rose chuckles.

"If you can just be okay, I swear you'll never have to clean again!"

"Please, please don't move," Iris murmurs, "Stay still, Rosie. Maddix, I need your shirt! Llia, apply pressure here. How could you do this to me? You always have to be the center of attention, don't you?! You can't leave us. We need you. *I* need you," She bends close and breathes a secret into Rose's ear. Pure astonishment washes over her features.

"Rose!" Maddix sobs.

"Oh no, Maddy, don't cry. I've always considered you to be like a brother. I will miss watching you squirm while talking your ear off. You make sure you take care of our sisters. They work too much; take them out occasionally and have a drink on me."

"Wait! Please hang on. Reo will be here to heal you. Just hang on a little longer! REO!" Llia yells.

"It's alright, Llia. I love you all. Thank you...for... being... my family!" Rose exhales one last time, her chest falling still beneath her bloodstained clothes. The warmth slowly fades from her skin as the first rays of dawn filter through the window, casting a gentle golden light across her peaceful features. The room falls into heavy silence, broken only by the quiet sobs of those who loved her.

"Rose, Reo! Hurry!" Iris shouts as she begins pressing on Rose's chest, desperation evident in her tone. Abruptly, Llia seizes her arm and frantically shakes her head. Tears cascade down around Rose's still form. Maddix squeezes his eyes shut, feeling the gentle material of his coat brush against his fingers as he covers her face. Clutching her palm in his, he sobs, his grief spilling forth in endless streams.

"She saved me! I-I couldn't save her!"

"You—you gave it your all, Llia. She gave herself up so you could survive. There is no greater love," Iris says, her voice cracking with raw emotion. They huddle together over Rose's body, shoulders pressed against one another as they form a protective circle around their fallen friend. Their tears fall like summer rain, dotting her pale face and the ground beneath them while the weight of their shared grief hangs heavy in the air.

After a short while, they dry their tears and listen intently to the fierce combat echoing beyond the walls. They meticulously gather their weapons before stepping out to explore the chaos.

Maddix remains beside Rose, gripping her hand with gentle reassurance while they exchange hushed words of comfort. Meanwhile, Llia limps toward the main door with determined steps despite her injuries, clutching her blood-stained sword with white knuckles as Iris follows close behind, her own weapon at the ready.

They exit and stand at the top of the entrance, the cool morning air hitting their faces as they take in the bustling scene of the parking lot below. The area is a macabre tableau, littered with the twisted bodies of fallen Yokai and pawns. Dark ichor mingles with blood across the cracked pavement, creating grotesque patterns in the dim light. Their eyes methodically scan the parking lot, darting from shadow to shadow and searching every darkened corner, but there is no trace of TJ or Reo's body among the carnage. A knot forms in Llia's stomach as she considers the possibility that they might be buried beneath the layers of rapidly decaying corpses, their flesh already beginning to dissolve into dark mist. Llia and Iris turn to each other, their warrior's composure crumbling as they embrace tightly. Their quivering lips and streaming tears speak volumes of their shared anguish and fear for their missing companions.

"Don't stare for too long, sis," a voice warns from behind. "It will haunt your dreams."

They turn and see TJ holding a battered Reo behind a statue by the door, pressed against the cool walls of the shrine. "We heard you calling, but we ran out of gas!" TJ says as they fall to the ground.

Rushing to their sides, the girls exchange glances of anticipation. Iris examines their wounds with a focused gaze, searching for any signs of severe injury. She examines Reo and notices he needs immediate care. With a firm grip, Reo holds his hand over his blood-soaked chest, his body marked with numerous cuts and bruises.

Llia holds him close, and Reo drifts in and out of consciousness, feeling her steady heartbeat and showering with her concerned breaths.

"Are you going to be okay!" Llia asks.

"Sure, it's not as terrible as it appears... actually, it's even worse!" Reo responds, prompting a laugh from TJ.

"I've done it. Myou is gone! But I worry she unleashed Penumbra. It was never about eliminating us, she merely required us to voluntarily arrive at the shrine to create the moonless night."

"I knew you could do it. She painted us into a corner, but you got all of us out alive." Reo says as he scowls from the pain.

"Not all of us... She—she got Rose." Llia cries.

"Oh God, no! Llia, Iris, I'm so sorry. Wait, where's Goose?!" TJ asks.

"He's fine. He's with Rose's body in the shrine. TJ... this may not be the right time, but we've lost a lot today, and I can't lose any more loved ones. Losing you is not an option for me. I'm going to tell my parents that you're the one I've chosen," Iris says. She finishes wrapping the last of the blood-soaked bandages around Reo's shoulder wound, her delicate fingers working with practiced efficiency despite the trembling in her hands. Turning her attention to TJ, their eyes meet in the dim light of the aftermath. TJ's broad smile breaks through the grime and exhaustion on his face as he pulls her close to his chest, feeling the rapid beating of her heart against him. He closes his eyes and savors the moment, breathing in the familiar scent of jasmine in her hair, trying to push away the horror of what they'd just survived.

"Will you marry me?" TJ exclaims. Llia and Reo's eyes widen with joy.

"Yes—yes!" Iris responds before they exchange a fervent kiss.

"Just one thing, though. I want kids, and you're gonna have to get a job to help support us."

"Oh, that's no problem. I've always wanted kids, and I don't think money will ever be an issue for us," TJ replies. Reo laughs at Iris' job request.

"What's so funny?" Llia whispers to Reo.

"He's richer than I am," Reo replies as Llia shares her surprise.

"Good," Iris exclaims, her eyes sparkling with joy. "Because I'm pregnant!"

TJ's eyes light up with excitement, his features radiating pure happiness. Their joyful laughter echoes through the air, reaching far into the distance, carried by the wind like chimes in a summer breeze. TJ smothers Iris in his powerful arms as they are all smiles, his muscular frame gentle against her delicate form. They all bathe in each other's embrace as they sit in the cool breeze, the rising sun casting long shadows across their faces while cherry blossoms drift lazily overhead, nature itself seeming to celebrate their moment of perfect contentment.

"That's what you whispered to Rose?" Llia asks.

"Yes."

"Good, that was good. I'm so happy for you both!"

"Thank you! I am happy for you two as well!"

"It's finally over. I've prayed for so long to have an honorable death, but you came and showed me how to live an honorable life instead," Reo whispers softly as he and Llia share a heartfelt kiss, their lips lingering in the warmth of the moment.

Above them, the inky black sky begins to dissolve, giving way to the soft, red honey glow emerging on the horizon, casting a warm hue over the world awakening around them. The first hints of dawn stretch their fingers across the landscape, illuminating the cherry blossoms that dance in the gentle breeze, while their hearts beat in synchrony, wrapped in the tender embrace of love and hope.

"There is something else, Reo. Apparently, the Orochi dragon is not dead, he is sealed away."

"Yes, in Mount Ryugatake. He was too powerful to kill, so they fed him something to make him sleep forever. But waking him up was always a long shot for Myou. It requires a lot of power to do that."

"You knew that and didn't think to tell me?!" Llia replies.

"Uh oh, their first fight as a couple," TJ says.

"We will talk about withholding information from me when you feel better. Just lay still and try not to die on me," Llia says.

"No promises." Reo winces in pain as he quips.

They rest in silence as morning's rays intensify. The survivors who sheltered in the shrine's garden step outside, squinting at the brilliant daybreak. Standing on the steps, a soft wind caresses their cheeks. Sirens echo in the distance, their sound increasing. Reo scans the assembly, observing the sunlight's vivid hues and the lively discussions surrounding them.

"Rose was an incredible person—I can't tell you how sorry I am," he murmurs gently, his voice carrying deep respect. Drawing her nearer, they watch as daylight gradually claims the heavens. Llia tucks herself against Reo's torso, soothed by his heart's steady pulse. The radiant light bathes them in its golden embrace. Suddenly, Llia's eyes fly wide, her attention darting to Reo's features as she notices his pulse accelerating. When she turns toward the rising sun, her stomach plummets.

Reo's gaze widens and his brows arch to their fullest extent. A wave of sorrow envelops him, his lips curling downward and tears beginning to gather in his eyes. The brightness from the red camellia sky fades as a vast shadow engulfs the light above.

She is free! Penumbra is here! We have failed. The Kokuten has arrived! That signifies Myou is alive, he thinks.

Llia shakes her head. *No, no, no, I killed her. I know I did. Wait, she said something right before I gave her the killing blow,*

Her fingers dig into Reo's arm as the darkness spreads across the morning sky like spilled ink. The sun's rays dimmed, then vanished, plunging them into an unnatural twilight. Cherry blossoms that moments ago danced in the golden light now withered and fell, their petals turning black before hitting the ground.

TJ pulls Iris closer, his jaw clenched as he watches the phenomenon unfold. The air grows thick and heavy with an ancient malevolence that makes breathing difficult. Around them, the survivors who had emerged from the shrine begin to panic, their frightened whispers cutting through the eerie silence.

"What happens when you fight a curse?!" Llia's voice cracks, her eyes fixed on the void consuming the sky above. The darkness swirls and pulses like a living thing, tendrils of shadow reaching down toward the earth.

She lets out a bitter laugh, tears streaming down her face as she answers her own question. "It fights back stronger than you could've ever imagined!"

The darkness above them continues its relentless advance, swallowing stars and clouds alike, transforming the world into a canvas of perpetual night. The temperature plummets and frost begins to form on the shrine's stone steps, crackling beneath their feet.

Llia remembers with sudden, chilling clarity what Myou's final word could have been after she plunged her blade into her throat. The realization hits her like ice water in her veins. Myou's disembodied cackle echoes through the dying sky, a sound both ancient and malevolent that seems to come from everywhere and nowhere at once.

Llia turns to Reo, her face drained of color, and with trembling lips repeats Myou's seemingly dying word—the one she had foolishly dismissed in their moment of assumed victory.

"She said Tsumi!" Llia exclaims.

The End

To be continued...

ABOUT THE AUTHOR

MARTELL L. HARRIS

L ong Beach native Martell L. Harris discovered his gift for storytelling in kindergarten. As the eldest of seven siblings, he mastered the intricacies of human relationships from an early age—a foundation that now enriches his work as an author of low fantasy, action, and suspense novels.

Drawing inspiration from literary giants like Alexandre Dumas, Anne Rice, James Patterson, Ian Fleming, and J.R.R. Tolkien, Harris has developed a voice that honors these influences while remaining distinctly his own. His writing combines Dumas's sense of adventure, Rice's atmospheric depth, Patterson's mastery of suspense, Fleming's action-packed precision, and Tolkien's world-building prowess.

Harris infuses his narratives with authenticity drawn from real-world experience. His extensive training in martial arts disciplines has equipped him with not only a deep understanding of strategy and conflict but the ability to craft visceral action sequences that pulse with realism. Yet what distinguishes his storytelling is the delicate balance between adrenaline-fueled moments and nuanced character development. His work features richly drawn personalities whose emotional journeys rival their physical trials, connected by dialogue that crackles with tension and reveals profound human truths.

In his debut novel, *Designed by Flaws*, Harris examines the complex interplay between bonds, honor, and love. His characters confront impossible choices that test the limits of loyalty and devotion, inviting readers to contemplate what it means to be imperfect yet unwavering in one's commitments. This distinctive blend of philosophical depth and heart-racing suspense has quickly established Harris as a compelling new voice whose readers eagerly anticipate his next creation.

Check out our online store for current deals, updates, and publications. www.TheNovelShelf.com

Connect with us on BookBub and Goodreads. We appreciate your feedback - please share your honest review on amazon, as it helps us produce more content; Thank you.